Blood Winter

Immortalibus Bella 3

SL Figuhr

www.slfiguhr.com
Email: info@slfiguhr.com

Follow SL Figuhr on Twitter:
https://twitter.com/SLFiguhr

Like SL Figuhr on Facebook
www.facebook.com/SLFiguhr.Author

ISBN-13: 978-0-9911498-6-5 (SL Figuhr Publishing)

ISBN-10: 0-991149866

LCCN: 2014953505

Book / E-book cover design:
www.celairen.com
https://www.facebook.com/celairen1

Manufactured in the United States of America

Acknowledgments

Edited by:
Lynda Dietz

Design by Celairen Art
www.celairen.com
using stock photography of
http://ybsilon-stock.deviantart.com/
and http://frankandcarystock.deviantart.com/
Cover Model: Danielle Fiore
http://daniellefioremodel.deviantart.com/

DEDICATION

Thank you to Bland (#1 groupie and fan), Iris (whose always believed in me), Michelle (my personal cheerleader,) Tom (for listening to all my whining), Maria (for providing the kick-in-the-pants I needed to publish,) to everyone whose stayed with me during my endeavors, and to all my new fans. I hope you enjoy the continuing journey.

CONTENTS

Prologue

Icy air streamed past the stone peaks, and a three-quarters moon played hide and seek with the clouds. Illyria stood on a small ledge, one booted foot propped against a lip of stone, inured to the freezing temperature.

The rivers reminded her of spilled ink, the main town and smaller villages along it blots. Inhabitants slept, some peacefully, others uneasily. Darker patches spoke of forests and valleys, an occasional faint twinkle marking the spot of hidden camps.

She brooded over past events. She and her allies had defeated their common enemy, but the feelings of wrongness and evil still lay over the land. How long would it take before the demon's taint dissipated?

Her right wrist ached and itched beneath the black leather bracers. Her body wanted to heal the scars, but couldn't, so every now and again she felt a twinge, reminding her she was demon marked.

When would payment come, if at all? Would she be forced back into the underworld as a slave? She had explored and then escaped from the afterlife, making herself what she was today. Or would she be used against her will to tear a rift open so demons could conquer her world? But these mental musings served no immediate purpose. She shoved them into a corner of her mind, to be ruminated on when other, more pressing, problems had been solved.

Illyria turned her thoughts from the recent past to her future. Her world, her domain, spread out below the mountain peak she stood on. It was her territory. She was its Master.

Mine, she thought and sent out with her power. *Mine. Do*

not trespass, lest death come for you. Was any of her kind left to hear the message? To pass the warning on? And what of Phillip? Was his mind still broken by the demon? Did he wander the world or had he met his Final Death at the hands of others?

A moment of grief and sadness washed over her at the idea. Two blood tears leaked out from beneath half-closed lids, leaving frozen tracks down her face before hitting the mountain and bouncing. It didn't matter if those she mourned had been friends, enemies, or unknown; they had all been kin. They deserved at least one moment of acknowledgment that at one time they had existed. She supposed that if she were the last vampire left, she could be the progenitor of a new resurgence should she so choose.

Once, the mental aether had been filled with noise from mortals and vampires alike, day and night. Enough clamor to drive one insane if one didn't learn how to dampen it. Now, the reverse was true.

The vampire cast her eyes over the crescent-shaped mountains, which sheltered the valleys and lowlands between their mighty heights.

She had dealt with the aftermath surrounding Lord Nicky's death. The immortals wouldn't speak of it. She made the king believe Nicky was alive, in hiding and plotting the death of the king. Maceanas was devastated by the duplicity of his oldest and dearest friend. He declared Nicky a traitor, and his life, property, and wealth forfeit.

A self-satisfied smile creased her features. The nobles fought among themselves to appoint the next advisor. The guilds and rich townspeople fought for more power and recognition from the king. The poor, the slaves . . . they just struggled to survive.

It didn't matter to her what the mortals who occupied the land thought. Let them fight over it, pretend they ruled it and those who lived there. She knew better—and soon, so would they

CHAPTER ONE

Martin paused in the hallway, hearing the murmur of voices coming from inside his father's former office. It was past midnight, and he knew normally his sire spent his nights with his lover, the duchess. He rarely slept at the family townhouse anymore. It did not sound like a female voice, however. The carved wooden door hadn't been properly closed, and a thin crack let a line of light and sound leak out.

The young viscount carefully moved closer to the small opening, avoiding the creaky spots in the floor. He angled himself so he could hear better, pressing up against the wall beside the small crack. *I'm not eavesdropping,* he told himself. *I'm just waiting for the right moment to announce myself.*

"You made a promise to me. Now it is time to keep it. You will mention to His Majesty I am the best noble for the role of advisor." The marquis' silky tone was cold.

"I am surprised you still desire the help of one you continually call weak," the earl spat back.

"I wouldn't, but your cowardice in political matters is well known. When the king hears your mewling support, he will know I am the correct choice." The scent of cigar smoke floated on the air.

"Your association with the traitorous advisor will speak more loudly than I on the subject," Sydney replied.

Martin could only imagine the look of thwarted rage on Jenabram's face as the man spoke. "We already discussed the matter. It is time you paid for the information I gave you. You will do as you promised—unless you wish to join your brothers?"

"Do not dare speak their names with your serpent's tongue!" The earl's voice held more rage than his son had ever heard.

"Neither I, nor the king, gives a damn about what you think of those events. It is ancient history. Now then, I expect the duchess will also support my claim."

His father's reply came crisply. "As I have stated—" He was brutally cut off.

"Don't whine to me! I don't care what you, or she, think. Just do it. I imagine there are worse fates than execution, especially if you hope to achieve your longed-for divorce." A chair creaked.

"Death would be preferable."

Martin strained to hear, nearly missing his sire's low voice response as a bell rang to summon a slave.

A bark of cruel laughter came from the marquis. "Consider the thought motivation." The sound of firm footsteps crossing the floor came clearly to Martin.

The young man hurried to hide behind a tall, ornamental vase. The door to the office was flung open a moment later, the irate face of the marquis briefly seen in the oil light, a cloud of cigar smoke trailing behind him. The man walked down the hall, intent on letting himself out whether or not a slave appeared. For a moment, Martin debated following, but thought otherwise as the doorman stepped from a side hall.

Martin had been handed a summons earlier that day by the butler, commanding his presence, along with the other nobles and townspeople of high status, to cast votes for candidates for the advisor's position. The young man couldn't say what made him so sure the duchess wouldn't back the marquis, only that he knew he was right. Tomorrow would tell for certain.

* * *

When Martin awoke, he asked after his sire, only to be told he wasn't present. The young man dressed with care. The gathering of nobles would be his first time participating in a royal election. The palace grounds bustled as his sled pulled into the courtyard. Martin followed a throng of older men inside the palace and toward the council rooms. The great council chambers echoed with voices. Clumps of people, mainly comprised of men, with a few women, stood scattered about the space. It was a point of pride among the nobles, to wear outfits in the fashion of their ancestors.

The more out-of-date the clothing looked, the older the title. Some members had managed to preserve their father's or great-grandfather's clothes. The young man could easily spot those whose titles had been granted within the past decade. They wore newer styles and didn't always adhere to their house colors. They also decked themselves out with more jewelry. Some of the people were minor nobles who had been elevated. Often it was a commoner or merchant who'd managed to do some fantastic deed meriting recognition.

Martin continued his stroll about the interconnected rooms. Most people chose to mill about the antechamber. Four stone carved fireplaces roared with flame in an effort to heat the space. Elaborate brass oil lanterns hung from brass wall sconces cast in the likenesses of past nobles. Overhead, six massive chandeliers of three-tiered metal held thick candles. The heavy brocade drapes around the windows swayed periodically from stray gusts of wind which found their way through cracks in the stone walls. They were tied back to allow the weak winter sun to filter through precious glass. The young man roamed the perimeter of the room, his boots thumping softly on the highly polished oak floor, after acknowledging his peers and betters.

As he had last night, he eavesdropped shamelessly while thinking, *This is becoming a bad habit. One my father would be ashamed of if he knew.*

He paused by a window, as if looking out over the dreary landscape, while listening. Baron Stavic, dressed in green velvet and lace, groused to a group of men, all barons themselves.

"That prick of a marquis stopped by a while ago, hoping to enlist my support for his bid to become advisor."

"I would not let him hear you call him names," one of the other barons with a thick, waxed mustache mildly suggested.

"I stand under the good graces of the duchess herself. What more support could a man want?" Stavic replied.

Quiet chuckles came from some of the men. "And what of when she falls out of the king's favor? Her cronies are not of high position," needled a man in puce brocade banded with egg-yolk-colored silk.

"Perhaps that is why they are her cronies," a different man

in black and violet finely woven wool put forth, "for then she will have no real competition."

"I would not call Earl Sydney of low standing," Stavic protested.

"Of whom do we speak? The elder, who has distanced himself from his family and his name, all because he lusts after the duchess? Or his heir, who has yet to prove himself worthy of his lineage?" the baron with waxed mustache asked.

Martin didn't stay to hear the rest; he moved on, strolling through the crowds. The intricately carved wood double doors leading into the major chamber stood open with royal guards to each side. A few nobles stood in clumps amid the tiered seats encircling the pit floor. He listened to the debates of which nobles should be nominated for the post as he prowled. Most of the young men he had grown up with had yet to inherit their titles and lands from their fathers, thus they had no say in the matters being discussed, and were not permitted inside. At the far end of the major council chamber, another set of doors remained closed and guarded. Martin knew from talks with his father, the great table of the inner council resided in the room beyond. Each chair's seat back around the long, massive wood table bore the crest of the noble to whom it belonged.

Martin strolled back to the antechamber. It seemed as if hours passed, but when he glanced at the water clock upon a mantel, only a quarter of an hour had elapsed. He occasionally amused himself by inspecting the tapestries which hung about the room. They depicted various kings and battles. After a few more minutes, the tramp of feet could be heard. The king's personal guards entered, followed by Aranthus and His Majesty. A servant carrying an elongated jug slipped inside the room before the guards shut the doors.

"All kneel and acknowledge your king!" the chamberlain bawled out.

Clothes rustled and a few joints creaked as the crowd complied, rising when bid. The king waddled inside, looking much larger, to sit himself in an ornately carved armchair, slightly elevated. It provided him with a clearer view of the long room. No one present could miss the ornate, jeweled gold goblet he held in one hand and drank deeply from at regular intervals.

His personal guard arranged themselves in a semicircle at his back. "We all know why we are here, so let's not waste time. I know there are still traitors in our midst; Nicky is still free."

No one moved. The king's voice, slurred by drink, shook, letting everyone know the rumors of his being perpetually on the brink of hysteria closer to the truth.

"For the past week, I have been inundated by those seeking to be named royal advisor." His voice firmed a moment with a tone of annoyance.

Glances and whispers were surreptitiously traded.

"I am tired of your sycophancy and squabbling. None of you, except for two, had the fortitude and bravery to consistently speak against Nicky out loud."

There was a low sound of hisses from different parts of the room, as if snakes were loose.

"Therefore, I have decided to suspend your privilege of choosing candidates for the position of advisor. I will make a decision on my own, and announce it when I feel ready."

Shocked exclamations rang out, their owners seemingly unable to prevent them from escaping at the king's words.

"You dare to defy me?" Maceanas screamed, sounding more like his old self.

Most of those in the room lowered their heads, bowing apologies and denials.

"Who among you dares to naysay me?" The king was now standing, fat face turning florid, goblet momentarily forgotten as his hands clenched into fists and he glared out over the crowd.

"If it pleases the crown, I wish to speak," a familiar drawling voice spoke.

Heads turned just enough to catch a glimpse of the Marquis Jenabram straightening from his bow.

"It does not!" Maceanas yelled.

Blithely the man continued. "Sire, that orphan," he spat, "brought shame to the entire kingdom. Please at least let your inner council of nobles put forth a few names of those we consider worthy for your deliberations."

All heads turned toward the king, whose red shade

deepened into a dusky purple. Those present who despised and hated the sneering marquis hoped he would be severely reprimanded.

"You dare ignore me? You dare to ignore my wishes?"

"I have never liked nor trusted the boy, Majesty. A feeling I never hid," Jenabram stated, "in which case, yes, I dare to make suggestions." His tone clearly implied any name the council put forth other than his own would be a mistake.

Heads swiveled back and forth, low whispers and murmurs rising against the silence.

"Then you should take comfort in the fact that is the only reason why I am allowing you to keep your tongue in your head, and your head upon your neck," the king screamed.

Both men had much the same look of rage, but Jenabram stiffened, making a deep, deferential bow.

"As for the rest of you, quit bothering me with your suggestions for a replacement. I want all able-bodied men out looking for that traitor and helping to rebuild my nation. Now get out of my sight and stay out!"

Aranthus thumped his staff on the floor after the king's pronouncement. His Majesty stomped off the small dais and out of the council chamber, surrounded by his personal guards, leaving a rising tide of voices at his back.

Martin hurried through the milling crowds, intent on reaching his father. He was surrounded by a group of outraged nobles, the duchess standing with a faint, amused smile upon her lips. She was the only noble present of the group who wore new clothes in her house colors of black, red, and silver. Despite it, she made the outfit seem as if it was as old, or older, than those around her. The tiara given her by the king sparkled in the oil light.

"Ridiculous," spluttered Baron Stavic. "Does His Majesty not understand the kingdom is on the verge of revolt?"

"Treasonous words themselves. I would be careful to whom and where you speak," the duchess mildly reprimanded the baron.

"When they begin storming the palace, and he calls for our personal guards to supplement his own, I intend to remind him of this moment," Jenabram savagely bit out. He turned to glare at the earl, speaking for his ears alone. "We would already have a new advisor if you had done as I said."

Martin didn't miss the comment; neither, it seemed, did the duchess.

"Done what exactly?" she calmly inquired. "Support your overinflated sense of self? Of your grandiose schemes?"

The marquis glared at her as the other men in the group continued to bicker among themselves.

"I have more right to be the advisor than any man in this kingdom. You will cozy up to His Majesty like you always do, and you will strongly suggest my name."

"Or what?"

"What?"

"Precisely. It sounded as if a threat should be in there somewhere."

He gave his habitual sneer to her. "Titles come and go around here, or have you forgotten? Without yours, you would be —are—nothing but a common whore. You think Sydney will still champion your mad schemes if you are condemned by the king? No. He will distance you the same way he does to all the other whores he's used."

"I think you are confusing him with yourself. Perhaps the real question should be, what would you be without your title? I think a rabid dog, which should have been put down long ago." Illyria traded barbs.

"Duchess, please," Sydney begged her in an undertone. "We must put aside our personal feelings for one another and work toward securing the kingdom."

He was ignored as his lover and the marquis finished up their personal spat.

"Father," Martin judged it safe to speak up. "May I have a moment? Please excuse me, my lords, duchess." He bowed.

They acknowledged him, drifting a few steps away as Sydney turned toward his son. "I am sorry your first chance to participate ended before it began."

"I am sure there shall be more opportunities." Martin found himself in the odd position of consoling his sire.

"Yes," his father conceded. "What was it you wished to

speak with me about?"

Martin made to reply, but all the doors to the council chamber were thrown open and the royal guards poured in. They shouted at everyone to move—to leave the palace or further risk the king's displeasure, possibly with a stint in the dungeons attached.

A few men protested, thinking the guards jested. They were proven wrong when they were set upon without delay and dragged off. After a few shocked moments, and some well-placed prodding of spears, the council chambers emptied.

CHAPTER TWO

The house lay still and dark. Mica opened the door to his room, listening for a moment, but all was silent. As best he could, he quietly walked down the old, wooden floor, but he still set off numerous squeaks. The once-immortal, weak from his continuing illness, paused briefly to catch his breath. As he sucked in air, his throat quivered, and a volley of coughing burst forth. The man did his best to muffle the sound, face turning red as he continued to cough. The bitch's office only a few more steps ahead, he opened the door to darkness.

Mica stepped inside and moved to the office's single, shuttered window, opening it. He backtracked to shut the door. Weak moonlight shone in, providing just enough illumination to outline the dark bulk of furniture and prevent him from stumbling into it.

He sat behind Illyria's work table, drew an oil lamp over to him, eventually got it lit. He had to wait for a wave of dizziness to pass. He must not be as well as he thought. A shiver overtook his wasted frame, causing the man to draw his thick wool bed robe tighter around himself. Mica opened the slim middle drawer, where various grades of parchment and vellum, along with quills, resided. He moved on to the left-hand side with sticks of sealing wax, ink, and sand. A small locked box rattled when he picked it up and shook it. *It could be a copy of her seal*. The right side drawer held a few pieces of correspondence.

Mica took them out and read each one, gleaning nothing of importance. He shoved the missives back, and sat drumming his fingers on the silky smooth tabletop as he thought.

Where would a lying, mistrustful vamp keep her secrets? In her crypt, was the first thought, closely followed by *not easily accessible*. She had to have a place nearby—had to.

Mica slowly stood, leaning heavily on the table top. He

waited for waves of dizziness and lightheadedness to go away. Taking the lamp with him, he picked a wall. It was cold, as not much separated the inner painted plaster from the outside wall. By pressing and knocking, he worked his way around the room until he eventually found an area which sounded different. It took longer than he liked to find the mechanism to open the panel, but behind it was an iron-banded wood door. Naturally, it was locked. He scowled, and began searching the room for something he could use to pick it. Mica knew his brother would be better at the task, but didn't think he'd agree to the act.

His brother. The thought made him angry. Colin let himself be sucked into that bitch's schemes, was even happy participating! He was teaching those of Illyria's slaves who wanted to learn, how to read, write, and do arithmetic. Mica was so engrossed in his search and sour thoughts, the voice startled him.

"Would the key help you?"

Mica jumped in shock, his heart pounding in sudden fear. He spun around to place his back against a wall. The oil lamp bobbed wildly from the movement before steadying.

Illyria stood half in, half out of the pool of light. One arm, clad in black velvet, extended, a metal two-pronged key held out in her fingers. A faint smile pulled one side of her mouth up.

They stared at each other for several moments. Mica blinked a drop of sweat out of his eyes. She suddenly stood before him. If he breathed too deeply, their bodies would brush against each other's.

"You—"

"Mica, what do you need that you feel you can't ask me for?"

"You—"

"Let us skip the insults. Sit down before you collapse. I'm not going to kill you. There would be no challenge in it; besides, I have too much respect for your brother to make an enemy of him."

Mica's head buzzed, his limbs shaking with the strain. He took several staggering steps toward the couch, only to feel his legs give out beneath him. He dimly knew the oil lamp was slipping from his grasp. The room spun, his stomach heaved, and he was sweating profusely despite the fact that shivers racked his body.

When he blinked awake from his brief faint, it was to find that Illyria had placed him supine upon the couch and covered him with a thin blanket. The oil lantern he'd nearly dropped sat upon a low table behind his head. His enemy held a small brass goblet out.

He sat up, too quickly, as the room spun. After it had settled back into place, Mica grabbed the goblet, gulped down the wine within, and held it loosely in one hand. She took the drinking vessel back and refilled it before placing it in his hand again.

"Let's try once more. What are you looking for? Gold? Blackmail material? A map with a big red X, marking 'here lies the evil vampire's sleeping lair'?"

"I hate you."

"Yes, darling, I know. My dear, white knight will sever my head from my body, yank my black heart out, burn the pieces, and scatter the ash to the four winds."

"I am not your anything. Where's my brother?" He meant his demand to come out strong, but in his weakened state it sounded whiney.

"Sleeping, I would imagine; it is the middle of the night." She stood, half of her in the glow from the oil lamp, the other half in shadow, no emotion showing on the smooth mask her face became when she was at rest.

"As soon as I'm well, Colin and I are leaving. When I have released Donny from his torment, I will come back for my vengeance."

"I would feel more threatened by your words if you weren't pale and sweating on the couch, looking closer to meeting death. Oh, and if you do die, tell him I said hello." A brief smile flashed across her lips, crinkling her eyes.

The man turned his head to glare at her as she dragged a chair over and sat before him, sure she was mocking him. "Tell him yourself, when I end you."

She smiled as if in fond remembrance. "It has been awhile. He might not remember me. Or may have another queen."

"Quit mocking me!"

Illyria raised a brow. "But I am not. I have met Death. I have been one of his queens."

They stared at each other. Mica felt tired; he knew he

needed more rest, but thoughts of Donny and the torment his protégé must be in demanded he rectify the situation.

"Colin and I are leaving," Mica began again, more to convince himself than her. "You will—"

She cut him off neatly. "All that you shall need will be ready. I'd hoped you would wait until you fully healed, and winter was gone. But, I know you'd rather sacrifice yourself for your noble quests than be reasonable."

Mica never saw her move. He blinked and she was gone; her voice floated softly back to him. "Please extinguish the light when you leave. The others don't deserve to be homeless because you harbor a grudge toward me."

* * *

A small lunch waited for him when Mica woke and rose the next day. He first soaked in a warm, herb-strewn bath. Fresh clothes, comprising of linen underthings, along with a shirt and pants woven of soft sheep's wool and dyed navy, lay waiting for him when he was done bathing. A pair of felt slippers, lined in wool, kept his feet warm. Mica didn't know if his brother had eaten already or not. No one joined him at table. Mary Elana served him, eyes downcast, mute. She ignored all his attempts at conversation.

The man dined well on a rich stew redolent of winter vegetables and venison, a thick loaf of mixed grain bread, and hot cider. A small fire burned low in the round, clay stove against one wall. The room's single window showed nothing but gray sky.

When he finished, he went in search of Colin, learning from one of the house slaves that his brother was at the palace. A look outside the frosty windowpanes in the sitting room showed snow-covered buildings, and long icicles descending from rooflines. High-walled paths were shoveled to allow movement, and patches of ice gleamed on them when the weak sun hit. The courtyard was a mess of trampled, dirty snow. Occasional squeals and other horse sounds filtered inside from the stable area. He remembered how cold it would be, and found the thought of going out deeply unappealing. Well, his brother had to come back for dinner. Mica needed a plan of how they were going to get to the ancient motherhouse, and then back to Donny's body.

He could spend his day calculating travel times, and how many supplies would be needed. Mica turned, making his way to a small writing room. It held a hinged-top, plain wooden desk and chair. A rag-stuffed cushion was placed for comfort on the seat. Oil-filled clay sconces on the wall bracketed the writing surface. A few steps behind sat a small clay stove. It had been laid with kindling, ready for whoever needed use of it. The air inside the room was chilly enough for Mica's breath to come out in a faint plume. He started a fire burning, and sat, arranging writing supplies and mixing up a fresh cake of ink.

Four hours later, Mica tossed his quill down in disgust. If his numbers were correct—and they usually were—it would take him at least a year to travel to the motherhouse. That didn't include finding food and water. He wasn't even sure how many towns and cities had managed to rebuild in the intervening years along the route he and his brother would have to take. He let his head rest in his hands, elbows propped up on the table. Another cough wanted to burst forth, and he couldn't prevent it. When it passed, he was left light-headed and panting for breath.

A trickle of fear filled him, but he ruthlessly squashed it down. He was fine. He would be fine. A little cough didn't mean anything. He rang a small bell to call a slave. Mary Elana answered, and silently brought him a goblet of hot cider upon his request. Mica was found much later by his brother, still working out the details of his trip. Wads of parchment littered the floor.

"Hey, how are you? The slaves say you've developed a nasty cough."

A brief scowl crossed Mica's face. "I'm fine! It's just a little —" He broke down into a hacking cough, leaving him once more struggling to breathe.

"You're not all right, bro." Colin knelt beside his brother, alarm evident in his features. "I don't think you're getting better. I think you're getting worse. Let me send for the royal physician."

"No, there's no need." Mica refused, finally able to get more air into his lungs. He felt drained, but refused to lie down. "I've been calculating our trip to the motherhouse."

Colin still knelt, and with great reluctance he stood and

leaned against the wall so he could be nearer to his elder brother. Mica laid out his plans, frequently having to stop talking just to catch a breath.

"Ok. Enough," Colin interrupted after his brother sat struggling for the nth time. He ran to the door and shouted for a slave.

When one came, he gave the person some instructions, ignoring his brother's protests. He walked back to Mica, who was clutching the writing top with both hands, head bowed as he fought for air.

"Shit! Mica!"

Mica feebly waved him off. He was unaware of his brother running from the room, calling for help as he fought to fill his lungs with air. He toppled from the chair with the force of his coughs, and managed to hack up a great deal of bloody phlegm upon the wood floor and rag-braided rug.

The effort left him dizzy and short of breath. Mica did his best to crawl over to the doorway, but could not find the strength to stand. Just the little movement he had done left him aching and weak all over. His chest pained him from all the coughing. He leaned back against the door edge, arms dangling by his side. He didn't remember feeling this weak and sick back when he had first been mortal.

The man would have laughed if he'd had breath for it. Of all the times to be felled by an illness which once could have been easily cured. He didn't realize he was passing out. Mica woke to the stench of unwashed flesh, piss, and a cup thrust under his nose.

"Get away from me," he feebly demanded.

"Drink it; it will help," Colin commanded his brother from somewhere nearby.

Mica shook his head, too weak to do much else, revolted by the filth-crusted hand that held the cup. Movement sounded, the nasty hand withdrew. A firm, masculine hand grabbed Mica's chin and tilted his head back.

His brother held the cup in his other hand, countenance grim. "You will drink this." He put the side of the cup to Mica's lip.

"No," Mica protested through clenched teeth, trying not to

move his mouth too much.

"Stop being so damn stubborn!" Colin pressed harder with the cup and his hand about his brother's chin. His voice lowered. "Don't make me get the duchess. I have a feeling she'll have no problem prying your jaws apart and dumping this down your gullet. She might even enjoy it."

Tears leaked out Mica's eyes, to his dismay and embarrassment. He gave up the fight, opened his mouth, and let Colin carefully pour the drink in a bit at a time.

"Good, real good. I watched the brew being made. There's nothing in here that'll poison you. It should help lessen the cough."

"Colin," Mica gasped out between swallows.

"No, don't say anything." He fed his elder brother more of the liquid, until it was all down.

He passed the cup off to Mary Elana, who had stood wide-eyed and silent the entire time.

"Help me get him up and to his room," Colin directed.

Mica saw a few of the house guards step forward and help him off the floor to support his stumbling steps back to his room. He didn't have a chance to thank the filthy, rag-covered person who stood next to the young girl.

* * *

Mica was expecting his brother, or a slave, with his supper tray. He was relegated to being back in bed. Whatever had been in the goblet Colin forced him to drink had helped some. He still coughed and wheezed and was weak, but he had managed to get several hours of sleep.

An icy hand touched his feverish brow, his eyelids snapped open.

"Get away from me!" He snarled, or tried to, before coughing.

As was her wont, she ignored him. Illyria brought a chair over to his bedside and sat down.

"Old friend . . ."

"I'm not—"

"New enemy. Do shut up and listen, please. If you don't

stop being so stubborn, and let people help you to heal, Donny will never be at peace. Is that what you want?"

"You bitch! Don't you dare speak his name!" He almost bent double with his coughing fit. When he had flopped back on the pillows that propped him up, she spoke again.

"You won't listen to your brother, and you call me selfish and heartless. You want to put Donny's remains to rest? You want to have your revenge on me? Then you will have to get better first. That means doing what you are told. Your brother thinks you mean to live as a mortal. Now you are getting a very painful reminder of how hard it is when modern inventions and medicine no longer exist. If you insist on ignoring the infection, it will kill you. Hate me if you must, but think of your brother."

She held the mug up to his clamped lips. He reached up and wrapped shaking hands around hers, but hadn't the strength to even try to push the mug away.

"Medicine, the same as the woman gave you earlier. Please, do resist. It's been awhile since I had a chance to force someone to do my bidding."

Mica watched her eyes turn honey fire, the faint luminescent glow beneath her skin, and a peek of her fangs as she grinned. He debated with himself a moment more before allowing her to help feed him the liquid. It tasted the same as earlier. He had a feeling he was safe from her only so long as Colin was useful and didn't cross her in any way. After the medicine came a clay mug with steam rising off it.

She carefully wrapped his hands around the warm mug, helping him bring it toward his mouth, and tilted it. The rich taste of chicken broth exploded on his tongue. He drank it down and let her take the empty mug from his hands.

"Would you like some more?"

"Yes," Mica answered in dull tones. He lay staring at the ceiling as she left and came back a bit later.

Once again, she helped him drink the second mug full of broth.

"There now, don't you feel better?"

"I'm not a child."

"Then quit acting like one." She set the mug on a small,

bedside table before leaning closer to fuss with the blankets.

Now what does she want? The man wanted her gone so he could try to sleep again.

Her face was its normal smooth mask, giving no hint to what her thoughts were. After he was tucked in, she rose and gathered up the mug and left him to rest.

CHAPTER THREE

Eron was not sure what had awoken him, but he found himself listening, lying still in the darkness, ready to defend himself if need be. There was only the relentless howling of the wind, the swish of snow, and the snores of the female warriors in the barracks behind his room.

After the bandits had burnt the first building during their raid, the second one had been hastily thrown up. It wasn't weatherproof by any means. Most days, the occupants woke to thin sheets of snow covering their blankets and the floor, and twice to ice. The large braziers which burned all night and day, tended to by a slave, did little to help alleviate the biting cold.

The building rattled from a particularly strong gust of wind, and he felt cold, feathery flakes land on his face.

Great, snow is leaking in again. The roof thatching probably needs repairing. Why did I agree to subject myself to the same conditions as the females I'm training? Oh right, I was stupid yet again, the immortal thought.

He tried to turn over and go back to sleep but couldn't. Eron forced himself out from under the covers, instantly regretting his decision as he started to shiver uncontrollably.

The man forced his feet into his icy-cold boots, strapped his sword to his side, took his cloak off the bed and wrapped it around himself, and cringing, slipped outside the door to the barracks. The wind nearly ripped the door from his grasp. He managed to force it closed before turning and observing the training ground.

Breath left his body as the cold knifed through him, and he fought to take air in. It burned his lungs and nasal passages.

"Next time, ignore your thoughts and stay in your semi-warm bed," Eron muttered to himself, breath leaving in plumes.

His eyes narrowed, already feeling dried out from the wind, and he was pretty sure his ears had instant frostbite.

He scanned the darkness before him, a slim crescent moon of no help. A sound came to his ears, perhaps the same one which had awoken him. He strained to listen as he cautiously moved, not wanting to hit a patch of ice and go down.

There! The sound came again, a faint snap, as of fabric rippling in the wind. He moved slowly, eyes doing their best to see in what little moonlight there was. He nearly walked over the cliff edge, and only just stopped himself in time. The increased tugging of the wind and the sound of the ice grinding past in the river far below alerted him to the danger he was in.

"Fuck me!" He was startled enough to shout out loud. *Good one, moron; now whoever is out here knows you are too. Brilliant.*

Strong arms wrapped around him and pulled him back away from the edge. He fought briefly before realizing they were like steel bands.

"You can let go. Even I'm not talented enough to be able to topple off the side from this distance," he deadpanned.

"Foolish man! You are free; you don't have to fake your death to leave. If you don't want to stay here, just say so. I will find someone else to take over the females' training." Illyria's voice held anger and bitterness.

Eron broke free from her arms and turned to face her. "That wasn't my intention. I thought I heard something, and couldn't get back to sleep. So I decided to see what it was."

"I am the only person awake who is out here. I doubt even the bandits are stirring from their holes."

"Well, now that I know you do your nightly stalking the perimeter of your land for trespassers to drain, I won't bother getting up."

"I do have guards for the job; why would you choose to inconvenience yourself?"

"I haven't felt like a popsicle in hours. I miss the sensation."

She ignored his joke, staring off toward the town, a faint furrow marring her brow. He shivered violently, wrapping his arms around himself while he waited for her to say something more, but she didn't.

"Popsicle status achieved. I'll be going." Eron started to turn away, but her voice stopped him.

"Come inside to my office, please. I have . . . concerns, and I would like your advice."

His breath plumed out, not expecting her to admit she didn't have all the answers. "You? Need help? Shocking! So that's why it's so cold: all the ice in hell has come here. Sure, why not? It's not like I've got anywhere else to be."

Illyria's office was warm, and bathed in the flickering light of flames from a stone fireplace. The immortal laid his wool cloak on the couch. A small, carved wood table in the corner held a brass tray with small brass goblets and a clay, wood-stoppered jug. Eron poured himself some of the liquid, bringing the bottle with him and setting it down on her worktable as he sank into a chair before it. She seated herself behind her table.

"Mica is much sicker than his brother realizes," she began.

"Death's door?" Eron joked.

The vamp's hesitation had anxiety growing inside him. Despite the fights the two men had had since arriving in Macinas, he didn't truly wish ill of his oldest friend.

"If he won't let anyone care for him, yes. I don't think he understands how close he is. I thought perhaps he would ask Colin to make him immortal again, but he hasn't."

"He may not know his own thoughts and feelings adequately on the subject," Eron replied. *It would be just like that mule-headed asshole to let himself die to prove a point.*

While her face showed no expression, her eyes held a deep pool of sadness in them. "He will not get a chance as things stand now. We must convince him to rest and try healing."

"Now would be a good time to show him the full extent of your powers and will. Make him do what you want. He's human. I don't care how much he may hate it, or what fights he and I have had. I'm not losing the stubborn ass."

"His stubbornness is one reason why it may not work. The other is his illness. I fear to take even the smallest sip of his blood, which would help me imprint my will on his. I . . ." Illyria trailed off, uncomfortable with her thoughts.

Eron set his goblet down. If she had this much reservation,

his friend's health had indeed dangerously deteriorated.

"I'm not making him immortal, not without his consent. Colin would agree, however much it might pain him to lose his brother."

Illyria looked down at her hands, eyes shaded by her half-lowered lids. "There is one other thing that might convince him to take his health seriously. But I would need his consent. And yours. And you would have to be willing to help."

He leaned forward, eyes narrowing in suspicion. "Which would mean?"

The vamp looked him in the eyes. "We retrieve Donny's soul gem ourselves and end his torment."

Eron kept his expression blank with a great effort, while inside he felt the stirrings of his darker side. "Why would you leave your empire-building for the length of time it will require? You may come back to nothing but ashes if certain people get their way."

Her smile was feral, eyes a blazing golden honey. "When they do, they will discover Nicky's wrath but a candle flame compared to the fire of mine."

The man regarded her a moment, weighing options in his head. "If I agree to help, I expect some compensation." He let his words hang a moment. "Nonnegotiable."

They regarded each other silently, she no doubt evaluating his offer. "What kind?"

"I will need to consider what I want, which will all depend on how you plan to achieve this goal and the amount of my involvement." The immortal kept his eyes steady on hers. "If and when we get Colin and Mica's blessing, I will tell you at the completion of our quest."

She nodded slowly, eyes gleaming while an amused smile tugged one side of her mouth up. "Very well. My blood oath on it."

* * *

A slave finished helping Mica complete his use of the chamber pot. A second slave finished remaking the bed with clean sheets. She left, taking the soiled linen with her. The first helped the sick man walk the few steps back to his bed. Mica leaned heavily on the man's arm, toppling onto the soft mattress. A violent coughing fit wracked his body. It was many moments before he could catch his breath enough to curl under the covers.

The remaining slave walked to a washbasin and cleaned his hands, mindful of the careful instructions his mistress had given him, even though he didn't believe half of what she said about germs. Next, he began to prepare the medicinal drink. A small table held a squat, bulbous oil lamp. Beside it was a metal trivet he placed over the top of the flame once it was lit. Next, a clay bowl he filled with clean water and set on top of the trivet. It took a while for the water to heat. While he waited, the slave sat down on a small wood stool before the table. He pillowed his head on his crossed arms. He dozed off, jerking awake at the sensation of steam against his cheek. The slave sat up, reaching for a pair of wooden tongs with which to pick the bowl up and pour the hot water into a mug. With that done, he set the tongs aside, taking up a covered clay jar and tapping out some of the contents into the water before stirring the mixture with a stick. The slave had started walking across the room to the bed with the clay mug when the door opened.

"Ah, Willeg. I will take that. Thank you for your diligence. Why don't you take a short break—say, half an hour—and then come back." His mistress dismissed him.

He bowed, handing over the mug, and left the room. Willeg noted the slave training the women warriors with the duchess, and his curiosity made him linger outside the closed door. The male slave, a new addition to the household, had been purchased from Gri a fortnight ago. His duties kept him close to the sick man's room. He did not have much time between working and sleeping to learn more about the raven household. Willeg pressed his ear against the sturdy wood door, hoping to find out what was going on. He almost fell into the room as the door was suddenly jerked open.

"Listening in when you've been told to go on break can be bad for your health." The dark-haired man's tone was grim. "Do as you're bid, or I'll have the warriors I'm training use you as a target for our bow and arrow lessons."

Willeg blanched. "Beg pardon."

He hurried off down the hall, the intricately woven wool runner muffling his steps. The slave knew he'd made no sound to betray his presence. One of them, either the duchess or the man, must truly practice witchcraft, like the gossips spread. The look in the man's eyes led the slave to believe he would ask for Willeg's life from their mistress. She would probably agree, too.

Eron closed the door, shaking his head in disgust after the retreating slave. "He's gone now. I don't trust him. Listening in at keyholes? Can you be sure he won't, accidentally or otherwise, harm our friend?"

Illyria gave the first genuine smile he had seen all evening, "I have made him very aware of what deliberate failure on his part will entail. I do like your threat—much more creative than the death I promised him."

"I have had over eight thousand years of practice." He approached the bed.

His friend glared at them both, but didn't speak as Illyria made sure he kept drinking the medicine. When he was done, she fluffed the pillows up and he collapsed backward.

"Aren't prisoners allowed to sleep at night?" Mica wheezed out.

"No, but patients are. For a small consideration I can upgrade your status," she replied.

"And this is why we can't have peaceful conversations," Eron butted in before they could further snipe at each other. "Old friend, you're dying. So shut the hell up for once and fucking listen to advice. And you," he rounded on the vamp, "stop with the snark. There're other people you can torment who I'm sure are much more deserving."

Both Mica and Illyria's mouths tightened in anger, but they gave short nods. Eron plopped down on the end of Mica's bed, as she sat in the only chair in the room.

"I have a question to ask of you, and I want you to answer me truthfully," Illyria began. "Is the reason you won't let yourself rest and heal properly because of Donny's remains?"

Mica glared at her, face going purple. Eron wasn't sure if he was angry, or trying hard to hold his coughs back. His answer came between hacks. "Don't . . . speak . . . his . . . name."

"Answer the question, damn it!" Eron barked out. "Your brother doesn't deserve to lose you because you're hardheaded."

"That, and Nicky."

"Would you trust me to retrieve the boy's soul gem and put him to rest?" Eron asked.

"I made the calculations. It'll take a year, at least." Mica motioned for some water.

Illyria poured some from the pitcher on the side table and handed it to him. They watched their friend's hands shake with the effort of holding and lifting the goblet to his lips.

"There is a faster way," the duchess idly remarked.

"Got a spare plane and fuel tucked away in your castle?" Mica squeezed out. He didn't like the flickering looks Eron and the vamp sent each other. "There is no way . . ."

"Mica, I don't know if you recall, but I have the power of flight. I can carry Eron to where ever he needs to go to see the job is done. It would not take long. Your friend just wants to know what Donny's soul gem looks like. The only problem would be in finding the correct spot where the warehouse once stood."

"No."

Eron shook his head, fighting back his anger. "Why not? It's what you want."

"No, I don't want her to know the location of the motherhouse. I don't want either of you knowing what shape his soul gem takes," Mica ground out, teeth clenched, veins standing out in his neck.

Eron propped one hand on his bent knee, leaning forward. "She can't get to them. Only we can." He hoped it was still true. After the guardian had answered Colin's summons and battled the demon, the immortal wasn't sure it, too, hadn't been destroyed. It had certainly seemed it at the time.

"No," the mortal insisted.

"Mica—"

"I said no. Get out, and leave me alone," the man further insisted. He feebly kicked his foot under the covers at his friend's leg.

Eron sat, silent, scrutinizing Mica while his friend coughed and hacked. The immortal stood up and walked two steps to Illyria. He put his hand on her shoulder, looking at his friend. Said in a pitiless tone, "Do it. Make sure you take the knowledge of what the gem looks like."

"No!" Mica's denial was filled with horror.

"I thought it a reasonable request to make of you, given how sick you are. Just remember, you brought this on yourself." Eron folded his arms across his chest.

"Mica." The siren whisper floated through the air as his field of vision filled with honey gold fire. Hands like steel bands clamped on his upper arms to hold him still. "Mica." His name a sweet song.

Dimly the mortal was aware he'd ceased to struggle as he sank deeper into those flames. One last "no" slipped from his lips as he was pulled down into the warm depths of the fire before him.

CHAPTER FOUR

"**D**oes it have to be a big gem?" Donny worriedly asked as he and his teacher walked along the city sidewalks. "'Cause I really wanna do this, only—well, you know I haven't got a whole lotta dough to spend."

"No," Mica replied. "You don't have to use a gem if you don't want to. But it must be made out of durable material. Many immortals create their pieces themselves, incorporating themes which have special meaning to them."

The young man perked up. He tore his eyes away from the crowds of people around them. "Can I ask what you used? Material-wise, I mean."

"I was a blacksmith, then a soldier, then a farmer. I used a little bit of metal objects from each of those occupations."

"I can't even begin to imagine what your soul gem must look like," Donny replied in awe.

Mica gave a quick smile. They continued walking, turning their conversation to mundane matters as the crowds of mortals grew thicker, going about their midday business. The older man led his protégé up to his loft. In his present lifetime, he chose to be a builder and restorationist. The bottom floor of the building currently housed a cafe offering specialty coffees, teas, and pastries. The second through fourth floors held two luxury apartments apiece. The loft had been tucked under the sloped attic eaves. Mica owned the whole thing, one of his earlier projects from before the area became gentrified. The men stepped out of a small elevator into a tiny foyer. The immortal led his friend inside and put a pot of coffee on. Donny wandered the space aimlessly. He had been here before.

"If you want to craft something, I know an artist who works with metals. She'll let us borrow her work space, and give you a good discount on the materials."

"Yeah, maybe. I mean, I dunno. I gotta think about it some more first. Okay?"

"No rush, just as long as you understand we can't do the ritual until the piece is ready," Mica reminded him, street noises from below filtering up through the half-circle windows.

Months passed since their conversation. Mica knew Donny hadn't forgotten about making a soul gem. His metalsmith friend said the young man came over after his workday and when he could on weekends, crafting his piece. The immortal only knew his protégé wanted it to be a surprise. Mica's memories of Donny sped up, then slowed down as if someone was searching a reel of film or an old DVD.

"So, um, here it is." Donny's voice was rough with suppressed nerves. He made a "ta-da" gesture with his hands.

The two men stood on a stained concrete floor, to one side of the metalworker's space. Around the perimeter of the room, different types of raw and found material had been stacked neatly. A lingering smell of propane hung in the air. For once, the shop lights blazed bright, instead of being turned down. Mica prowled around the object, inspecting the welds. The piece was crudely crafted, an amateur attempt. Finally, he straightened up and smiled and clasped his protégé on the shoulder.

"It's a fine piece, and a worthy endeavor."

Donny let out the breath he had been holding, a sheepish yet proud smile breaking across his face. "I know it's not the best, and kinda hard to make out what it is."

Mica shook his head. "That matters not; only the amount of time and effort which went into it."

The young man nodded. "So . . . when can we finish it? The . . . you know . . ."

"I have to gather the ritual mixture first. While I do, you may choose another immortal besides myself to witness the ceremony if you want."

"Naw." Donny shuffled his feet, face going red. "I don't know any other, besides your brother, I mean, and Eron."

"It can't hurt to ask," Mica mildly replied, gesturing for Donny to take his soul gem with him.

The young man picked it up reverently. It was meant to

look like a futuristic racing bike, done in various metals. Those who merely glanced would only think it a haphazard piece, poorly made.

After a while, Mica lost his grasp on his thoughts. They receded from his mind. The once-immortal found himself floating in a pool of honey. Dimly in a recess of his brain, he knew that wasn't right. From nowhere in particular, a ribbon of crimson cut a lazy path through. He watched as it swirled and blended, turning the warm color a darker shade. The man closed his eyes, took a deep breath in, held it, and sank beneath the surface.

"Mica." The siren croon was back, cutting through the thick liquid. "Mica. Wake up. Dream time is over."

A familiar male voice came to his ears as if muffled with cotton. "What did you do to him? You weren't supposed to make him worse. Did you even get it?"

"Mica!" The siren became a shrieking harpy.

The man opened his eyes, not realizing he had shut them. He looked at the two faces peering at him as he licked his lips. His mouth had a strange taste to it. Had he bitten the inside of his cheek? He tasted musty copper, dank air, and decay. The last made him gag, which turned into more coughing.

When he felt he wasn't going to puke, Mica realized the persistent pains in his chest were dulled, and it wasn't quite a struggle to breathe.

"What the hell did you assholes do to me?" the mortal rasped out.

"I had to give you some more medicine. Your cough became worse. If it tastes bad, I'll speak with the woman who made it and ask for a fresh batch," Illyria lied.

Eron poked his tongue into the side of his cheek, striving to keep a neutral expression. Behind them, a knock sounded on the door. The person entered as bidden. The slave, Willeg, was back.

"We'll leave you to rest. And Mica, for your brother's sake, let my slaves and me take care of you until you're healed." Illyria stepped away from the bed, taking her leave.

Eron hesitated. "Seriously. Try." He turned, walking out of the room, closing the door behind him.

Illyria stepped from the shadows as the wood gently

thumped shut. "I know what you need to look for."

"Great. Now to plan when we're going to do this. Why did you give him a taste of your blood?"

"To better insure he forgets what he told us. That he lets himself be taken care of so he heals," she smoothly replied.

37

CHAPTER FIVE

Eron felt exhilaration flow through his veins, even as he kept his arms clasped tight about Illyria's waist. He blinked the sting of tears out of his eyes from the biting wind. Below them, the earth lay in a darkness it hadn't known since before the start of the Industrial Revolution. He had only just awoken from his brief nap, cradled against her body as they flew. They descended in a rush of wind and disturbed sand.

The bulk of the mountain range rose before them. Behind, what had once been grasslands was a desert. The clear air let constellations be seen in all their bright glory, the sand and rock already cool beneath their boots.

"This would be so much easier in daylight."

"Joined Mica in his quest to see me dead, have you?" she replied.

Eron snorted. "I'm practically blind. I thought with my directions you would set us down closer."

"I have come as close as I am able, having never been to the place. We are on the remains of a road. I am hoping you will be able to tell if it is the correct one."

Once, the land at the base of the mountain range had held a small village. The people, by and large, herded goats. A few tended small farms, laboriously keeping them watered, either by a system of canals, or by toting jars of the precious liquid drawn from a small tributary of the great river to the west. In the fading light, nothing but sand, piles and hills of it, could be seen. The remains of the village were buried beneath its shifting bulk. The immortal unslung his pack and untied one of the torches he had strapped to the bottom of it. Next he took flint and stone, working on getting it lit. Once the spark caught and burned bright, he replaced the pack. In spite of his directions, age and the elements had worn away many of the markers which had dotted the ancient road, traces of which could only be seen because many hands had labored to chip it out of the mountain side. He had to search long and hard to find any remains of the stone markers.

"Help me look for three infinity rings entwined," Eron commanded.

He did not know how long they searched before her voice softly called out, "What about bones?"

The immortal came over, holding the torch up in an effort to let more light spread over her find. Behind a rock declivity was a jumble of human skulls and other bones along with the faded remains of paint. They finally found a nub of rock which might have once been carved. Beside it was a jumble of rocks of various sizes that had faint marks on them. It was hard to tell if they were natural, or man-made. He started walking up the road, knowing she was behind him.

In some spots, they had to clamber over fallen rock, or jump across gaps. A few times Illyria had to fly them across wide sections of the roadway, which was missing, having crumbled into rock slides. They continued in silence, the air slowly becoming colder as night wore on. After about a half hour, the road ended in a flat spot of rock-covered debris. The light from Eron's torch let the two seekers discover the stones comprised of petrified metal. On the far side, twin pillars with the immortal sigil carved into them announced the presence of a path. They crossed the distance and started upward. Another half-hour walk brought them to the first in a series of rock-cut steps leading up to a small ledge. The centers were nearly worn away from centuries of use, so they had to use the edges. Once on the ledge, Eron paused to catch his breath and gaze out over the darkened land below. The wind blew cold.

He fancied he could hear screams of terror, the whinny of horses, the pounding of hooves and the clang of metal from raiders, on the wind. If he closed his eyes, the scene would spring to life behind his lids, along with the smell of sweat from man and horse, mixed with the coppery scent of spilled blood. Eron would not let himself be dragged into his memories of when he was mortal.

"Is anyone up there?" he asked Illyria, jerking his chin

toward a bulge in the mountain that squatted like a wart on a face.

After a moment she replied, "I cannot tell. All is blank, quiet. If any still live, they could be sleeping."

Or dead. The stray thought flitted through his mind, much like the bats above them. Eron turned and continued the climb after lighting another torch off the dying remains of the first. The stairs led into a tunnel with another ten-minute climb, letting out on the first of a series of plateaus. Once grass, scrub brush, and trees had grown to be eaten by the goats the order had kept. Now, it was barren and bleak. They continued on, past remains of raised beds where vegetables and fruit had been coaxed out of the thin, rocky soil, and watered from now crumbling, dry stone wells. When the night was half gone, the two seekers reached the last of the stairs. Eron held his torch up, knowing it was useless. The wind blew harder, sounding like the moans of the dying, making the flame dance and splutter.

He took in a deep breath and began his ascent. Eron looked up at the front of the motherhouse. Its carvings had almost worn smooth in some spots. The large door had dried out, the wood bleached white from the sun, and the iron rusted and flaking. He pushed gently, the bottom of the door scraping across stone, crumbling as it did.

"Hello?" the immortal called out for form's sake. "Is anyone here?" His voice reverberated in the silence. The order would never let the doors fall into such disrepair unless there were too few remaining to replace or repair them.

Illyria stepped up behind him, scanning for blank spots, finding none. "I think perhaps they are all gone."

He closed his eyes wearily for a moment before opening them back up. "Once my kind built this place, it never has, to my knowledge, been left empty. Come on."

He led the way farther inside, the torchlight showing trash, decay, and the remains of modern civilization. The air hung heavy and still, with a musty odor. Eron slowly explored the public rooms, Illyria by his side. The area showed signs of animal use. Even the dormitories were devoid of human remains. What had once been personal belongings were left behind, making it hard to say if raiders or elements had created the mess. The two immortals spent the few remaining hours of nighttime prowling the extensive buildings, looking for survivors. Eventually, Eron led them both back to the entrance hall.

"Sun will be up soon. Will you promise me you won't explore if you wake before I do?"

"As you wish."

* * *

Eron woke to blinding sunlight streaming in through the portals where window glass had once been. Mostly the entire entrance hall was bathed in a golden glow. He didn't see Illyria, and wondered where she had hidden herself to keep from burning in the sun's rays.

"Where did you all go? My brothers and sisters," he muttered to himself as he explored farther than last night.

There had been a mix of immortals and trusted humans, some of whom would undergo initiation, who had lived here. Everything had been left behind. Eron began to search more systematically. It was late afternoon by the time he finished, and the immortal concluded the motherhouse had been abandoned. Until he entered the outer chambers to the Cave of Soul Gems.

Bones, clothing, and mummified parts lay scattered about; a few bodies had scraps of skin and muscle still clinging.

"What the hell?" Eron scowled in rage. "I never heard about a fight taking place here."

He walked around the remains, sun shining through cracked, dusty plastic domes in the ceiling. The immortal pushed open another pair of doors, and strode past more bones and scraps of cloth. It was impossible to tell who had been human, and who had been immortals. On one wall, graffiti had been spray-painted over scenes of the Rituals of Becoming and Undoing: a large wolf's head in profile, snarling and showing teeth, the three banded infinity rings a collar about the stump of its neck.

A string of curses slipped past his lips and Eron punched the wall, relishing the pain that came as his bones broke.

"Damn Immortal Wolves! Where are you now? Huh?" he screamed into the silence, listening to his voice echo. "Who killed you? Or are you hiding? You fucking cowards!"

The more he stared at it, the more it seemed the graffiti started to glow and become a living thing. The head turned and snapped its jaws at him. A blinding flash of light seared his eyes, along with lances of pain. Eron slammed into the wall behind him as a flashback engulfed him.

* * *

The immortal sat tied to a chair, flesh burning and aching from the beating he had taken, blood trickling and staining his clothes and the floor. The door to his left opened, and booted feet approached, stopping before his hanging head. Eron felt a hand grab hold of his hair and yank his head up. He stared through swollen eyes at the person before him.

"Five thousand years and you still can't train your soldiers in how to beat a person properly," slipped from his split lips.

The man holding his head up laughed, letting go of his captive's hair. Eron kept his eyes on his old friend and general. When he could stop his mirth, the man spoke. "You don't think I'd let the seasoned troops have the first go at you, did you? You've gone soft—forgotten the lessons you used to beat into us, Abi Dari."

"As have you. Time was you'd have killed me since I'm a useless, pathetic shell of what I once was, Telal."

"I might still, old man. "

"What stays your hand?" Eron asked, knowing his former general, whom he had raised to kingship, all too well.

"Power of a kind we never had." A mad light seemed to shine in the man's eyes.

"We were the Alal. Who had more power than us? Did I not give you the secret to life eternal? Did I not give you my crown? My kingdom? My wealth, in thanks for all your service?" Eron asked.

"Only because you knew if you didn't, I would defeat you, send you to your Final Death," Telal stated, voice tinged with resentment. "The day you abdicated your place to me was the day you became less than worthy."

"If you're not going to kill me now, what are you wanting? As you have noted, I am nothing," Eron replied.

"I need the help of my sarrum, the old one, the one you used to be," Telal said, his manic grin morphing into a serious mien. "There is a child, an eternal one, who possesses powers greater than Ummum. He believes I do his bidding, when it is the other way around."

The laughter escaped; Eron couldn't help himself. Even when his old friend snarled and beat him near death he kept laughing between his grunts of pain. He only stopped laughing when it interfered with breathing. The immortal lay on his back, still strapped to the chair as his old friend explained his plan to him. When he was done, Eron realized the betrayal of their kind would eclipse all the evil he had done in his past. He remembered the glorious rush of being worshipped as a god. He hadn't the taste for it now, but if he didn't pretend to, there would be no way he could protect those he cared about, much less his own life.

"If I agree to this, Telal, what will I be? What will you have me do?" Eron asked.

"You will be our sarrum again. We will be reborn as Immortal Wolves. We will cull the weak and the unworthy, and their eternal lives will help the wizard. They will tremble in fear," Telal stated.

"Well, if refusal means my Final Death, then I will be sarrum again."

* * *

Eron kicked open the last set of doors in rage, a grim smile tugging the corners of his mouth up as they crashed against the tunnel walls. He lit a torch and strode forward. The tunnel wound its way deeper into the mountain. He came to the point where the Guardians should have been.

"I, Eron, the Destroyer of Nations, come in peace. I wish to remove the soul gem belonging to Donny. Please grant me entrance." He spoke the phrase automatically and waited.

Nothing. No wash of acceptance or feeling of rejection. He put a foot forward and waited and when nothing happened, he stepped farther inside. No Guardians rushed to impede his progress; it seemed they really were gone. Eron wondered if Colin had realized what he was doing when he'd called the Guardians forth to help his brother from being taken by the demon Nicky had trapped. His rage became tinged with panic and worry. Before the Cave of Soul Gems and Guardians, and the motherhouse, all immortals hid their gems as they saw fit. Eron realized the place was no longer a safe and secure spot for the immortals' trapped souls.

Sweat dripped from his brow, even though the temperature in the cave held at a steady, pleasant sixty-five degrees. Niches, carved into the stone from floor to ceiling, were empty. He remembered the last time he had cause to visit before he had gotten tangled up in Telal's schemes. Each and every one had been full, so that those who lived here worked on carving another cavern out.

* * *

The noonday sun beat down upon the sand and rock. Irrigation canals ran from a small tributary river, which were used to water the fields. Mud brick huts stood in a cluster, a small village. Most of the work was still done with tools their ancestors would recognize, and animals. There were a few modern vehicles of indeterminate age, mostly held together with rust and baling twine. The jeep Eron traveled in left a long trail of dust and sand behind as it bounced and jounced across the landscape. A short main road, filled with potholes, went directly through the center of the village. The smells of mud and manure assaulted Eron's nose as he drove through and toward the motherhouse's road.

Because of the tumultuous history of the area, the road leading to the compound had to masquerade as something more. One branch led up and over, trailing off into a single-vehicle-wide path. The other ended at what appeared to be a lookout point and a shallow cave. To one side was a goat path.

Eron carefully steered the jeep into the cave and gently bumped the back wall. He applied some pressure, and the blackness gave way, forming a metal plate he could drive across. Half an hour later, he was parking and walking the rest of the way up. The stone face was being washed, the door and hinges being oiled and polished.

The people working nodded respectfully to him, and paused to let him pass inside. His friend was hanging out in the entrance hall, talking with those who served the immortals. He broke off his conversation to greet his friend, and led him up to one of the guest rooms.

After a quick wash up to get the dust and sand off, and a fresh change of clothes, he met Mica's brother back at the entrance hall. They quietly conversed as they walked toward the most heavily guarded area in the motherhouse.

"How many of us are there?" Eron asked Colin.

"A little more than four million," he answered proudly, sweeping one hand out before him. "As you can see, we have to expand, even with the reuse of niches from those who have gone to their Final Deaths."

"Even with a world population of six billion, we are growing steadily. Perhaps too much so," Eron commented as they passed the men and women working determinedly with pickaxes and other tools.

Rock dust filled the air, and his guide hurried to lead them past, deeper toward the very first cavern.

"Some of the members would agree with you. I have heard talk of a splinter group breaking off. They call themselves the Immortal Wolves. Problem is, we don't know who is a wolf for certain and who isn't."

"But surely the Guardians . . ." He fished for more information.

"Eron, you know as well as I that anyone can come and go freely. We are not here to limit how many soul gems they take out. If they know the names of the immortal(s), and are allowed passage, well." He shrugged. "We ask for them to leave a record of who they have come for, but it is voluntary. We tried to enforce our brethren before to comply but that led to greater attacks and rebellion. So we went back to the old system."

They exited the series of interconnected caves, walking back toward the main area. Colin opened a door into a warmly appointed room and let Eron enter before him. The scents of old parchment, wax, and leather lingered. A few men and women in their early twenties to late thirties sat at desks, working to repair and preserve old records. They barely looked up as the two men passed by them. Eron waited while his friend unlocked another door at the back of the room. It opened onto a long hallway lined with doors.

"Storage areas for the records. I want to try and put everything on computers. Catalog it, photograph it, cross-references," Colin said as he locked the door behind them and led Eron back toward his small office.

The desk was stacked with papers and books, even old photographs. The immortal cleared a chair off so his friend could sit, continuing to talk as he did so.

"I figure, we place the main servers in a secure spot at one of the auxiliary houses. We can have a small desktop unit that can be run off of the existing solar power grid. There's a satellite uplink which will let me update the records. That would be an ongoing, recurrent cost."

Eron listened to Colin's excited voice rattle on, amazed his friend had no idea of the part he would play in the immortal's history. He listened intently, nodding in all the right places. Eron almost felt bad for what he was about to do, but then he remembered how many of them there were, and knew the ranks would only grow if something weren't done about it.

* * *

The torch flickered as Eron climbed iron steps, his boots ringing on the metal and along the catwalks. Mica had told him where Donny's gem rested. The light flickered inside an empty space.

"Shit!" The immortal swore. "Maybe he didn't remember the spot correctly. Or I'm not in the right place."

Eron fished the piece of parchment out of his pocket Mica had written the location of the gem on along with a small, hand-drawn map. He carefully checked the map and his location over. Nope, he was in the right place. There was even the young man's name crudely carved into the stone beneath the niche.

"What the fuck?" Tension and fear ratcheted inside him. He had to force himself to remain calm. Perhaps his old general had sent someone to retrieve the boy's gem.

The immortal looked in the surrounding niches, empty save for dust and insect carcasses. He turned and strode along the walkways, letting the torch light fall inside the spaces as he passed. Nothing. Lots and lots of it. It took several minutes to reach the area he remembered Cassiopeia had placed her gem at. Empty. Had Telal managed to find her? And ended her life? Or had she asked someone she trusted to give her the Final Death?

He rested his forehead briefly against the stone, fingers gripping the edge of the niche. "You were the third. The mother. Did you get tired of life? Did you ask an old friend and protégé? Or did you place your trust in the wrong person?"

Eron would never know now. He had enslaved her once, treated her so cruelly she'd tried to kill him just to escape. She had eventually tricked him into gaining her freedom, and started an army to end him.

"Yet here I am. And you are gone. The only other person who shared those ancient times with me. Perhaps you are the lucky one after all. The smartest of us in the end." He pressed a kiss to the carving of her name in remembrance.

Before he left, the immortal detoured to the spot where Telal had placed his gem. The niche was empty. A grim, satisfied smile curled the corners of his mouth up. He had thought that had been a dream, another piece of the nightmare part he had played. The proof was before him. He had ended the man.

* * *

"Eron," the voice whispered in the dry darkness.

The immortal awoke with a start on the remains of a wooden bench. Honey gold eyes hovered near him.

"I'm sorry."

He felt her icy hands close around one of his and squeeze gently as her eyes came to his level. As his eyesight adjusted to the moonlight streaming in, he saw she crouched next to him.

"Immortal Wolves." He spat. "Do you remember them

now? Our role in it?"

She blinked, still holding his hand as the fire of her eyes came and went. "In my dreams, my nightmares, as I lay resting since we arrived here. Are we to fight over what we have done? What we have caused?"

Eron didn't reply to her questions. "Ash remains in the spot Mica placed his gem. Colin's and mine are still there. The Guardians . . ." He swallowed his anger back. "Gone. And almost all of my brother and sister immortals. I only saw a handful of soul gems left. I didn't realize how great the destruction, how many were used for the experiments after we had been cursed." He flung his right hand out to encompass the semi-dark room. Ash was a thin film on the floor and piled up in drifts in corners. Fragments and finely ground grit crunched underfoot from where clay and stone tablets had been pulverized. The hallway which had once led to the storage rooms showed the remains of a great conflagration which had scorched the whole length of it black. Ragged holes in the walls spoke of explosions.

"I saw, bits of it. Donny's gem?"

"Gone."

"Perhaps it was moved, re-hidden when your kin realized what was happening?"

"The bodies of those who once lived here were all in a central location, as if herded there. No unnecessary destruction beyond everyone's soul gems and what was needed for the records."

"Then all this was in vain? If his gem is not here, it is possible he has been laid to rest." She spoke what she meant to be comforting words.

"I don't understand who else might have known. All those who were there that night were cursed. I doubt the Fae would have concerned themselves with the remains of one they believed in the end had participated in the death of their king." The old habit of lying came easily.

Illyria remained silent, still crouched by him, holding his hand. Eron was surprised to find how much he cared about the destruction of his kin, even though it was at his hand and on his orders, and he was capable of shedding tears. He let the grief wash over him in long waves. It had never taken him long to mourn. His was intense but brief.

"How much night is left?"

"About half; do you want to go back now?"

Eron considered. He was immortal since the earliest recorded years of civilization. There had been long periods when he fell into a funk and despaired, even considered ending his life. It was one of the many reasons he had become an Immortal Wolf. It was time for a mass cleansing of humans, vampires, immortals, and whatever else might lurk on the edges. He regarded the woman before him; they had done their best to end humanity's downward spiral. Yet, everything clung and struggled to live, just as small and despicable as ever. They were all just filthy roaches.

"No." He shifted suddenly, bringing his free hand to where he could barely see the outlines of her head, and tangled his fingers in her hair. "No. I'm not leaving until it is finished. We'll find and remove what gems remain to another cave, hide them, and seal the place. Help me. Help me attempt to find where the warehouse was the night we were cursed. Help me make sure Donny is at peace, then we will go back and face Mica. Together. This is my price I ask from you: share your blood and power with me, take of mine in return. Let us continue what we started."

"As you wish," she replied.

CHAPTER SIX

Sydney woke alone—again—in Illyria's bed. A single, small oil lamp burned on a table near the middle of the room. He petulantly flung the covers off, not caring how cold the room was, and getting up, snatched on his robe. The earl walked across the icy wood floor to a drape-covered window, moving aside one panel. The sky was a liquid silver, the sun's rays struggling to break through the cloud cover.

He let the drape fall shut, and turning, walked over to the bell and rang it. It was several moments before a yawning slave answered the summons.

"Food, drink, and water to wash with," Sydney tersely commanded. "My usual. And have my horse made ready."

The slave bowed and quickly left. Chadrick paced back and forth, forming in his mind what he wanted to say to his lover when she returned. Where was she? What was taking her so long? Why did she have to take her former slave with her?

None of those questions looked to be answered by the time his requests arrived. He'd never anticipated he could again ache inside with longing. Sydney had thought all capacity to love had been lost to him with Alise's passing. Within three-quarters of an hour, he was swinging into the saddle of his mare and trotting across the bridge to the sheriff's office. He stabled and cared for his horse himself. Sydney let himself inside the kitchen to find the cook already working on breakfast. The man was an older, peg-legged ex-sailor. He grunted a hello as he went about his work.

The earl passed through, farther into the building and to the cramped office he shared with Saizar. The night porter had remembered to light a fire in the grate, and an oil lamp. His lordship picked up a taper, lit it from an existing flame, and proceeded to light the other lamps. The whole building shook from an especially forceful gust of wind, whistling through the countless cracks and holes, blowing out his taper. Snow drifted inside on the air's wake, coating everything. A rumbling of voices, curses, and feet overhead let him know the men were awake.

He was not in the office long before the night porter dashed inside, sheaves of parchment and clay tablets clutched in his hands. The cook must have taken a moment to warn the young teen.

"M-m-m-morning, s-s-s-sir," he stuttered, thrusting both hands out to the earl, who sighed to himself.

"Thank you, Ben." He took the proffered mess, setting it down on the desktop. "If there is nothing to report, you can go eat and sleep now. Consider yourself off duty."

The teen jerked his upper body down, then up, and clumped excitedly toward the dining hall. A faint tremor shook the walls, and the pounding of booted feet let him know the men had dressed and were coming downstairs. Chadrick sat down, quickly sorting the mess before him, and began to read through it all, hoping to finish by the time the men would be ready to train.

* * *

The lawmen were running around the training yard, carrying logs upon their backs, when the day porter appeared in the doorway to the sheriff's barracks with a middle-aged man behind him. Sydney didn't stop calling out encouragement as the men ran, but only watched as Saizar walked over to speak with the person. After a few moments, he indicated he needed the earl. Sydney bawled out for the men to keep running as he joined the two men.

"My lord, this man is from a small, nearby village." Saizar introduced them. "He takes care of part of the king's forest."

"M'lord." The man bowed.

"What can we help you with?" the earl asked.

"Well, I was out in the forest as I am most days, and I happened to overhear a group of men. There sounded to be four or five of them, just from the voices I heard. They were hunting illegally, and planning raids on the villages nearby. I knew I couldn't take them all on by myself, so I went back to get some help. We tried to track the men, but lost the trail when it started snowing." He shifted uneasily, as if expecting to be blamed for failure.

"Continue," Sydney gestured.

"So, after the storm let up, we tried searching the surrounding countryside for traces of their camp. We did find it, in an abandoned serf's croft, only they weren't there at the time. We returned to our village, only to find that the men must have been waiting for us to leave, as the place had been raided." The forester clenched his hands, breathing heavily. After he got his emotions under control, he continued.

"Ours is a small village, just a dozen crofts. The bastards had set fire to everything. My son," he sniffled, then spat a glob of phlegm upon the ground. "My ten-year-old son was gutted. Our young women were missing, the rest of the people killed. You must send men after them!" He finished his tale with an enraged demand.

"Where is your village?" Sydney asked.

The man gave them directions before trudging off, back to the remains of his home.

"I doubt there is much we can do," Saizar began after the person left. "But it would be helpful for the men to ride out and learn what little there is from what remains."

"Agreed," Sydney replied. "We should probably travel to the other surrounding villages. They may need help or warned of the danger."

"I will get the men and horses ready. If you will see to our supplies?" Saizar asked and received confirmation.

* * *

The sheriff and his men followed the broken path made through the snow drifts to reach the small village. They could see and smell the smoke from fires before the destroyed crofts came into view. Carrion birds had already arrived, and they flew up from the bodies of slaughtered animals, calling out their displeasure at being interrupted in the midst of their feast.

The scent of blood and guts hung heavy on the crisp air. One of the villagers could be seen trying to save the meat before it spoiled or was consumed by birds. The lane ended at a churned piece of mud-, blood-, and snow-covered ground before a small church. It too bore testament to having been burned, but the fire had since gone out. Two rows of bodies wrapped in coarse linen lay before the entrance. As the horses clopped forward, throwing up ice and mud balls, a rumble sounded. Off to the left of the men, one of the stone crofts tumbled down, the mortar no match for the heat of the flames that had engulfed it. Saizar called out for his men to halt. The few village men who had survived looked up warily from what they were doing. Soot streaked their faces and clung to threadbare clothes. Many of the men sported injuries. They regarded the lawmen in anger.

"Hello. I am Saizar, sheriff of Macinas. These are my men, and Earl Sydney. Your forester sent word to me of the attack. We are here to lend what aid we can, and learn more of what took place."

A few of the villagers ignored him and continued with their scavenging work. One spat and another stomped over, shouting angrily as he came.

"Bastards! Go back to your cozy town! A pox on you and that disease-ridden, whoreson king!"

Saizar heard the low snicker a few of his men gave and only shook his head at them. "Will one of you please tell me how to find the forester?"

Another torrent of abuse came from the angry villager. It didn't last long before they saw the forester himself come huffing out of the tree line, following a well-trod path. He hailed the sheriff's party and came up to them.

"Sorry. Dan lost the most. Both his daughters were taken in the raid, and the rest of his family slaughtered."

"A hard thing for any man to bear," Saizar replied. "Will one of your men take some of my men to the last spot you found evidence of the raiding party?"

The forester's head bobbed and he motioned to one of the men who had ignored them. He came over reluctantly.

"This is Ned. Ned, the sheriff wants to be shown the croft we found that the raiders had used."

"Don't see what good it'll do. If our men couldn't find 'em, what makes you so certain they will?"

The sheriff spoke. "We will be better able to dedicate more time and effort to the search. If you will, take four of my men with you. They will need to know every scrap of information you can recall about the raiders."

He turned in his saddle and called out the names of those he wanted to go, one of whom included a tracker turned slave before being sold to the sheriff's office. The small party had been told what to do beforehand, so they each took the lead rope of an extra pack mule. The men and mounts moved off into the forest, the dark gloominess quickly swallowing them.

"If you will be so kind," Chadrick addressed the forester, "what and which direction are the nearest villages to yours?"

"My lord." The man bowed, and pointed toward a narrow road, barely wide enough for a cart, which ran past the church and into the forest. "If you follow that road, it will take you to the next village. From there, they can tell you of any more nearby."

"Thank you," the earl replied.

Saizar called out for two of the men to stay behind with the earl while the rest were to follow him. The forester, along with some of the other men who had finally stopped work and drifted over, watched as the lawmen split. All but one of the remaining pack mules went with the sheriff and his group. They clopped off down the road. The forester looked avidly at the nobleman and the two lawmen who'd elected to stay behind. His amazement grew as the men swung out of their saddles.

"Have you a name, sir?" the earl inquired of the man before him.

"Yes, my lord. William Stoutoak."

"As the ground is too hard to dig, what have you in mind for your dead?"

"We have come to the agreement we will burn them. Two of our men are gathering more wood as we speak," William replied.

"We will stay and help with your task. I do not know what your food or shelter situation is. If you are amenable, the palace will shelter, feed, and provide clothing for anyone who stays there," Chadrick informed the man.

The forester's face became wooden at those last words. "I

will let the survivors know of the king's generosity. Thank you."

"Guts," Sydney turned to the former butcher, "help to see what can be saved from the slaughtered animals. It is cold enough to keep the meat frozen. Samson, help with gathering wood for the pyre."

The two men bowed and started off to their appointed tasks. William had already trudged out of sight behind one of the smoking crofts. Sydney led the horses underneath a pine branch, and got them settled before helping.

* * *

The next morning dawned cold and gray. Sydney and his men woke with the remaining members of the village in the church. Fur and wool blankets crackled with ice as they stood. Bones ached from the cold which had seeped up from the stones as they slept, even with using pine branches and straw as bedding. The lingering stench of smoke mingled with scents of horse and dung. The lawmen ate a cold breakfast of jerky and hard biscuits as they went about the task of feeding, watering, and grooming their mounts. The village men had already left the church to check on the funeral pyre.

Sydney and his men, leading their horses, stepped out into an icy morning. Behind the mountains, dark clouds could be seen stacking up as if something held them back. There would be more snow, possibly a blizzard, come nightfall. The funeral pyre had burned out. Some of the men used crude rakes and shovels to scoop up the ash and deposit it into any unbroken clay pot they could scavenge. One man moved among the burnt out crofts, trying to retrieve hidden food stores from dirt cellars. By the amount of swearing, he was not having much luck.

Guts checked on the remains of the animals he had been able to help save. They were all frozen solid, dangling from branches of a big oak, macabre ornaments. All the men moved quickly; a sense of urgency prevailed as the lowering clouds continued to build up. What had started as a breeze slowly grew stronger as the day advanced.

By midmorning, the village men, with the exception of Dan

and a few others, had decided to gather what little was left to them and start toward town and the palace. Their eyes still shone with a mixture of grief, rage, and some resignation. Sydney wished them luck, watching as they trudged out of view, pulling a sled, hastily cobbled together and piled with frozen animal carcasses, behind them.

The earl and his men set their horses to trotting on the road the rest of their party had taken. The wind reminded them of beasts, roaring in agony, and it blew hard, as if trying to stop their forward progress. The men pressed on, and by nightfall managed to reach the next village. A young boy, set on guard to look for them, brought the exhausted men and horses through the crude defenses to a tiny tavern. After caring for their mounts, the men tromped inside the tavern where a hot meal awaited them. The place was crowded, despite the howling wind, swirling snow, and stinging needles of ice outside.

Saizar and the lawmen were not there, having moved on to the next small village. An elder, bent almost in half with age and leaning on a staff for support even though he sat, spoke for everyone.

"Your sheriff has confirmed the rumors we've all been hearing these past months. So a foreign duchess has defeated Lord Nicky." He paused to spit on the floor at the name, as did the rest of the villagers. "I know the fat asshole on the throne doesn't care about us beyond his precious taxes. So it has to be the woman who's never met us, his latest toy, who sends us help."

"She has already proven herself to be a worthy successor to the title," Sydney assured the gathered assemblage. He briefly outlined what she was doing.

"Time will tell," the elder replied. Grumbles followed his statement. "As you saw from our defenses, the bandits have made attempts to raid our village. Only a few of the groups were made up of people we don't know. Most of those who raid do so because of that bastard Nicky and the old sheriff, with their ruthless tax collections and unjust laws."

"I will carry your complaints to the new advisor. If there is nothing we can help you with immediately, we will leave in the morning," the earl assured the people. After a few more bits of conversation, the lawmen were shown to a room for the night.

CHAPTER SEVEN

Lady Sally sat in her room, sobbing. She felt an outcast amid her own friends. She, who had once been their leader. After the events with Lord Nicky the night of the Harvest Festival, few of her friends wanted to visit. Sally thought at first they meant to offer her solace, but it was soon made clear they only thought of her as a novelty. In a fit of anger, the young woman had quarreled with the few girls whose parents still allowed them to associate with her. Thus, she found herself housebound and friendless. To add to her misery, her father presented Sally with a list of suitors for her to choose from. How was she expected to pick a husband from the worthless candidates her father claimed were the only ones available? Her parent wasn't even going to stay for the interviews; he was too busy playing lawman, helping peasants. Peasants! It was disgraceful, especially since she needed his help more than they.

She wished Dennala had been allowed to remain her minder, but the slave had entered banishment with her mistress. She may have been across the yard with her mother in the dowager cottage, but for Sally's purposes, it seemed farther away.

The young woman walked to her privy chamber, and tried to repair the damage her tears had done before she opened the door to her chamber. The guard outside stood blocking the opening.

"Yes, m'lady?"

"I need a request sent to my mother, asking her to please visit me on the matter of my suitors."

"Yes, m'lady. I will send a page. Will that be all?"

She hesitated, then shook her head and disappeared back inside her room. She wandered over to the window; snow swirled outside, occasionally hiding the view. If only she knew where Lord Nicky was, she would run to him. She didn't believe the gossips and rumors of his disgrace which said he was a traitor and had left the country.

* * *

Lady Sally sat primly in the receiving room, wearing her second-best day dress, a somber navy wool with starched white collar and cuffs. Her hair was in a single braid, coiled at the back of her head in a bun. A bustle from the hall, and sounds of a sharp voice heralded the arrival of her mother. Lady Elizabeth entered the room at the same time as a kitchen slave bearing a tray of food and drinks. The countess was in one of her new, shapeless sack gowns, with a length of white linen wrapped around her head and neck. It made the stark oval of her face stand out more. Lines of age carved deeply upon her skin, and her eyes seemed to have sunk in their orbits.

"Mother, thank you for coming." The young woman stood and curtsied to her parent.

The elder woman swept a glance over the offerings suspiciously, her eyes chilly as the weather outside. "Bribery? It seems your father's efforts at finding you a proper teacher leave much to be desired."

Sally bit her lip to keep the angry retort from slipping out while her cheeks reddened. "I only thought to make your visit more pleasant, Mother."

A cold eye pierced her daughter, who resided into silence. Elizabeth seated herself and flicked her fingers at the waiting slave. The girl poured a goblet of spiced wine and placed some victuals on a plate before setting both on a small side table. Sally reseated herself, folding her hands demurely on her lap.

"What is it you want, Sally?" came the curt demand as the countess removed her thin white deerskin gloves. She left them lying in her lap as she picked up the goblet and sipped.

"My suitors . . ."

"What of them? If they are not to your liking, you have only your disgraceful behavior to blame. I do hope you have not dragged me out into the abominable coldness on a petty fantasy."

Sally sat, stunned at the uncaring tone. Her bottom lip quivered, and tears welled up in her eyes. She quickly brushed them away; her mother despised scenes.

"Father and Martin insist I cannot marry Lord Nicky. I fail to see why not. Why can't the king command him to take me as his wife?"

Elizabeth's nostrils flared in annoyance, and her voice came out sharper than normal. "Lord Nicky has been declared a traitor to the crown, his crimes so monstrous they have been forbidden to be spoken of. He has fled the kingdom. Your unfortunate liaison with him makes you . . . suspect. If it weren't for your father's and my intervention, you would have become a royal prisoner—a fate which would not have ended kindly. "

"But . . . but—" The tears she had been fighting back spilled out.

"Kindly stop sniveling. I cannot abide overly emotional scenes."

"What am I to do? Have you seen the list of prospects Father has for me? I can't marry one of them!"

Lady Elizabeth took a sip of her drink, and coolly regarded her daughter over the rim of her goblet. Her unfaithful husband had graciously consented to give her a copy of the list. She despised him for humiliating her, for the shame and degradation he continually brought to their family by openly flaunting his affair with that wretched duchess. But, she was forced to admit, he had done his best to find suitable candidates for their daughter. Even if that meant a merchant's son or two populated the list.

Sally quietly cried into an embroidered linen square. It had been a month since she had been with the former advisor. Since then, her moon-flow had come. The physician who was tasked with her health declared she was not pregnant. His words had sent hatred for him throughout Sally's being. His words meant there were no obstacles to her being married by winters end.

"I do not see the problem with your father's list. I suggest you pick the least onerous out of the bunch. And Sally, do not think by marrying, you will be free to engage in extramarital affairs as your father does. Should you disregard my advice, I will disown you."

"Mother!"

"I have nothing more to say."

"But . . . but—"

"No, Sally."

"Can—can you at least give me your opinion on which one you think best?"

Elizabeth's mouth thinned as she glanced at one of the causes of her daughter's pain. The scroll sat between them, half a dozen names on the list. She picked it up, unrolled it, and read over the information yet again.

One man she considered too old for the simple reason when he died, her daughter would be free of any guiding hand. A second man she rejected as too young; he would not be able to tame Sally's wayward tendencies. That left four men, which included a fairly well-off merchant, a member of the royal guard, a second son of a second earl, and lastly, the fifth son of a baron with a small manor and lands.

She debated the merits of each man, listed next to their names by her husband's steward. Elizabeth handed the scroll over to her daughter with her recommendation.

Sally's face, which had been hopeful up to that point, fell. Her upper lip curled in disdain.

"But Mother! He is merely a Mister! And—and—he lives in the countryside!"

"You asked my opinion, and I have given it." She turned to command the slave who still stood waiting quietly, head bowed and hands clasped before her. "Have my cloak and muff fetched immediately. I am taking my leave."

The slave bobbed a curtsey and hurried off. Sally let out a wail.

"But Mother!"

"Stop it! Stop it right now! It's time you grow up. You chose an action, now you must deal with the consequences."

Elizabeth bundled herself up for the short trek across the yard as her daughter continued her wailing. She left the mansion to the sounds of weeping and her own bitter thoughts.

Damn Chadrick for this mess. I will never consent to a divorce, no matter how many times he goes begging to the king. At least my other daughter is someplace where she cannot embarrass us.

* * *

Lady Sally sat sulking as Crystal arranged her hair. She was already dressed in a modestly cut gown, which was at least an improvement over the shapeless sacks her mother would have wanted her to wear. Her father still was not back from gallivanting around to useless, poor villages. Her maid brought her what rumors she could, which wasn't much. Displaced villagers from the outlying lands of the kingdom straggled in. They claimed empty or abandoned shops and homes. The nobles jockeyed for position of king's advisor, despite His Majesty's threats on the subject. The duchess, whom Sally blamed for every misfortune she currently endured, was still away. The last of her possible suitors was due to arrive this afternoon.

Once her slave finished with the plain hairstyle, she escorted her charge to the receiving room.

A different slave opened the door to admit both women. "Lady Sally," he announced to the skinny man shifting on the hard wooden couch.

She stared a moment in dismay; her body slave, Crystal, gave her a sharp poke, forcing her to enter. The man stood, wide-set eyes roving up and down her frame.

Sally stopped three feet away, and curtsied as protocol demanded while he bowed to her.

"Your ladyship, I am Baron Richard von Winesburg. It is an honor to meet you. The descriptions of you did not do you justice." His lips twitched.

She was horrified at his attempts to smile. It looked as if he were having spasms. *I cannot marry him.* "Thank you, my lord," she gritted out.

They both sat, she on another hard couch across from him. Crystal seated herself unobtrusively in a corner.

Lord Richard cleared his throat, his protuberant Adam's apple bobbing. She refused to speak, sitting and staring at him expressionlessly. The minutes ticked by as he opened his mouth and closed it several times, reminding her of a carp. Sally took careful inventory of his outfit. He was dressed in a winter fashion from seasons past. His dark hair showed signs of being hastily combed back into place. It didn't fully erase the marks a hat left. He wore thick-soled riding boots.

The sound of a door opening intruded on the otherwise silent room. A kitchen slave bearing a tray entered and set her burden down on a nearby side table. She then took one step back, lowered her head, and stood with hands clasped in front of her, waiting for instructions.

Sally started to scowl before catching a glare from her body slave. She forced her lips into a smile.

"Would you care for a drink of mulled wine? Or a bite to eat?" The young woman asked, as she had been instructed.

"Ah." The man gave a quick sideways glance to the offerings. "Yes, thank you. I should enjoy that immensely."

Lady Sally carefully poured a goblet full, handed it over with a linen serviette, and using the tongs provided, put a selection of meats and cheeses on a small plate before offering it to him.

She then served herself, thankful neither he nor she would be able to converse while eating.

To her horror, after a few mouthfuls, the baron began chattering. The sight of the half-masticated food left her slightly sick to her stomach.

She gave a delicate, imperceptible shudder at the man's poor manners.

"Your father, Lord Sydney, thinks we would make a good match."

Pieces of food dropped out while he talked, landing on his baggy gray pants.

"Is that so, my lord?" she murmured, keeping her eyes downcast so she would not have to witness him eating as she delicately nibbled and sipped.

"I have a small country estate to the west of town. It produces flax."

O, Great One! Not another dirt farmer. He probably has an ugly, small shack, with no comforts, Sally uncharitably thought. She remained silent.

It didn't seem Lord Richard noticed, or perhaps he took it as encouragement. Once he got started, he babbled endlessly of his days, and of what they entailed.

She sat with a tiny, frozen smile on her face, and occasionally nodded her head or made ambiguous noises.

Finally, the baron wound down. His face wore an eager-to-please mien. She would have gotten away with remaining silent until his last few words.

"After all, I think it an excellent partnership between us. You will be able to get away from the town and the gossips with their unsavory rumors. A few years, and the birth of some sons, and you'll be considered respectable again."

"Wha-wha-what?" she stuttered, dumbfounded at how brazenly he spoke of her disgrace.

He either ignored or didn't pick up on the clues of her dismay. "Yes. I mean, that is why we are here, is it not?" In his eagerness, he leaned close, causing her to pull back as much as the couch would allow.

"I admit, I had not considered taking a tainted woman as a bride."

She felt her face flush red, and her temper rise. How dare this ugly, skinny, country, no-account baron cast a slur upon her. Without pausing to think, Sally opened her mouth and let his lordship know exactly what she thought of him.

His eyes bulged in outrage, and he stood abruptly as her body slave scolded her from the corner.

"I did not come here expecting to be insulted, considering how precarious your situation is. I shall tender my regards to your father, and explain to him I have changed my mind."

He stormed from the room, snapping at the Sydney slaves to have his horse brought around, his final insult clearly heard by the seething girl and her slave. "I am not spending a minute more wooing a mannerless slut."

Sally leapt up from the couch, intending to charge out into the hallway and scream what a poor substitute for the advisor he would make. All the slaves present in the room sprang to action, grabbing her. While the young woman fought them and hurled imprecations. They bent her over the back of the couch while one of the male slaves set to guard her came into the room. He proceeded to whip his charge's buttocks with a willow branch.

* * *

Martin and the Sydney steward sat straight-backed at the dinner table, quietly conversing during the meal. Sally cried silently, tears streaming down her face as she carefully shifted, trying to find a spot which didn't hurt. Her buttocks felt as if they were on fire, and stung fiercely, making sitting still an agony.

She half dreaded, half anticipated, the lecture she was sure to receive afterward, confident her brother would understand her position. To her dismay, once they were seated in her father's office, she wasn't given a chance to explain. It was another humiliation as her brother listened to Crystal's report of the suitors. And her charge's behavior.

"Sally. I sympathize, but unless you plan on being a total outcast, you will have to choose one. Father seems to believe you understood perfectly what your punishment entailed. Baron von Winesburg was the last man who showed honorable intentions, and you gravely—and unforgivably—cast slurs upon him."

"It's not fair! I am older than you! Why should you be allowed to tell me what to do? Didn't you hear me? He lives—"

"Father doesn't care where he lives. Our laws support the men, no matter what their age may be. No, it isn't fair, but that's the way it is. Your life is to be devoted to your husband."

"You pig! I suppose you'll expect the same of your wife?" Sally shrieked.

Her brother sighed and shifted uncomfortably. He did not like this part of being an earl. "Sister, I expect when I marry, the lady will be a proper wife. Honestly, I don't know of many men who don't expect it."

His sister crossed her arms beneath her breasts and pouted. "I won't marry them! Not one! I'm an earl's daughter! None of them is worthy of my hand!"

"That may have been true had you remained pure, but you chose to lie with a man before being wedded. As a noble born, your worth is considerably diminished. Baron von Winesburg has already spread around town about your lack of manners, and how unsuitable you are."

"But Martin! He called me—"

"Out of the six suitors Father has been able to convince to take an interest in you, four have written to withdraw their suit. Do you know who that leaves? Two. Two suitors." Martin's sapphire eyes, so like their father's, pierced her own lighter blue.

"I don't care. Lord Nicky—"

"Sister, don't be a silly goose. He can't marry you. He is a traitor to the crown. If he attempts to return, he will be arrested and put to death immediately."

"No." Sally vigorously shook her head in the negative. "No. It's a lie! That duchess is lying! She thinks she's going to steal him from me! He said we were meant for each other!"

Martin sighed, wishing more fervently his father wasn't away on law-related business. She glared at him.

"Sally, you will not speak falsely of the duchess." He knew his father would not approve of his sister's accusations.

She uncrossed her arms, hands in fists as she leaned forward and screamed at her brother. "She ruined my life! And Father doesn't care because he can't stop rutting with her! Mother was right!"

The slap across both sides of her face came as a surprise. Her cheeks stung along with her buttocks.

Her brother stepped back, breathing hard, eyes glittering in anger.

A shocked, strangled sob escaped her clamped lips.

"Sally, it's true you are older than I by several years, but you are impudent and unwise. Most girls your age are already married, with families. Father will be further disappointed in you. As head of the household, you are forcing me to make choices I would rather not. But I will, because I am duty bound to do so. You will be remanded into the care of your slave. You will be sequestered from any visitors. Unless you have a preference, I shall write tonight to the suitor I think would best suit you and inform him of your acceptance of his proposal. I suggest you begin work on your trousseau immediately. You are dismissed." He rang a bell to summon slaves.

"What? Martin! I'm your sister! How can you be so mean?! I hate you! No! I won't! I won't!" Sally's shrieks echoed throughout the mansion as she was hauled to her room by the house slaves.

CHAPTER EIGHT

The lawmen rode into town on weary steeds. Behind them plodded a small crowd of starving villagers. Most only had the rags on their backs and a few guided animals as thin as they. A two-wheeled cart rattled and creaked at the rear. It held those too sick or elderly to make the journey without help.

As they made their way through the remains of Macinas, a male voice floated toward them on the semi-still air.

"Repent! Repent, I say! Sinners! The Death Lands wait for us. The Emperor of Death and his minions are eager to drag off those who turn from the Undying Lands. Who has brought this evil upon us? None other than the foreign harlot. The scarlet whore. The duchess. Her house is made of ravens. Birds of ill intent. Birds who feast on carrion." He stopped to take a nip from a jug at his feet before continuing.

"No, I say; no! And our king? He does nothing! He feasts and lies with his harem of whores. He has forgotten his people. He has left you to your misery and starvation. And what of the nobles? The merchants of wealth? They all have sold their souls to the Death Lands. They throw their scraps out into the streets, as if we are dogs. We are not. We are men, women, and children who have been spit upon and forgotten for too long. Come, join me so we may rid our town of such a pestilence. I have food and shelter for those who will join and be born anew."

Saizar groaned as Priester Joseph and Brother John came into view. The two holy men stood on a frozen pile of slush. The elder man shook his fists, alternately at the town and toward the palace. The younger was laying his hands upon the heads of people who kneeled in the snow before him. When they stood, he dipped into a basket at his feet and gave them a misshapen loaf of bread and small, dried fruits.

Saizar brought his horse closer to the earl's, using a lowered voice to comment. "I like this not. I know the people have been looking for someone to blame, but it seems more a way to stir up trouble."

"I will warn the king and those I can about the danger that's brewing," the earl promised.

The lawmen tossed worried looks at the raving man as they rode past. He did not fail to notice them, and flung a hand out at the pathetic sight.

"See? They bring more trash, more refuse to pick over our bones. They will steal what little is ours." Priester Joseph pointed his finger, his body trembling—whether from cold or outrage, the lawmen didn't know.

Saizar made a motion. Guts and Merrit broke off and rode up to the priest. They were eye level.

"Here now, it's one thing to preach your religion, but you are trying to incite a riot. Those people are just as much in need as those who live here," Guts firmly spoke when the priest drew air in.

"Liars!" He hissed at them. "Men of law you are not. You are just more wolves, covering yourselves in sheep's wool and claiming you are not predators. I know what you are." Spittle flew from his lips, a crazy madness lighting up his eyes. "You will not silence me. I have a right to speak the truth. You may have slandered Lord Nicky, driven him to run for his life, but you will not do the same to me." He gesticulated wildly.

Merrit didn't like what he saw. Those who had come to worship listened to the priest. Many of them nodded, a few voiced low agreements. "Priester Joseph, we do not deny your right to preach. We are only asking you don't incite a riot. There are many people, noble and commoner alike, who are willing to help those in need."

"Do not listen to him, my faithful. He lies. They all lie. They have serpent's tongues," the priest screamed.

Guts nudged his horse around the slush pile so he faced those milling about. "There is help if you need it. The palace will feed and shelter you, as will the duchess. Times are hard for everyone. But if you attack fellow townspeople, we of the sheriff's office will have no choice but to arrest those who do. Please, if you need help, seek it at the palace. Thank you."

Guts and Merrit rode off, back to the sheriff's office, taunts from the crowd and threats of the Death Lands from the priest following them until they rode out of sight.

* * *

Sydney led the displaced people over the bridge and up the hill. "You may set up camp on the greensward. There are only a few homes which are not occupied inside the town itself. The palace will see to feeding you."

Eyes, dulled by hunger, sickness, and the unending cold, only stared at him. Sydney did what he could to see they had feed for the animals, and tents for shelter donated from the former army stores. He sent for the town healer, and even helped to build bonfires at which the people could warm themselves. Once this was done, he started back down the hill, meaning to stop at the family town home.

* * *

"Is there anything else I can get you, my lord?" Sydney's valet asked as he completed brushing off his master's coat.

"No, thank you, Roger," came the weary reply. The earl turned from his mirror, a costly piece not many could afford. His father would never have stooped to such vanity. Chadrick had originally given it as a present to his first wife.

Sydney walked downstairs, the thick wool runner in his family's colors muffling his steps. His skin showed signs of the bitter cold and relentless winds. The white in his hair had grown a little more, and to him, the sapphire of his eyes seemed dull. The nap he had taken upon arriving at the mansion only made him feel more exhausted instead of refreshed. The earl paused outside the door to the dining room. Martin had requested his mother's presence. Sydney would not let himself be upset by his wife's malice. He entered the room in time to hear Elizabeth's harangue.

"It's disgraceful. There is no reason why we should be dining in near-darkness."

"Because, Mother," his son calmly replied, voice only betraying a little exasperation. "We don't know when ships or supply trains will be able to get through. I would rather conserve what lamp oil and candles we have, than waste it. There is sufficient enough illumination to see what we eat."

"I know very well what supplies we have. It was not all that long ago your **father**," she spat, "threw me out as if it was I who was trash, and not that whore of a duchess. If our stores have grown so low, it is because you allow them to. It means you are too lax with the slaves."

"I will not be wasteful when others go without. Our stores are no more depleted than they should be through use."

A slave silently stepped forward and pulled a chair out for the earl. He sat and motioned for his goblet to be filled.

"Ah, Father!" His son broke off the discussion, relief evident. "I am pleased you and the others made it back safely."

A displeased snort came from the countess.

"Thank you," he replied.

Martin signaled for the food to be served. A hearty fish stew was brought around, with bread. The family sat and ate in near-silence. The drapes and tapestries swayed from gusts of wind through cracks in the stone and wood-paneled walls. A small fire crackled in the grate, not doing much to warm the room, half of which, along with a long, polished table, lay in darkness.

While the slaves cleared the dirties in preparation for the next dish, Martin attempted conversation. "What was the state of the villages, Father?"

"Oh, who cares about **them**!" His sister tossed her curls. "Martin has been an absolute beast while you were away!"

"What can we expect from him?" Elizabeth said to no one in particular. "He would rather chase after infamy than glory."

Sydney took in a careful breath, reminding himself to keep his temper as he turned slightly to reply to his son. "Most have been decimated. Only a few have managed to repel the bandits."

"The marquis has been at the palace every day these past few weeks, helping His Majesty when our king will permit it. **He**, at least, has his priorities straight. I will not be surprised if he is named advisor. If you had just stayed here and done the same . . ."

Elizabeth droned on. Her family made an effort to ignore a favorite new subject of hers.

"Martin wrote to the most horrid suitor! He promised him I would marry him! Father, I can't!" Sally wailed.

The slaves silently placed new plates and brought out a platter of mixed vegetables in a heavy sauce, meant to disguise the shriveled state from being in storage. More bread accompanied the dish.

"My sister insulted one of her suitors. He then spread about town what she had done. Four of the six immediately wrote to withdraw their suit." Martin tossed a warning look at Sally.

She ignored him, continuing on. "Now my brother says I'm to be a wife of some **flax farmer**!" Her nose scrunched up in disgust. "He has no table manners! He—he—he's a beanpole! He's **ugly**! He lives in the **country**!"

"My sister, Meanna, agrees with me. You must forget about that—that duchess, and the sheriff's office. I expect you to be at the palace come daybreak, asking the king to assign you a task. You must not come home until you have redeemed yourself in his eyes. He must see you as a viable candidate for advisor," Lady Elizabeth firmly instructed her husband.

Martin gave a sympathetic grimace to his sire. "Does this mean we should fear more attacks from the bandits? I don't suppose you heard . . ."

A third time plates were changed, and another dish came out. It consisted of bread pudding with its own sauce, smelling of brandy.

"It's not time for dessert, you stupid slaves!" Elizabeth could be heard berating. "Martin! This is entirely unacceptable. I expect to have a proper dinner when I am here. I do not care what you do when I am not in attendance."

"Oh, I'm sorry, Mother. Did I not tell you? I have instructed Cook to keep our meals simple," Martin quickly replied.

His mother stared for a moment, speechless, then let loose with a volley of criticisms.

"Father! Did you hear what I said? The country!" Sally repeated in horror.

Sydney sighed, counting the minutes until he could politely

excuse himself and leave his mansion.

CHAPTER NINE

Jenabram's mansion shone with light, and music could be heard emanating from inside as highborn and rich merchant guests feasted. His blatant unconcern for those he considered beneath him angered those who starved outside. He added to his insult by having his slaves dump the scraps from his nightly feasts outside his mansion to be pawed through by the desperate.

Kendall sat regally in his chair, a golden, jewel-crusted goblet of wine in one hand, with his ever-present sneer as he presided over the elaborately laid dinner table. His guests could not help but note the new suit he wore, the height of fashion. Nor could they miss the small fortune of jewels and precious metals which winked at them in the light from shirt studs and cuffs, including a cravat pin, several heavy rings, and his newest affectation: a diadem around his carefully coiffed head.

All four of the marble fireplaces, carved to represent some of the more disturbing legends of half-people, half-machines which had lived before them, roared with flame and heat. Overhead, massive chandeliers burned perfumed oil, throwing more heat and light about the room. Six-armed candelabra with beeswax tapers sat surrounded by hothouse flowers. Over a dozen slaves in formal attire in almost-constant motion moved about the room as they saw to the guests' needs.

Baron Stavic, in a new suit of tailored velvet and brocade, frothing with lace, was babbling inanely to anyone who would listen. "Of course, I am still keeping tabs on the royal food stores for Her Grace. Does anyone else find it very odd she had to suddenly leave on a trip? And in this weather? What could possibly be so important for her to risk her life?"

"It seems she is showing her silly, female side. What have I always said? Women cannot be trusted with important matters; their little brains become full and they can't handle the

responsibilities," Sir Dalton replied. He was not a supporter of the marquis, but kept his true opinions of the man to himself.

He thought it best to appear distant, yet cordial, to those with higher standing so he would not miss any information. He had clothed himself in an outfit which had been reworked from out-of-date fashions. It was simple, yet elegant and functional.

"Really, Sir Dalton, I object on behalf of all my kind," Baroness Rothsbury protested. Her chins quivered.

The old knight snorted. "'Tis true, after all, you are in charge of rationing food. Work for a woman, keeping her menfolk fed properly."

Her large bosom heaved in outrage as her reply was lost in the babble of voices. Whatever advantages she enjoyed as a crony of the duchess was not being spent on new outfits, given the slightly faded state of her dress, three seasons out of date.

"Does anyone know what was really found beneath the palace? Did anyone see the traitor Nicky actually leave?" another minor noble by the name of Flouten asked.

Jenabram himself wondered such things. "It is rather convenient the only reports come from the duchess, a recently freed slave, and a pair of foreign merchants."

"Are you implying she knows more than she is letting on?" Flouten demanded as his faded lace cuffs revealed his hands with a flick of his wrists.

"When one thinks upon it, her sudden departure is highly suspicious. I wouldn't be surprised to discover she is a plant. Put in place by the orphan himself to dispose of the king and steal the throne." Jenabram signaled for more wine as he let his insinuations take root.

"If so, she is going about it in a rather strange way. She helped expose the former sheriff and the corruption which ran rampant through his office," a noble whose name escaped the marquis called out.

"I'm sure we will find it a calculated move designed to bring her closer to His Majesty." Jenabram swallowed half the contents in his goblet, giving his listeners time to ponder his words. "We don't need a person like that gaining more access to the throne."

"Or someone who is only known to be concerned for his own prestige," Sir Dalton, who had been listening in, muttered to Earl Sydney. In a louder tone he asked, "Whom are you suggesting we support for the role of advisor? His Majesty did make himself quite clear on the subject of meddlers."

"Pah," Kendall spat in contempt. "I have it on good authority he spends his days like all the others: having the harem entertain him, and eating—when, of course, he isn't obsessing over assassins."

"He has had good reason of late to be concerned about such things." Sir Dalton spoke up.

"Of late?" The marquis pretended shock before slipping back to his customary tone. "It is all he ever concerns himself with, even above his constant rutting with his harem. No, we will just have to tell His Majesty he has a new advisor and present it as a fait accompli. We must be united behind the person."

The marchioness, gowned and bejeweled as elaborately and as expensively as her husband, noticed the slight shudder Chadrick gave at those words. He purposefully ignored the pointed look the marquis directed his way.

Flouten was not to be put aside. "We tried that already. Or has your famous wit become addled from all the wine?"

Blue eyes glittered in anger. "I am not suggesting we put forth a selection of candidates. We only need one. Me."

"I say! That's rather presumptuous of you."

"No, it is smart," Jenabram replied, the anger in his eyes slowly kindling to fury at the stupidity of those sitting around his table. "The king already trusts me. The town folk know of me and my customs. They know what kind of advisor I shall be. A known quantity is preferred—nay, required—over an unknown." He drank the last of his wine with a self-satisfied smile.

"I would not be so sure. There may be another noble who is just as capable," Flouten insisted.

The withering glare his words elicited gave him a small pause, but the man continued. "What about Earl Sydney?"

Chadrick hastily swallowed his mouthful of wine. "Oh no, I have no desire for it," he demurred, without supporting the marquis' claim, a move which earned him a searing look of hate

from the marquis.

"We don't need another traitor next to the throne. Have you all forgotten his brothers? Executed for their crimes." Countess Sydney's chilly voice cut through the babble. She was sitting near Lady Anne, every motion and word she made calculated to remind everyone how a high peer of the realm should behave and dress.

The earl winced inside, wishing he had not come. His wife had apparently decided turning their children against him was not a sufficient enough punishment. She did her best to attend every gathering and event the nobles hosted, whether she liked them or not, spreading her malice and spite.

Sir Dalton cast a disapproving look toward the woman, as those trying to toady to the marquis sniggered in delight.

Chadrick noted the new outfit she had on, an expense which should not have gotten approved. He briefly wondered if his seceding control of the family fortunes over to his son a mistake.

The intricate ballet of slaves, food, and dishes continued as another course was served. A wine, picked to complement, was poured. Five different courses and wines had been served, and it appeared more was still to come.

The marquis continued extolling his virtues, all the while making subtle jabs at Sydney, whose only wish was for the dinner to end, a sentiment he seemed to hold almost continuously when he dined with his peers while the duchess remained away.

CHAPTER TEN

Henrik shivered as he polished dented pewter mugs and washed out wooden ones. The half-burnt tavern had yet to be rebuilt. He wondered, as he always did lately, if he could nudge out the current owner and become the tavern's sole proprietor. The clientele of the Bloody Knuckles seemed to have gotten even worse, if such a thing was possible, now that the old sheriff was dead. The ex-soldier kept his conversations with the patrons on innocuous subjects. If they wanted to try and engage him in the more outlandish speculation floating about the kingdom, he let them rattle on, adding noncommittal noises. In this manner, he learned all kinds of tasty tidbits. Henrik picked his marks with care, dropping hints he was a trusted intermediary for all kinds of trading. For a small consideration, the barkeep would arrange meets with buyers and sellers. A few more coins slipped to Henrik gave the customer access to choice rumors. He also learned which of the bandits who now frequented the tavern could be trusted to carry out illegal acts in complete secrecy.

From behind the kitchen door, came the sound of Jenfry cursing out her daughter's replacement. After a moment, the child came into the bar area, sniffling and wiping at tears and snot.

Henrik watched as the child made her way out into the maze of pathways shoveled out of the snowbanks. He wondered vaguely where she was off to. His answer came several hours later. The child dragged a basket of food, and behind her, the mad priest walked, tugging on his long, greasy beard and wearing his customary scowl.

The barkeep held the kitchen door open for the child, calling to Jenfry, "The crazy priest is here."

She snorted and began berating the small girl. Henrik let the door shut and took his position back up.

"My usual," the priest snapped out.

Henrik didn't bother hiding his distaste for the man as he filled a mug and thumped it down before him. Joseph refused to gossip, and if any tried to engage him in conversation, he would immediately begin preaching and trying to convert the unlucky soul into becoming a member of his church. Henrik had tried a few times to speak of certain people and their sinful ways, hoping the madman would unknowingly let slip information. It only worked once, and the outcome was so small, it made the hassle the barkeep had gone through not worth doing again.

The priest mumbled over his mug, probably some blessing, before greedily gulping it down and waiting for another. Halfway through his second mug, the child came out with a loaded tray. She had to carry it with both hands, and even then it looked as if she struggled to keep from dropping it. Henrik took pity; he relieved the child of her burden and set the bowls of stew and burnt bread before the priest. The child hurried back into the kitchen with the tray.

After the priest had eaten and the bowls sent back, Jenfry came out with her threadbare cloak on. "Mind the place. I'll be back," she curtly commanded the barkeep, as if he didn't know his job.

Henrik made no reply—only narrowed his eyes as the two set off. He knew they were taking advantage of the duchess's absence to harass Jenfry's daughter. The fat owner made no effort to keep her voice down when she bragged to the whores in her employ about her visits. At this time of day, there usually weren't any patrons. Henrik finished his task, then crept up the stairs. He listened for any movement behind closed doors which might signal the whores stirred. All was quiet. The former soldier picked the lock on Jenfry's private sitting room door. If all went well, he would be able to continue his search for the deed to the tavern, and the profits the owner hoarded.

* * *

Jenfry had no trouble entering the Duchess's grounds. Priester Joseph's ranting and raving as he stood in the middle of the nobles' street distracted the guards. As she came upon the courtyard, the sounds of mock battle could be heard drifting from behind the mansion. One of the entrance doors to the mansion itself stood open, and from inside came the steady chink of chisel on stone. Jenfry continued toward the stable area. Behind the day's manure pile, which hadn't been carted off yet, was a garbage pit. Her daughter claimed she liked to visit the horses, but Jenfry knew she lied. She knew her smart-mouthed former stable slave was probably trying to seduce the girl.

Jenfry kept her beady eyes on the kitchen doorway. She huddled farther inside her cloak, making sure to keep hidden in the shadows cast by one side of the stable wall. Jenfry's daughter walked around the manure pile, scraps pail in hand. She saw the shock and panic spreading across her daughter's face before the girl stopped her forward momentum. Mary Elana stood as if frozen.

"Daughter! Come here and greet your poor old mother," Jenfry demanded.

The girl stood trembling, shaking her head in denial.

Her mother walked the few paces toward her daughter and grabbed her by an arm. The girl barely resisted, and her mother shoved her roughly into the corner made by the stable wall meeting the stone boundary wall of the property.

"Now then, child," her mother began, eyes glittering with malice, "let us have a nice little chat."

The girl's eyes remained wide in shock, her breathing fast and shallow, fists clenched tight around the handle of the pail.

"Rumor has it your mistress manages to stay the king's favorite. So here's what you're going to do for your dear old mother. You're going to volunteer to accompany the slaves when they go to fetch wood and food for the household. You'll make sure some of it finds its way to me. If you don't," she dropped her voice even lower, "the good priest will stand outside the whore's gates preaching against her, and everyone who lives here, until you do."

Tears spilled out of Mary Elana's eyes, snaking down her face. Her mother's grip tightened painfully around her slim wrist as she jerked the girl closer to her.

Jenfry's sour breath blew over her daughter. "You think I

won't? Your mistress is an adulterer, a whore, an unclean soul. What do you think will happen when the king withdraws his support, and another takes her place? Huh? I'll tell you where you'll be, begging in town and whoring alongside her."

Her mother ranted on while Mary Elana cried harder and harder. She tugged, trying to break the bruising grip around her upper arm. Jenfry only tightened her hold.

"Stupid bitch! I can get in here anytime I want. It doesn't matter how hard your mistress tries to keep me away; she can't. Doesn't speak so highly of her, now does it?"

Spittle hit Mary Elana's tear-frozen cheeks; her breath wheezed in terror. The girl's mother had now taken to slamming her daughter's unresisting body off the stone wall behind them. Jenfry's voice rose higher as she spewed her hate, and Mary Elana's panic grew. If anyone found out her mother was here, they would tell Her Grace when she returned. She might even be angry enough to dismiss the young woman from her post. Mary Elana couldn't let that happen; this was the first time she'd felt safe. She was fed, clothed, and warm. No one tried to grope her, no one berated her for no reason. She couldn't lose the comfort of her new home.

In a blind panic, Mary Elana swung the pail she still clutched upward as her mother slammed her against the wall. The hard, cold metal clipped Jenfry on the chin, snapping her head back from the force. The slops in the pail rained down upon both women and the ground. The young woman felt her mother's grip loosen, and she bashed the pail on her mother's head on the downswing.

Jenfry staggered backward, shock, disbelief, and pain in her eyes over the unexpected attack from her mousy daughter. Mary Elana scrambled for the small opening presented between her mother, the manure pile, and the stone wall. She slipped on the ice, started to go down, flinging her arms out in a desperate bid to stay upright. Mary Elana's hand, and most of her weight landed heavily on her mother's shoulder. As the young woman pushed off and away, the momentum caused her mother to lose her footing on the treacherous ground. Mary Elana didn't bother to see what happened; she bolted around the pile and toward the stable. If she had glanced back, she would have seen her mother land backward in the manure.

The young woman let the side door slam shut behind her. The horses nearest the noise startled, whinnying and shifting in their stalls. The girl ran toward the middle of the stables. She didn't know when she had let go of the pail. She skidded to a stop, breath whistling in and out, chest heaving from a combination of fright and adrenaline. She had the dim thought that perhaps she could hide in a stall until her mother left the grounds.

A high pitched nicker, and banging on a stall door drew her gaze around. Windstorm had his head and neck stretched over his door toward her. His lips moved as he sent a torrent of sound her way. His antics looked like he was blowing kisses at her. Mary Elana stared at the stallion a moment, then broke out into hysterical giggles.

It was thus how Domiano found her. "Um, hey . . ." He waved to catch her attention. "Are you hurt? I saw from the hayloft how your mother attacked you. I was on my way down to help."

She shook her head, giggles fading until she caught sight of the stallion, and then they started up again.

The stable master turned to see what she found so funny. "Stop that," he commanded the stallion and walked closer to the girl. "Ignore him. He likes to flirt with all the pretty females; thinks he's gonna get lucky."

Her giggles finally subsided, the realization of what she had done causing her to gasp in panic and blurt out, "My mother! She'll have me arrested and-and thrown in the dungeon to rot!"

"No, she won't," Domiano fiercely replied. "She attacked you. She isn't even supposed to be inside the gates. Stupid guards." He muttered the last.

The girl shook her head. "Yes, she will. She'll find a way."

"You think your mother can outwit Her Grace? Despite what she was yelling at you, she can't. You're safe here."

"She said she can get inside anytime."

"No. If the guards had been doing their duty, she wouldn't have. You need to tell Her Grace about this. She will speak with the security and make sure they don't slack in their duties."

"I can't!" Mary Elana blurted, cheeks reddening. "I don't

want to get anyone in trouble. They'll hate me if I tattle on them."

"It's not tattling," Domiano insisted. "You mention what happened—what she bragged about being able to do. Her Grace will investigate the matter, and the guards will be so worried about how your ma slipped past them, they won't think to blame you."

The girl stood with shoulders hunched inward, arms crossed over her chest, hugging herself. "But what if they still do?"

"You worry too much," the man replied. "I'll see that they don't. Come on, let's find your pail and get you back inside. You can't work all covered in stinking scraps." He took an oil lamp off a nearby hook and held a hand out to her.

Tentatively, Mary Elana placed one of hers in his warm, work-roughened grip. He led her outside into the gloaming. Voices were shouting from near the front gate. The two young people could make out Jenfry and the guards having a confrontation.

"See, they have caught her sneaking around. They'll tell Her Grace and you won't have to worry about getting them in trouble." He let go of her hand as he stooped down.

The scrap pail now bore two dents. The girl accepted it back, and let the stable master escort her to the kitchen door. She slipped inside, shyly thanking him. Luckily, Cook didn't notice the length of time she had been gone.

"Unto the Great One! I said to toss the scraps into the garbage heap! Not try and wear them," the man bellowed, catching sight of her. "Go clean up and change. I'll not have smelly, dirty slaves at my table."

"S-s-sorry. I slipped . . . on the ice," she meekly answered as she set the pail in its assigned spot.

"Hrmph," he snorted, turning back to stirring an enticing-smelling stew and thus effectively ignoring her.

CHAPTER ELEVEN

The mansion grounds and those who lived there were slowly waking. The great gates remained closed and locked, something which would change within an hour or two. Illyria landed in the deepest patch of darkness she could find, the wind from the river tugging at her and Eron's cloaks. A few flakes of snow drifted lazily out of the sky, which was slowly turning silver as the sun rose behind a thick cloud cover.

The two made their way inside the house. Noises made them aware the slaves were beginning a new day. With her blood in his veins, Eron noticed he could see much better in near-darkness. It was an unnerving sensation at first, but now it just fascinated him. A faint light glowed from underneath a closed door.

The two immortals stopped; Eron knocked. He had to repeat the knock several times before Colin opened the door. By his mussed hair and clothes, along with the creases on one side of his face, he had been sleeping. His eyes grew wide at sight of his friend, a brief look of worry passing across his face before he stepped into the hallway, closing the door behind him softly.

"I am glad you both made it back. Was your trip a success?" he asked.

"Yes. How is your brother?" Eron replied.

"The medicine the herbalist gave seems to be working. His cough has lessened, and he no longer has to struggle to catch a breath."

"Good. Let me know when Mica is awake and alert so I can fill him in on what happened," Eron requested. "We just got back. I'm going to grab some sleep, if possible."

"Sure," Colin agreed, and turned the knob to go back inside the room. He paused before blurting out, "Are you sure you're all right? Your eyes look weird."

Shit! Eron thought while out loud he said, "Yeah, too much sun and no sunglasses." He waved goodnight and headed toward Illyria's office, meaning to nap on her couch.

* * *

Mica sat before Illyria's worktable, the first time he'd been out of bed since passing out weeks earlier. Just being near her and Eron anymore made his skin crawl. He felt revulsion toward them. Two small leather sacks sat before him on top of the table. Eron was talking, and had been the whole time. The sound made Mica feel physically nauseous.

"Shut up," he finally ground out. "You make me sick. Both of you. You're lying. I know you are. I don't know how, but I know there're things you're not telling me."

"Mica, I don't know who started the Immortal Wolves, or how they managed to infiltrate the motherhouse, or how they found and killed almost everyone," Eron smoothly lied.

Colin sat on the couch, sipping hot cider. He remained quiet, observing and occasionally making notes in his journal.

"They still have to be alive! I can't believe you left our soul gems unprotected." Mica turned, eyes blazing in fury, toward Illyria. "And as for you, if it hadn't been for your infernal meddling, the Guardians wouldn't have been consumed by that-that demon! Donny wouldn't have had to suffer the way he did!"

"What did you think would happen? From all accounts, your quest was already a disaster," she countered.

Their bickering continued. Eron turned away from his friends and leaned toward Colin. He held out a piece of folded parchment, which the other man accepted.

"I moved the remaining gems to a safer cave, one that, to my knowledge, only I know of. I made a map of it for you, and included the names of those immortals whose gems still remain."

"Thank you." Colin smiled, showing he didn't align with his brother and his recriminations.

"The wolves destroyed everything, Colin. All your hard work over the past centuries, while you lived at the motherhouse. Whoever they were, they were thorough. All the records had been

85

destroyed. They burnt them, blew them up, pulverized them even. Honestly, I don't think any of the wolves are alive. If they were, we would be dead. I wish I knew who finally figured out who they were, and how they managed to stop them."

His friend nodded. "So it is your belief they meant to end us? All of us?"

"Yes, it's the only idea I can think of which makes sense. If anything, there may be one or two left who had no one to end his or her eternal life. It's possible the list holds that person's name." More lies and half-truths flowed from his tongue.

Colin tucked the parchment away in a waistcoat pocket, and resumed sipping his beverage. "This young protégé Mica is upset about: I take it whatever disaster befell him did so because of something Her Grace was involved in?"

"More or less."

Mica's brother slowly nodded and looked over at the arguing. It seemed to have ended. Colin placed his goblet aside, stood, and walked the few steps to stand beside the worktable. "Your Grace, as our quest is ended, so is our need for your support with it."

She inclined her head to the immortal, and he paused before continuing.

"I have been thinking these past few months. I would like to stay and help the town."

"Colin, no!" Mica roared.

He was ignored. "While I make a passable merchant, my true passion is learning, and the quest for knowledge. My talents would be best served as a teacher and recorder of deeds."

"We are not staying," Mica snarled. "Those two are perfidious liars and murderers, and will get us killed. We'll take our parchment business elsewhere. We'll find a kingdom that isn't tearing itself apart."

"I'm sure His Majesty would be delighted to have a man of learning reside in his kingdom. How can I help you?" Illyria ignored Mica's ravings.

"I should like to start a school. It will be small at first but will grow in time. I am willing to teach anyone who wishes to learn: reading, writing, arithmetic, philosophy," he offered.

"Excellent. I will see you have access to the king for your proposal." She smiled and turned to his brother. "Mica, Colin is a grown man. I understand if you want to continue your journey elsewhere. I would advise you hold off for another few weeks. You are not fully healed, and hopefully, by then the snows will let up enough to make travel possible." Her tone became thoughtful. "Although I doubt the mountain passes will be cleared until a few months beyond that time."

"I'm not letting you get your claws into my brother," came the heated response.

"Short of kidnapping your own brother, it doesn't seem you have a choice in what he wants. This is a fight you will not win, Mica. Take the time I am offering to finish healing, and think of what direction you want your own reborn life to go," Illyria coolly replied. "Now, if you two will excuse me, I have estate business to discuss with Eron."

Mica glared, fists clenched with impotent fury. He rose a little shakily, as sudden movements tended to make him dizzy still. He snatched the bags containing the ashes of his and Donny's soul gems and stomped from the room, childishly slamming the door shut behind him

Colin sighed, apologized for his brother's behavior, and exited the room after picking up his journal. Eron turned toward Illyria.

"When does our world domination start?"

"When I decide how best to go about it."

"You mean 'we.' When we choose. I know you must be bored with your intrigues. All these idiots, bungling up yet another chance to begin anew."

"Quite certain of it, are you?" she asked.

He merely smiled and took a long drink of cider, eyes intent on hers.

"Oh, very well. I admit it has been hard to not just strangle them with their own intestines. The bandits don't provide as much sport as they used to."

"Which leads back to my main point: hostile takeover or continue weaving webs?"

She sat staring off into the fire as he sipped, waiting for her to speak. He knew what he would choose, but given his past exploits, thought it might be time to try a different tactic.

"Both. The king will make me his advisor. We will rid the kingdom of the worst offenders, and rule the rest with an iron fist."

"As my queen commands," he mocked, raising his goblet to her in a toast before finishing the contents.

CHAPTER TWELVE

Raina stood near the back of the audience chamber, next to a pillar. Sleep-deprived, exhausted guards stood around the room's perimeter. His Majesty sat on his throne, all the harem women kneeling in rows around it. Aranthus stood at the bottom of the stairs leading up to the platform, every noble and merchant of importance packed into the space before. Behind and to the sides stood members who helped record and see to the running of the kingdom. The rest of the space was filled with peasants and the poor, hoping to get a chance to beg of even a few crumbs from the king's table.

Maceanas was shouting, gesticulating wildly as spittle flew. "How dare you keep secrets from me! I am your king! I should have been informed of such duplicity the moment it became known! I shall have you all stripped of your titles, whipped and fined! You have put my life in danger!"

He raved on; the young woman couldn't really see anyone's faces very well from her position, only a few profiles. The heat from so many bodies made the room unbearably hot, and many sweated freely from it and a combination of nerves and other emotions. Raina glanced toward a guard; his face turned an ashy gray. As she watched, his eyes rolled back in his head and he collapsed, metal armor ringing against stone.

"What happened?"

"Is he dead?"

"Maybe he was poisoned!"

The mutters rose and slowly rippled toward the front of the room as fellow guards darted looks between them, wanting to go to their fallen comrade, but not quite willing to risk the king's wrath.

"Silence! Silence I say!" the king screamed from his throne. "What is wrong with him?"

The royal physician was trying to make his way through the

crowd; people parted to let him through and then eagerly crowded in behind him as he knelt next to the fallen man. Raina watched as he lifted an eyelid up, held a small brass disk under the nose for breath. After a few moments, he stood and called out into the eager hush of listeners.

"Sire, the man is merely exhausted near unto death, nothing more. I prescribe rest for him, hearty meals, and in a day or two he will be fit for duty."

"What? What? A day or two? I need him now! I cannot be unguarded! I don't care how you get him better, but I want him back guarding by morning! No excuses or it's your head!" the king bellowed.

The physician could only bow and murmur acceptance as his apprentices began to drag the man from the hall, his armor producing shrill noises from the contact with the stone floor. The crowd turned back to the king.

Aranthus banged his staff upon the floor to quiet those who still whispered amongst themselves.

"I am offering a reward of a thousand gold pieces to any person with knowledge of the group operating in my kingdom under the head questioner's leadership which leads to an arrest and execution."

A gasp rose, voices rising briefly, then falling off as the chamberlain banged his staff against the floor. The king continued, "Another thousand gold coins will go to the person who can bring the traitor known as Earl Nicholas, former royal advisor, to me alive, for questioning. Aranthus and Mathias will record whatever is said in the utmost confidence. However, should any think to make false claims and profit from them, he will be flogged, then hanged."

More gasps and shouts rose from the crowd, and it took longer for the noise to die down.

"Today, I confer royal power and authority on my new advisor: the Duchess Illyria Maison du Corbeau. She is to be obeyed as I am obeyed. To refuse her is to refuse me. Any who ignore her requests will be considered traitors to the crown and kingdom. Now go!"

A moment of tense silence filled the hall as His Majesty's

words filtered throughout the collective consciousness. A few of the nobles and merchants forget themselves, yelling in outrage and derision.

"Guards! Arrest those dissenters who continue to speak against my proclamations!" the king screamed.

Almost all the voices dropped off except for a few who were extracted from the crowd with a small amount of hassle.

"Does anyone else care to voice their opinions? Take them to the dungeons to rot."

The protestors were clubbed into silence and dragged off. The king stood and everyone made their obeisance as he left the throne room. Once he was gone, the crowd broke into smaller knots of people. Slowly some of the groups shuffled toward the door and out, voices rising in displeasure or outrage over the new appointment once they were outside. Sycophants eager to curry favor moved toward the duchess. The young woman kept to her spot, watching who passed, eavesdropping.

Priester Joseph spat upon the floor. "The Death Lands will take you all for your sins." He stomped from the hall.

She noted a few of the nobles hung back, including Baroness Rothsbury. They all gathered around a man with black hair and silver wings at the temples who stood next to the infamous duchess. Her Grace had a small smile of satisfaction on her face.

Raina shifted her weight from foot to foot, as the nobles filtered out. She almost missed a dark-haired man skulking behind a pillar, shadowing the earl and the duchess. The man and woman came toward her, and she stepped into their path, dropping a graceful curtsey. "Your Lordship, Your Grace. A moment of your valuable time, please."

He frowned. "I am not accepting women, especially young ones, into the sheriff's service."

"I am not applying. I have information . . ."

"Then you should be telling it to the chamberlain, or Mathias."

The duchess was looking at her in a disconcerting way as if trying to peer through her eyes and into her mind itself. "Chadrick." She lightly touched his arm, eyes never leaving the face of the woman before her. "What is it you wish to speak of?"

Raina lowered her voice, not wanting to be overheard by the other nobles. "Baroness Rothsbury gave me some old accounts to go over, several months back, to see if I really knew what I was doing. I've . . . found some discrepancies. It's been weeks since I brought them to her attention. Since then, I have not been allowed near the books again. I would not bring it up, but I have felt as if I am being watched."

"What do they have you doing now?" the duchess asked.

"Copying last year's census and matching it to those who are known to have survived so far under the royal census taker."

"Do you remember which accounts had the problems?" the earl asked.

"Yes. For the most part, they were kitchen records, except for one set dealing with the Lord Advisor's expenses. The former advisor," she hurried to add. "There were . . . items on it of a questionable nature and amount."

The two nobles exchanged glances before the woman spoke. "Thank you for alerting us. We will make inquiries." The young woman was dismissed.

She curtsied again as they made to move on, but the elegant woman paused and half-turned back. "Raina, should you hear rumors of unrest and starvation, come and tell me." Then they walked out.

Raina was shocked at the use of her name, never having told it to them. It confirmed some of the whispers swirling around town about the foreigner.

* * *

Sydney escorted Illyria out of the palace, walking with her down the hill. "My love, with this appointment, surely you can ask the king to grant my request."

She turned her head toward him, calmly replying, "I will try my best, but I don't want to be seen as abusing my post the way Lord Nicky did."

A sinking feeling took hold of him; all the doubts and nasty words Elizabeth had flung at him rose to the forefront of his mind. *Had the duchess used him? Did she love him? He was afraid to ask, not sure he could stand knowing the truth.*

It was as if she knew his thoughts, for she tucked her arm around his, snuggling close. "Do not despair, my love. It would be best if you petitioned him again, yourself, without trying to involve me. Perhaps your lady wife would be amenable this time to supporting it?"

Sydney shook his head. "No. She will do everything in her power to block it. She wants me to suffer, to deny me any chance at happiness. She thirsts for vengeance." There was nothing more to say on the subject. *I can do nothing to alleviate her hatred of me. She continues to nurse it as she has for years, shortly after we were wed.* He was pulled from his thoughts by the duchess's voice.

"His Majesty is correct in thinking there are more traitors lurking."

His disappointment with her answer to his request made his reply harsh. "All this talk of traitors! When will it end? When we are all dead? Or just mindless slaves with no will or thoughts to call our own?"

She fully faced him, touching his arm and stopping their forward momentum. "I understand how this can be a terrible reminder of what happened to your own family, your brothers. Please, forgive my poor choice of words. I should have said, we must make sure there are no others taking advantage of their positions the way Nicky did."

Sydney scowled at nothing in particular over her shoulder, not sure he could meet her eyes.

"I am counting on you to help me. I need your incorruptibility, your honor, your love of the kingdom." She tried to catch his eye as he bowed his head, studying the icy, snow-covered cobbles.

"Is that all you need me for?"

"Of course not. Will you come back with me? Surely there is something at my home I can tempt you with," she replied.

He felt the cold air pierce his lungs, almost painful, as he gave himself time to think and decide. "Yes, I should like that very much."

CHAPTER THIRTEEN

Dascis sat at his desk, his feet propped on a hot stone in an effort to keep them warm. He could feel the heat lessening. The wood inside the fireplace was getting to the point where he would have to stand and add more. Two oil lamps burned at the top corners of his desk. He had long since sent his clerks and apprentices home.

The rotund man dipped his quill in the ink, and continued recording recent events on parchment for inclusion into the official records. He was jarred out of his work by the sound of heavy pounding on the outer door to the Royal Records offices.

"Damn it all!" he roared as a fat drop of ink marred the pristine sheet. Quickly he worked to mop it up, to lessen the damage, but it was too late. He would have to scrap the page and start over. Nothing must mar the official records.

The pounding came again, relentless enough that he thought the door would soon be smashed inward. No one but slaves and various minor officials visited him in his offices, and they only to fetch him for the king or for other royal business.

It was too late to be needed, unless . . . That woman!

Dascis heaved himself away from his desk, snatched up a lamp, and hurried toward the receiving room. When he got to the door, it was shuddering. Quickly he opened the peephole to yell, "Give me a moment, damn you!"

He slammed it shut without waiting for a reply, and worked the locks before drawing the door open. A strong gust of wind blew in, ripping the door from his hands, nearly braining him as it slammed against the wall.

He held the oil lamp up, squinting against the snow blowing in. "Who is it?"

"The royal advisor, Duchess Illyria, seeks an audience." The slave gestured behind him at a black coach with silver trimmings.

The records keeper scowled, annoyed with how every new advisor had to bother him. While he wished to be left alone, he thought it best to get the interview over with. "Well then come in and be quick about it!" He tried to shield the oil flame from the wind, which was bringing snow in that fast piled upon the floor.

A footman opened the coach door, and Her Grace stepped down and strode forward. Her long, dragging bustle skirt made a path in the snow. Behind her, the coach moved off, the driver maneuvering it under the building's steep overhanging roof in an effort to keep snow from piling on top. The footman jumped off the rumble seat and hurried to toss blankets over the horses to keep them warm during the wait. The duchess stepped far enough inside so her retinue, comprising of the slave who had banged on the door, and a heavily cloaked and hooded person, could also enter. Despite the short walk from carriage to the door, her black cloak was covered in a thin layer of snow.

"Good evening, Dascis. Thank you for taking the time to see me." As she spoke, she removed the cloak, handing it to the covered person, and started to work off her black leather, rabbit fur-lined gloves.

He bowed. "Er, yes, of course. The pleasure is all mine," he could only mumble as he shut the door and relocked it before turning to face the advisor.

She wore a tailored, knee-length in front, long-tailed red coat with silver buckles that crisscrossed and a stiff standing silver lace collar with three points that curved outward. The cuffs had two inches of intricate black embroidery on them. The layered red and black bustle skirt swept the floor in back and came down to mid-thigh in front. She wore thick red tights, and shiny black knee-high leather boots with a tall, thick heel. Her hair was in an elaborate updo, and she wore a half crown along with jewels of rubies and black gemstones.

"Er, congratulations on your new position, Your Grace. How may I be of service to you tonight?" He gave a servile bow, something in the way her eyes blazed with a honey gold fire warning him to proceed carefully.

"Thank you. I am hoping your reticence to gossip and

questioning nature will be able to help me. Is there a spot we may sit and talk?"

Damn it all! "Of course. I am afraid only my office has warmth and light."

"If there are chairs we may sit on and room for us all, then please show us the way," she graciously replied.

Double damn! He gave a weak smile, and turning, led them to his space. Once they were seated, the slaves on chairs just outside the door, he at his desk and the duchess next to it on a high stool, the room seemed cramped.

He placed his feet on the stone, which had gone cold. Grumpily he rolled up the scroll he had been working on and placed it in a reed basket for a clerk to scrape clean and reuse. He should have gone home hours ago, despite the bleakness of his small rooms.

"Dascis, I am given to understand you hold all records for everything which happens within the kingdom. Not just of personal exploits, but of financial as well."

"Of course." *What the Death Lands is she up to*?

"I am trusting my request of you will remain within these walls, and go no further."

His brows raised in inquiry. "Naturally."

"I need an accounting of each royal office: who is in charge, the number of slaves and paid workers, and their yearly expenses during the previous advisor's term. I shall also need the same for the royal army, the palace, and copies of all taxes paid to the crown."

The record keeper's mouth dropped open in shock. *Impossible*! He had to clear his throat several times before he could speak. "And you would want this when?"

"A week."

"Right. Shall I hand deliver it with a bow as well?" The sarcasm slipped out before he could stop it. He was angry she thought she could waltz into his office as easily as she had the position she now occupied, and think he would jump to her tune.

"The bow is not needed, but I would be most appreciative if you brought it to me in person." The calm manner in which she ignored his colossal rudeness had him rethinking his next words.

"I can supply what you need; however, I cannot do so alone in the time frame you give. I would need to use some of my clerks and copyists."

"How many?"

Dascis sat and made rapid calculations in his head of who he thought he could trust, for surely if word leaked out, she would take actions against his office. What those might entail, he had a feeling he didn't want to experience.

"Two clerks, to fetch and replace the material, and at least four copyists."

"I will want to meet those you deem responsible and trustworthy enough for the job before you begin," she replied.

He bristled in outrage, "There is no need. I would stake my life upon my choices!"

She tilted her head to the right, reminding him of a bird of prey before it struck. "Are you certain you wish to stake your life? For I shall ask for it if you are wrong."

A tremor of fear wormed down his spine, and despite the growing cold in the room as the fire burned down, sweat popped out on his brow and trickled down the back of his neck. She did not rave and rant as the old advisor was wont to do, or spew a torrent of threats. That, along with her simple statement, made him believe she was in earnest.

They stared at each other, only the rustles of the shifting slaves breaking the silence.

"I . . ." He had to blot his forehead and back of his neck with a handkerchief and moisten his lips with his tongue. "If you will consent to stop by tomorrow evening, after the bulk of the workers have left for the day except for the ones I need, you may inspect them."

A small smile flashed across her placid features. "Very good. When your task is completed, you may ask a favor of me. I trust our terms will be acceptable?"

He automatically nodded, wanting nothing more than to lock up and go home. The duchess made a gesture to one of the men. The slave exited the room at a trot as she stood. Dascis took this to mean she would be leaving. He escorted her to the receiving room, unlocking the door as she wrapped up in her cloak and tugged the gloves on.

"Until tomorrow night." She inclined her head in good-bye.

He opened the door, bowing from the waist up as he did. In a swirl of snow and a blast of cold wind, she left. Dascis closed, locked the door, and leaned his back against it a moment. He was not looking forward to the next day.

CHAPTER FOURTEEN

Snow fell thickly, adding to the layers already coating everything. A week had passed since the king had made his demands for information. Everyone wanted to be the person to collect what for many was the equivalent of three years' income. The young woman shivered, pulling her cloak tighter about her. His Majesty, in another fit of paranoia, had relegated all non-palace slaves and personnel to the streets.

The cold seeped into nooks, crannies, and bodies. Each morning brought another few corpses claimed by winter or murderous, desperate townspeople. Raina had managed to secure a room for her and her brother to share at an inn.

The Baroness Rothsbury had approached the young girl when she'd showed for work, and told her she was being reassigned. The woman scowled; clearly the noblewoman had been confronted by the duchess about the accounts Raina found, and the baroness was taking out her ire on Raina.

She supposed she should be grateful she still had a job, given the circumstances. Raina put another log into the fire pit near her, trying to ration the small pile of wood she was given to keep warm, and nudged the ink bottle closer to her oil lamp in a futile effort to keep it from freezing.

"I don't know what to do! We're starving!" the mother before her wailed. Her brood of children crowded around her, huddling for what warmth they could manage.

Raina's fingers were stiff with cold, her feet and nose numb with it. It was a month into the winter season, but already mutters flowed about the brutality of it. She tried to write down the names and ages of the children and their mother, the ink a thick sludge.

"The brothels aren't hiring! And the slavers say they don't have enough buyers." She broke down weeping.

Raina sighed, the story all too familiar. "I will put you on the list for food and shelter for today."

"Today!" the mother shrilled. "What am I gonna do tomorrow? Stand in line again, hoping we survive another day?" She spat suddenly at the young woman, who moved enough for it to hit her shoulder and slide down the sleeve before freezing.

"I am sorry. His Majesty prevents me from doing more." She apologized and held out a wooden chit.

The woman snatched it out of her hand and spat on the ground. It crackled as it hit. They were quickly jostled out of the way by the next group of people in line. Raina swallowed, trying to calm her racing heart. She had two guards nearby, but knew they would not be much help should matters turn ugly. At noon she had to take a break, unable to endure the cold anymore. Hateful words and curses followed her retreating back. She hugged the satchel with her parchments, inks and quills to her chest. The walk up the hill took an especially long time due to her frozen feet.

Raina was glad when she could sit down by a fireplace in a corner of the palace and thaw herself out. She ate and drank what the slaves presented to her, nothing fancy: bread, stew, and hot, spiced wine. After her lunch, Raina was walking back outside to resume her post, head down, when she crashed into someone and they nearly fell.

"I'm sorry! It was my fault for not paying attention to where I was going," the young woman gasped out.

"Pardon me, I should have been more careful." The young man smiled at her, sapphire blue eyes crinkling at the corners.

His hands still had hold of her arms from when he caught them both. She stepped back, and he let her go. "Sorry."

"Thank you for catching me, my lord; with your pardon, I must get back to my job," Raina said with a little curtsey.

He bowed his thick head of glossy black hair. "Of course." He stepped out of her way.

Her walk back to the little hut wasn't quite as dismal, but the line of shivering, angry townspeople queued up outside had her lips pressing together. Before her downfall, she wouldn't have cared much about those of lesser status, but now that she was one of them, she felt indignant over the injustices they had to suffer.

* * *

Dawn came with wails of distress, cries of rage. Raina left her brother huddled under the covers of their shared bed and descended to the inn's main floor.

"You should go back upstairs, barricade yourself inside," one of the inn keep's sons informed her.

"Why? What is happening?" she asked.

"More deaths. A blizzard moved through overnight. A lot of people didn't make it, including some who had heat and shelter. Those who are without having begun to rampage. They're busting down doors, raiding for food. Some are even killing the owners and taking over their homes."

Raina felt fear race through her as the noise became louder. The sons guarding the door tensed, and braced themselves. A moment later it shuddered under the weight of pounding fists and feet.

"Bastards! Let us in!"

"I've got children freezing and starving! I know you have food and fire!"

"Open the door!"

Shutters closed over the windows rattled violently, causing all inside to jump. "Da!" one of the boys called out.

His mother appeared, spotted Raina, and hissed. "Are you daft, girl? My family can't protect you and our inn! You'd better get your brother and get out! Hurry! They haven't come around back yet!"

Another forceful rattle of the shutters and door caused her to jump. Raina whirled around and fled up the stairs, eyes wide in terror.

"Hilel! Hilel! Get up!" she screamed, bursting into their room.

Her little brother mumbled and burrowed deeper underneath the covers. The woman could hear the insistent pounding, the voices of the mob. She was thrown into a flashback.

* * *

"Rose! Get the children to the safe room!" Lord Smirkin bellowed to his wife.

He and his knights formed up in the courtyard and on the walls of their castle, archers shooting at the attackers.

Raina stood frozen in a shadow on the upper walkway of the main keep, unable to answer her maid's or mother's cries as they looked for her. The gates burst open under a battering ram, men in armor with blue- and white-checked surcoats poured through. A few fell to arrows, but the attackers answered in kind. The two sides met in a clash of blades and war cries. The opposing force kept pouring inside the ruined gates, with a group on horseback.

"Kill all who resist!" came the cry.

The young woman watched in horror as defenders she had known all her life fell. Her father and his closest men-at-arms were forced back toward the main keep. Some of the attackers broke off to grab fleeing women, throw them down and rape them. The fight was now being raged beneath her hiding spot. She didn't realize she was crying, clutching her elbows with opposite hands.

She shook out of her paralyzing fear as the wooden walkway shuddered. Her father was forced up the stairs, fighting the entire way.

"Father!" she cried.

"Raina, run! Run now!" he yelled to her, redoubling his efforts against his attacker.

"Bitch! Don't go far! I claim you as my prize!" screamed the young nobleman attacking her father.

"Raina, run!" Smirkin yelled, which turned into a sound of pain as a sword found a weak spot in his armor.

"Father!" she cried again as he slammed back into the wall.

"Run, Raina, run!" He bellowed with what breath was left to him.

She finally did what he said, turning and fleeing along the walkway toward the main door. The baron's son laughed behind her, metal clinking as he gave chase.

* * *

Raina shuddered, realizing she was curled up in a ball on the inn floor, tears streaming down her face. The pounding had not let up from below, and now a cracking sound joined in. The door would soon give way.

"No! Not again! Never again!" The young woman didn't realize she had spoken out loud.

She forced herself off the floor and into motion. She grabbed the money pouch she had hidden with her earnings and shoved it into her satchel. She threw her new, thick wool cloak over her shoulders and secured it. Then she grabbed up her brother's cloak and shoes, ripping the bed covers off him. He cried out in protest.

"Get up, Hilel! There's a mob at the door."

"I'm tired. I wanna sle . . ." he trailed off, eyes widening in fear at the sounds coming up from below. He whimpered in shock.

His sister forcefully grabbed his legs and shoved his shoes on. She yanked him off the bed, tossing his cloak around his shoulders and quickly fastening the pin shut before scooping him up. Raina managed to stagger out the door with her brother before his weight was too much and she had to put him down.

"Run, Hilel, run!" Raina snatched his hand and yanked him after her.

They could hear the heavy thud of feet on the stairs, the cries from the fighting going on below. Sister and brother fled down the hall toward the rear stairs, a male bellow behind alerting them to the fact they were spotted. The two didn't recall how they made it down without tripping and falling. The kitchen door stood open, cold and snow swirling inside from the wind. The fire in the big fireplace flickered wildly, casting monstrous-looking shadows about the room. They ran outside, immediately blinded by the pelting ice and snow.

"Raina!" Hilel cried, words snatched away by the cruel wind.

She would not let go of his hand, no matter what. The young woman turned right, dragging her brother after her. If they could get to the bridge with its palace guard, maybe they would be safe.

* * *

Brother and sister sat shivering on a hard bench near the roaring fireplace. A silent slave had long since departed, after setting down a tray with hot, spiced wine, and meat pastries. If it hadn't been for Viscount Martin's intervention, the angry townspeople would have killed them both.

"Raina, I wanna go home," Hilel whimpered. "I don't like it here. I'm always cold and hungry."

She sighed, too tired and dejected to explain yet again why they couldn't do what he wanted. After a few more minutes of whining, her brother finally lay down and curled up into a tight ball and fell asleep. The young woman sipped at the wine, looking about the plain room, to her an oddity given this was an earl's mansion. Neither he nor the countess, or even the young ladies of the house, had come to speak with her. The rumors of upheaval in the family must be true. Eventually, Raina stood up and wandered about the space, peeked out the heavy drapes at the icy street and inspected the few religious-themed knickknacks.

A brief knock sounded on the door, the black-haired, sapphire-eyed viscount entered.

"I'm sorry to have left you alone for so long. I hope the slaves are accommodating to any needs you have?"

She inclined her head gracefully, "Yes, my lord. Thank you." She paused. "And thank you again for saving my brother and me. It's a debt I shall owe you."

He looked slightly ill at ease. "Yes, well. I would be a cad if I didn't help someone who needed it. There is nothing owed." He coughed into his fist before continuing. "However, I am afraid you will be forced to find other lodgings. The mob, it seems, destroyed the inn you were staying at."

A sinking feeling began in the pit of her stomach. "Of course." Her words were curt, angry. *Now what can I do? That was the only affordable inn that had room.*

Viscount Martin picked up on her agitation. "Forgive me; if I may, have you another place to go? I don't recall seeing you around town before. I mean, you're not a local."

"No, my lord, I am not. I am just a displaced merchant

104

from another land who got caught up in events after I decided to permanently relocate here."

"Ah. I'm sorry my homeland is giving you such a quick look at how troubled it is."

She gave a strained smile. "If it is safe to venture outside, my brother and I shall be going."

His brow wrinkled in worry. "I don't mean to be presumptuous, but as you already know, it isn't safe to stay in town. Might I suggest you try the palace first? If you are doing work for them, they should find a spot inside to house you."

Raina remained silent, not quite concealing the quick shudder. She didn't trust the rumors of the king's moods, which said he behaved more and more irrationally. The palace could be more dangerous than the townspeople. The young man picked up on her discomfort and stood thinking as she woke her brother and shushed his whining.

"If the palace is not agreeable, I believe the Silver Thorn still has some rooms, or you could beg for lodging at the duchess's. She is a good friend of my father and me, and is equally concerned with the well-being of those living here. If you tell her I sent you, she will provide housing for you and your brother until events calm down."

Not bloody likely a powerful female such as she would want another single, free born young woman around all the time. I'd be looked at as competition, she thought with a quick scowl, having known a few two-faced, catty bitches before. The inn he mentioned was still out of her price range.

"It can't hurt to ask; she is not as mean as some make her out to be. If it weren't for family problems, I would invite you to stay here. Unfortunately, they prevent me from extending the hospitality of my family's home." He bowed to her, then opened the door and stood aside as the two homeless made to leave.

The young woman paused in front of him, "Thank you, my lord. I will keep your counsel in mind."

He smiled at her. She felt a different kind of flutter now, but squashed it and quickly exited the building. Once outside, the sharp, icy wind buffeted brother and sister, instantly sapping the warmth from their bodies. Hilel sniffled, whimpering in discomfort, and pressed tight against her side as they descended the mansion's front stairs to the street. She turned right, down the steep incline, and tried not to slip on the treacherous, ice-covered stones. By the time they crept within sight of the Silver Thorn and the bridge, snow fell relentlessly and the wind howled past. An early dusk settled over the land from black storm clouds. The cold made any idea of trying to find another decent, affordable inn seem an insurmountable task.

"Raina! Carry me! I can't walk! My feet burn. I'm so sleepy."

She just wanted to cry; she also shivered violently. Raina almost walked into the cold stone wall, blinded by the sudden blizzard. With a groan, she hefted up her brother, who didn't seem to have the strength to wrap his arms around her. They and his legs dangled. He felt like dead weight, and only moaned when she tried to speak to him.

"Hilel!" she screamed in his ear. "Wake up! Don't sleep! Please!"

Tears froze on her cheeks as she tried jouncing him and nearly lost her grip. Raina tried to redistribute his weight, causing him to slip from her arms and drop onto the new layer of snowfall.

Fruitlessly she tried to rouse him, and when that seemed impossible, to pick him back up, the ice underneath causing her to slip and slid and crash down beside him.

"Help! Someone! Please help!" She tried to shout, words whipping away in a shrieking wind.

Tears and snot covered her face in a thin crust. She managed to turn Hilel onto his back and get herself onto hands and knees, then stood.

Reaching down, Raina snagged her brother under his armpits, and attempted to drag him along the wall; there had to be a gate somewhere. She almost passed it, except one of the iron hinges snagged her cloak and ripped it, letting her know it was there. She pounded, kicked, and shouted as hard and loud as she could. She was ready to give up when one side creaked open and two massive men looked out at her.

The sight of them would usually have sent frissons of fear and panic throughout her, but she forced them down. Now was not the time to give in to her emotions, not with her brother's life in danger. They shouted at her, but the wind made it impossible to understand. One came over and picked up her limp, snow-crusted brother while the other beckoned to her. Once inside, old crumbling buildings cut out some of the wind as a third slave shut the gate. She followed the man carrying her brother as he brought her down the frozen mud drive and around a small house. Immediately the wind slammed into them, causing the party to stagger against the buffets toward a door. Raina had a brief glimpse between swirling, driving snow, of the town sitting far below.

The slave led his charges inside a cramped kitchen, where a woman even younger than Raina with frightened, wide eyes and the demeanor of a rabbit shut the door, the sound of the storm instantly muffled.

A fat cook barely looked up from his chopping. "Don't just stand there, girl! Go and get Susafan and inform your mistress."

The girl scurried off, flinching at each word.

"Best lay the boy in our sitting room by the fire. Thaw him out. Looks half dead to me," the cook replied unhurriedly, dumping his work in a pot. "I'll send in something hot." He set the pot on a hook over the fireplace and moved toward a pump and basin.

"Follow me," the guard slave replied in a deep bass voice.

She had no choice; now that it seemed she and her brother were safe for the moment, she felt all her senses dulling. The slaves' sitting room turned out to be surprisingly comfortable and cozy. A cheerful fire crackled in the iron screened hearth, radiating warmth. A wealth of oil lamps lent a rich glow, dispelling any gloom. Hilel was laid down on a couch near the fire, the sudden warmth a shock.

"He can't stay in his wet clothes," Raina stated with determination, expecting an argument of some sort.

"Then you'd better get 'im out of 'em, shouldn't you?" the man replied as he walked toward and out the door.

"What . . . I need something to wrap him in!" she called after, without receiving a reply. "Asshole," she muttered and wiped at the thawing snot and tears on her face.

She took off her cloak, snow falling in piles on a braided reed rug, and worked on her brother's clothes. A knock on the open door announced a middle-aged slave woman.

"Hello. I am Susafan, Her Grace's body slave. Mary Elana told me about the two of you."

She clucked her tongue, shaking her head, her gray-shot brown hair in a coiled braid at the back of her head. She shut the door with one hand and advanced, kneeling beside the boy.

The body slave placed a pile of what looked like towels and blankets next to her.

"Let me. You should get out of your things, too—don't want to end up sick from cold," she commanded in a warm, yet firm tone.

Deftly, quickly, her work-roughened hands peeled Hilel out of his soaked, snow-crusted clothes and shoes, wrapping him snugly in blankets after drying him off. She turned her attentions toward Raina.

"Well, come on. Hurry up." Her tone brooked no nonsense.

Raina complied, thinking the woman had a gleam in her eyes which might soon precede her doing the job. Susafan handed towels over, and worked on drying the woman's hair herself as Raina dried herself off. The slave used the last of the blankets to wrap around her, and sat her down on a couch opposite her brother's. A knock came on the door, the slave calling out to enter.

Rabbit, who must be the one Susafan called Mary Elana, carried wooden buckets over and set them down where indicated. The slave tested the temperature, nodding in satisfaction.

"Put your feet in; thaw them out before you lose your toes. Wouldn't hurt to stick your hands in, either," she replied critically, eyeing Raina's blanched extremities.

Blushing furiously at being treated as if she were a child again, the young woman did as bid. The hot water made her moan as pain tingled almost unbearably throughout her feet and hands. Susafan had gone around back of the couch and was now brushing out Raina's long, chestnut hair.

"What exactly was a young lady such as yourself doing out in such nasty weather? Don't you know how foolish it was? You nearly died, and your brother as well."

A sudden surge of rage had her snapping, "There would have been no need for us to be searching for new lodgings if it weren't for this cursed town and the wretches inhabiting it."

There was no reply, only the occasional tug as snarls were brushed out. She felt the woman's hands beginning to braid her hair.

"You speak well. Not a slave," the older lady mused. "A coddled daughter of a rich merchant?"

"No," Raina gritted out. "Who I was is of no importance. Not anymore, and especially not here."

Another cluck of disapproval came from Susafan. She walked around to face the woman, finished with braiding. "A word of caution, young mistress. Those who reside in this house will neither cause nor bring harm to you or your brother. Her Grace will not allow it. She will, however, expect answers to her questions in exchange for her hospitality. I suggest you speak truthfully with her, ere you come to regret any duplicity later."

The slave gathered up their wet clothes and shoes and crossed the room, opening the door and saying before she left, "Cook will have a hot meal brought in for you both. When you have warmed up, eaten, and your things are dry, I will take you to Her Grace."

Raina sat, scowling at the closed door, lips compressed.

CHAPTER FIFTEEN

Raina hurried across a palace courtyard, the clack and clatter of wood all around. She paused briefly, seeing orphaned young boys and a few girls playing with wooden swords and shields. Others scrambled over and around the piles of snow. She knew her brother was one of the groups pretending to be soldiers, and just hoped he behaved himself. After watching a few minutes, she turned, shifting the bulky stack of accounts in her arms before continuing on. Raina passed through halls and rooms, each guarded, even if not in active use. She came at last to the great doors leading into the council chamber. The guards opened them for her, allowing passage. The young woman noticed His Majesty in attendance. She made a deep curtsey to him, noting he ignored her obeisance. As Raina retreated the correct distance—for it would not do to immediately present her back to the king—she noted his rumpled robes of state and general unkempt air. She also caught a whiff of alcohol.

The young woman approached the council table, a noble in each seat, with Her Grace, newly appointed royal advisor to the king, seated at the head of the table which was stacked high with scrolls, wax and clay tablets. Standing behind her was a man with dark hair and eyes. His gaze swiftly but effectively sized her up before returning to watching the rest of the gathering. Merchants and craftspeople crowded the large space, making it seem smaller than it really was. Men and a few women argued with her, while several copyists sitting to the sides scribbled furiously to record every word, listening in fascination.

"You cannot do such a thing! It's bad enough those women are aping the men, but to demand that! No, I will not stand for it," one of the wine merchants bellowed.

"Even Lord Nicky, bastard he was, knew what a woman's place is."

"Gentlemen, are you perhaps forgetting recent events? We have lost many people, including men, to the weather and the bandits. We must have replacements if the town means to survive. We cannot wait until spring and hope for travelers. My proposal is very simple: those who want to learn will be given the chance. If you don't want your own kin involved, by all means, forbid them from partaking."

"No, it's a dangerous precedent you are setting. What will male newcomers with the required skills do when it is found a woman does male work?" another outraged male demanded.

"I am sure some of the women will be glad to give up their new, temporary roles when the day comes. Remember, all that I do and implement is not permanent, but merely a way to get us through hard times."

"I still don't like it." Almost every person present supported the complaint, adding to it.

The noise swelled, and for a moment it seemed a riot would break out, but a furious pounding of a staff, and Aranthus's continuous calls for silence kept actual violence at bay. Those present didn't stop their arguing until they noticed the palace guard tossing people away from the crowd and clubbing them, at which point, all present realized the king was screaming at them.

"Traitors! How dare you?! How dare you disagree with my chosen advisor? I will have you hanged. I will strip you of titles and wealth. Treasonous fiends." His Majesty frothed about the mouth, spittle flying, face mottled purple and red from the force of his shouting.

Raina saw how the people quickly quieted while debasing themselves toward the king. Eventually, he leaned back in his throne, motioning them to continue, his enraged stare and clenched fists keeping order as his people turned back to the discussion.

The duchess inclined her head regally toward Maceanas, a smile of thanks pulling her lips up, to which he gave a curt nod in return. Raina caught the swift smirk which crossed the face of the man behind her chair before his expression turned neutral again.

Her melodious voice brooked no disagreements. "Your objections are noted, but we will continue. We have no other choice. We must adapt and change where necessary; otherwise, we may as well abandon the town instead of clinging to the way things were done and slowly dying. Sir Dalton, have you any more word on the remnants of the royal army?"

"No, Duchess. After going through the records, and asking about, I have come to the conclusion there are none and have been for some time."

A new round of voices rose at his revelation.

"Unacceptable! We cannot be unguarded! We barely have a sheriff's office."

"And the palace guards are tied up with His Majesty's delusions of assassins creeping about the palace." A few people forgot themselves and called out, only realizing their mistake when said guards grabbed hold of them and hauled them, some desperately apologizing or protesting, to the dungeons.

"We could hire mercenaries . . ." her grace suggested blandly, no hint on her face the forcible removals caused her worry, "or convince the bandits . . ."

The protests became even more vigorous until she let the subject, and a few more townspeople carted off, go.

"Sir Dalton, it would be an immense kindness if you could discover where the army has gone off to. Surely some are still alive, hopefully not all in hiding. We do need protection, since the bandits are only going to increase their bold attacks as winter continues. We need to re-form the army. Sir Dalton, I expect you to take inventory of the armory, and come up with some suggestions for achieving the goal."

He huffed and chewed one end of his luxurious white mustache. "I shall try."

"There is no 'try.' You will do as bid or I shall find another who is willing," Her Grace snapped out.

Raina continued sorting out her load on a small side table, keeping her head down as she eavesdropped and waited for her turn. Her eyes burned from hours staring at numbers, hands cramped from holding a quill, back aching with long hours sat hunched over a desk. After a few more minutes, the room emptied as the people, grumbling among themselves, left to start the tasks they'd been assigned. The young woman realized His Majesty and the guards had also taken their leave.

"Your Grace," Raina curtsied.

"Yes, Raina. What has your investigation discovered?"

The young woman held out several thick scrolls. "Here is the census, along with those declared dead from the recent attacks. The second scroll is everyone asking for food and shelter. As for the rest: the royal storehouses have been severely depleted. What was supposed to be inside isn't. The only explanation I can find is both of the main men in charge stole what they could and sold it for profit, which they must have pocketed. If no more people show up begging for shelter, we will have enough to last us through the winter."

"Come spring?"

"No, Your Grace. Not unless ships come bearing supplies."

"The royal treasury? Does it have the funds should such an event happen?"

The young woman hesitated a moment, fear fluttering in her stomach, but so far the duchess had shown herself to be understanding and didn't blame those for things which were not their fault. "I am not sure; the way the numbers are adding up now, only if we put the building off. I have a lot of work left to do, and the records are confusing and misleading."

She understood immediately what Raina referred to. "Keeping a second set of numbers has been a time-tested method of stealing funds. I shall speak with the head of the treasury and determine who is behind the problem." She held her hand out for the scrolls. "Has Aranthus passed on the state of the kitchen stores?"

"Yes, Your Grace." She waited while the duchess read, before passing over the rest of the material.

The young woman did her best to conceal a yawn behind her hand and not fidget. It was hard, the only sounds in the room crackling from the fireplace and scrolls being opened and rerolled. Raina felt unease prickle along her skin, though she could not say why. Despite this, she felt herself nodding off, only to jerk awake and stumble awkwardly.

"Thank you, Raina. Get some sleep. You are of no use tired."

The dismissal was plain. She curtsied again and left the

room. Once outside, the anxiety she felt lessened with each step she took away from the council room, a feeling she would usually stop and examine, but exhaustion rolled over her mind, making thinking and staying awake an effort. Raina knew she needed a quick nap after checking on her brother.

CHAPTER SIXTEEN

The king paced inside his royal suite of rooms, his continuous state of inebriation momentarily swept away by events in the council chamber. While walking back to his suite, he heard the voices of mobs in the shrieking wind, the swish and clatter of ice, bandits trying to force their way inside the royal palace. Maceanas's thoughts so unnerved him he broke into a run, and entered his chambers to the sound of his personal guards clinking and clanking behind him. In his paranoia, he forgot who they were and what they did. The men turned into an invading army chasing him down, intent on killing him. The guards before the royal suite's doors saw the panic on their Sire's face, which accompanied his mad screams to be saved as he hurtled inside the room.

Aranthus and the trailing guard stopped before the closed doors and confused men before them, winded from their run through the corridors.

"Halt! What business have you?" they demanded.

"Have you gone as mad as His Majesty?" The chamberlain berated them between heaving gulps for air.

The two guards' faces showed uncertainty, but they did not uncross their pikes to allow access.

"How can we be sure you have not turned traitor?" one demanded.

"If I had, would our Sire not have already demanded our execution?" Aranthus replied, mustering a glare as his thudding heartbeat slowed.

The guards took a moment to think. One replied, "He has not had time to give the orders. Until then, we cannot let you pass."

The chamberlain spluttered, hands tossed up in the air in disbelief. Behind him, the rest of the personal guards clinked and clanged as they shifted.

"Imbeciles! Out of the way!" was what he finally managed to get out.

The guards on duty resisted, despite the anxiety and uncertainty on their faces. Aranthus had a feeling the fear which had first gripped the king all the past months and still held him in its sway was now infecting the rest of the palace staff. The knights behind him muttered, apparently not keen on engaging their fellow men who refused them entrance.

"Fine!" Aranthus snapped out, worms of worry twining in his gut as he backed up, keeping his eyes on the two men before him who had lowered their pikes. Their intent was clear.

The eunuch was not about to let himself be skewered by a couple of jumpy men. It would be better to accept the king's wrath later after he managed to calm down, than to die now. He drew himself up, outrage in every line of his person.

"When His Majesty has calmed down, send a slave to inform me so I may attend our king."

The guards still kept their wary stance as the chamberlain and the men behind him turned and walked off down the hall.

* * *

"I want my guards! I cannot be unguarded! Where's my chamberlain? Someone get me Aranthus!"

A slave slipped outside, grateful for the clean air and a chance to escape the king's growing madness. The two guards on duty cast sideways glances at the slave. Before one could make a comment, the man trotted down the corridors, passing more guards who stood at attention, ostensibly to keep marauders at bay.

It took the slave nearly three-quarters of an hour to find Aranthus, by which time he was sweating profusely in fear of what kind of punishment the king would order for him due to how long it took to find the chamberlain.

When both men arrived back at the royal bedchamber, His Majesty was in the middle of a full-blown rage. One of the guards opened a door, and an empty clay bottle which had been thrown shattered behind the men, who had ducked to avoid the unexpected missile.

"Your Highness. I am here. What is the will of my king?"
Aranthus entered, speaking soothing words, oozing deference as he
knelt with head bowed submissively.

"I want my guards. Do you not hear those noises? Bandits!
Assassins are trying to get in and kill me!"

The chamberlain noted this was not one of the usual fits
Maceanas had. This one appeared to be much worse. He spotted
slaves and harem women cowering behind or under what furniture
was too large to be tossed about. An especially fierce gust of wind
rattled the wooden shutters over the windows. The king shrieked in
terror and commenced tossing the remains of chairs toward them.
Most of the pieces bounced off the walls, to land harmlessly on the
floor. But one or two hit their mark and the tinkle of shattering
glass could be heard.

The king gave a long scream, hands reaching up to grip his
hair. "Guards! They've made it inside my room. Help me."

The two men poked their heads inside, as the slave cowered
behind Aranthus's bulk.

"He's gone right mad, hasn't he?" one of the men muttered
to his fellow guard.

"I think I'd rather be outside patrolling than dealing with
this," the other muttered back.

The chamberlain sucked in a worried breath, but pasted a
calming smile on his face, while quietly instructing the slave,
"Find the royal physician and tell him to come at once. When you
have done that, send a messenger to bring the advisor here. Tell her
it is of the highest priority."

The slave bolted, glad to be out of the stinking room and
the mercurial moods of the king. The guards watched him go with
no small amount of envy on their part.

Aranthus proceeded farther inside the chamber, talking in
soothing tones as one would to a frightened child, hoping the
physician hurried.

* * *

Illyria and Eron arrived at the palace to find the halls and
corridors filled with gossiping guards and palace slaves. One of

Mathias' men escorted the pair. Greetings and questions died at sight of the fierce expression on the advisor's face, and her firm pace which had people scrambling out of her way.

"Should I find any of you not going about your duties when I return, I shall find more work for you which will keep your idle hands busy and still your wagging tongues," the duchess snapped out without pause.

Behind her, the crowd straightened from their curtsies and bows, hurrying to act busy. The guards at the entrance to the royal wing snapped to attention, already pulling the doors open for her to pass through.

Once shut behind, one man whistled low, commenting, "I'd give a week's pay to see that fight."

Illyria arrived to find the inner guards holding the doors open eagerly for her. Commingled voices reached her ears clearly. She swept inside, adroitly avoiding the debris which littered the floor.

A thunderclap of sound from her slamming her hands together put a halt to the arguing.

"Majesty, I am told you have concerns regarding your safety?"

The king hurried over and gripped both her hands in his tightly. "Thank the Great Spirits you are here. I need more guards. Don't you hear them? The bandits? They're trying to get inside and kill me, just as they did my family."

Behind him, Aranthus rolled his eyes and the physician snorted loud enough to make his own opinion known.

"Then we should not linger here where they can find you. I will send for more guards before we move you to safer lodgings," she replied.

"They should already be here! It's treason! They are in league . . ."

The advisor cut him off neatly. "Nonsense. They are no doubt busy chasing the bandits away. I will send my own guardsman to personally bring more men here."

The king glared suspiciously at the man standing slightly behind her; he bowed solemnly, the barest hint of a mocking smile hovering about his mouth.

Lowering her voice, and turning her head, Illyria said to Eron, "Take the royal physician with you and have him bring a drink which will put His Majesty to sleep. If he objects, remind him I will replace him first chance I get."

Eron gestured to Dr. Greggson, and together the two men exited the room while she worked on getting the king to at least sit down until reinforcements arrived. Aranthus hurried to straighten the heavy chair His Majesty favored. The king sat, hands clutching the armrests, jumping at every little sound.

Advisor and chamberlain drew off a few paces, yet still in sight of the king.

"Dr. Greggson is bringing a sleeping draught. When it takes effect, I want His Majesty's chambers thoroughly scoured clean. We will work on getting him bathed and properly barbered when he wakes."

Aranthus sucked at his teeth. "He will not like your duplicity when he wakes. He may strip you of position and title."

"A chance I am willing to take. His unsettled mind is affecting the staff and, in turn, those who shelter here. We have enough problems with food and wood stores running low, without added problems."

"I will do as you wish." His tone implied that despite his fondness for her, he would make sure any blame landed on her alone.

It wasn't long before Eron and the physician returned. It took ten minutes of soothing and coaxing before the king would drink the concoction presented him. Once he did, it took a further fifteen minutes for him to grow drowsy and compliant enough for the men to lead him to the royal bed and lay him down. The sheets stank of sweat and sex, but they covered the king up anyway.

"Ladies," Illyria turned to the harem women present as snores rose from His Majesty, "if you would be so kind as to return to your rooms, I shall be along shortly to speak with all of you."

The women fled, most grateful to get out of the room, only a few irritated they had to take orders from the elegant woman.

"When he wakes, what then?" Aranthus wondered.

"Dr. Greggson, how long has the king's . . . preoccupation . . . with being attacked grown since Nicky and Rablias's treachery was exposed?"

The man thoughtfully stroked his beard, eyes narrowed. He still hated the new advisor for making him treat the unwashed masses, but had seen enough of her efforts to weed out those taking advantage of their positions to tread with care.

"I have been spending most of my time treating the townspeople"—he still voiced his complaint—"instead of the king, so I am uncertain. He has these fits; they come and go. Usually, if I am around, I can stave them off before they get to this level."

She ignored his jab. "Have you an apprentice?"

"I wouldn't trust him with so delicate a task as His Majesty's health. But he knows enough to be effective in other areas," Dr. Greggson blithely replied.

The twisted smile she gave was the only comment to his blatant maneuvering to get out of treating the townspeople. "Very well, doctor. I release you from the dreary duty of caring for the peasants. In return, you will keep His Majesty calm and complaisant. Use what you must, be it drugs, wine, or women. I'm sure, since you have achieved your goal of no longer having to waste your . . . talents . . . on the citizens, we will not have a repeat event of what just happened. Your apprentice can take over treatment of the townspeople. If I hear any word His Majesty is roaming the halls unsupervised while in the grip of madness, I shall hold you solely responsible. We must not let any harm come to him, nor let him be the cause of any during these states. I trust we understand each other?"

His face bloomed red at her implications. "Implicitly," he gritted out, bowing stiffly before excusing himself so he could gather his supplies.

Aranthus had already sent the exhausted slaves who'd been inside the room to take a rest and meal break. New slaves filtered inside, and began the laborious task of cleaning and straightening the royal suite. Illyria and Eron stepped outside and walked a few paces down the hall.

"Why don't you just kill him the way you've done with everyone else?"

"I need my puppet a while longer, until I have replaced key positions with those who will be loyal to me. If the doctor keeps him drugged and quiet, he will serve my purpose."

CHAPTER SEVENTEEN

The royal treasurer and his underlings had broken off work to eat a late midday dinner in one of the gloomy outer rooms which made up their offices. He didn't like the sudden prying into his accounts, as he thought of them, by the upstart little foreign girl, no matter who had ordered it.

He was confident she hadn't discovered the methods by which he carefully bilked the crown of its income and gave it to himself instead. His wife had sent a slave with a meat pie, a flagon of ale, and a sweet pastry made of dried summer fruits. As was Tanner's right, being in charge, he sat in one of two padded chairs before the crackling fireplace. Anson sat in the other across from him. The rest of the workers sat shivering at their high-legged desks. They each took turns warming themselves by the round wood burner placed in the center of the room.

It was this mood of smug satisfaction the sudden appearance of His Majesty and the duchess, with royal guards, ruined.

Some of the underlings jumped, spilling food or drink. Tanner choked on a swallow of wine before he could sputter out, "What the— Who the hell!"

"Kneel before the king!" Aranthus bawled out.

Diners scrambled to swallow down their meal, and hurried to make their obeisance.

Boot heels clicked on stone as a person stalked over. Tanner could see his own face in the highly polished black leather. A scroll dangled before his face; he took it as the king's slurred voice commanded, "Rise, as you were."

A frantic scraping of wood on stone commenced as the workers obeyed. They sat but did not eat; instead, they stared avidly at the woman advisor. Today's events would make for exciting retellings at home. The duchess and the king stood out against the drab gray stone and dark wood furniture in their finery.

"Confiscate everything. If it has writing or numbers on it, I want it," the duchess ordered, turning to Maceanas.

"Stop right there! No one touches the royal books without my permission," Tanner bellowed before his underlings could obey.

"You dare saith thus to your king?" His Majesty bellowed in anger. "You will do as you are told."

Tanner hurriedly unrolled the scroll, eyes pinging back and forth across the page. His outrage and panic grew. He had to keep calm, though, if he wanted to survive this unwelcome and unannounced inspection.

"Majesty," he began, only to be rudely cut off.

"Keys. Now," the duchess snapped at him, holding her hand out for them while the bulk of the guards fanned out to search the rooms, grabbing tablets and parchment, even scraps of paper, stuffing it all into sacks they carried. Those who weren't so engaged closed and barred the doors and stood with their backs to them.

"These keys cannot and will not leave my person. As I," he emphasized, confident the king would support his decision, "have been commanded by His Majesty."

An amused smile lifted one corner of her mouth as her eyebrow quirked in unison.

"And your king is commanding you to do as my advisor wishes. It has been far too long since I last saw my treasure," Maceanas announced, eyes wandering about the room.

Anson noted the king's pupils were dilated, and a faint scent of herbs and wine wafted from his person. He narrowed his eyes in sudden suspicion. The scent was familiar—one he had smelled before when his child had been given a calming drink before a nasty cut on his head had been sewn shut. He tried to catch his supervisor's eye, but the man stared intently at the advisor.

Tanner forced down his growing panic as that damn woman addressed the workers. "Finish your dinner, and afterward I will be speaking with each of you. You will not be allowed to leave the premises until some questions have been answered."

The treasurer's displeasure grew. "Outrageous! There is no need . . ." At sight of the royal scowl, he realized he dared not protest further within the king's hearing range.

"My apologies, Sire. I shall need my assistant and one of the copyists to help with the locks and traps. If Your Majesty will follow me, please." He bowed low before turning and entered the first of many chambers which led farther inside.

Five minutes of locks and disabled traps later, the great carved and gilded doors of the vault swung inward. The royal treasurer touched his torch to a pool of liquid which shimmered in its stone trough on each side of the open doors.

Flame ignited and raced along the surface, following the channels which waited. They all stood and watched as the vast space slowly revealed itself under the line of flaming oil. At the far back, the separate lines of fire met in a large round bowl with a highly polished bronze disk behind it which reflected the light toward other disks positioned about the room. The ceiling was lost in darkness, and the rough walls revealed the space had been chipped out of the mountain.

Illyria could not understand what type of system the treasurer used to group things, unless it were one called "utter chaos." Chests, barrels, sacks, and other storage items lay in piles. Amid all the clutter stood worn, ancient statues, some made of marble, others of precious metals and jewels. She half expected a dragon to come roaring out from behind the large bronze disk at the back of the room.

"I trust there is a method somewhere in all this, of which I am merely ignorant?"

The displeasure in the advisor's voice caused Tanner and his second-in-charge to shift and dart looks at each other.

Beside her, the king frowned. "I do not recall ever seeing my wealth so . . . diminished." He took a few steps forward, sweeping the area with narrowed eyes.

"The Royal Harvest Ball was more expensive than those held in the past, especially with the addition of the peasantry." Tanner made excuses.

The king's eyes swung toward the advisor.

"I am unaware of there being enough townspeople left after

the raid which would have caused a significant depletion of funds for the ball. If I might, when was the last time you visited the royal vaults, Majesty?" Her Grace delicately probed.

Maceanas's brow furrowed in thought. "It has been . . . well, awhile," he admitted. The king stepped down the three stairs into the chamber itself. He strode over to a collection of chests spilling a mixture of silver, gold, and bronze coins.

A smug smile creased Tanner's face, as he made a hand gesture meant to signify: there is your explanation.

The advisor wasn't about to let him off so easily. "Which says the crown's expenses have been exceeding income. The other explanation is the records I hold."

"You are mistaken, and no doubt poor at arithmetic, as all women are." Tanner's tone was patronizing. "The only expenses fulfilled today or in the past have been of the normal variety."

The duchess brought up a leather folio she had been holding by her side, undid the clasp, and let it fall open on her left arm. The flickering light caught the half-crown she wore as her head dipped down, selecting parchments. Tanner's resentment grew. Lord Nicky, utter bastard he had been, had never dared to wear any sort of headgear which even hinted at being a crown the way that damn woman was.

"For your consideration, Sire: a total of Lord Nicky's expenses during his tenure as advisor, per year."

Aranthus took a copy, as did Tanner.

She brought out even more parchments, naming them as she passed them out. "What Nicky claimed to be yearly personal versus official expenses according to the records he kept. Also, the same for the sheriff's office, and Jake."

Both men's hands were rapidly becoming full as Her Grace continued on for each office and official in the kingdom which received royal funds.

"The last set of copies you hold is of what the royal treasury pays its workers, according to the claims they have made. It is possible it is out-of-date, as I had to request a copy from the royal records keeper. Be that as it may, given the state of this room, it would be wisest if we did the yearly reconciliation now, and increased security measures. If I might have the royal books, they will show the income and outlay. We can then put these allegations of misappropriated funds to rest." The duchess acted as if just the mere act would not be a massive undertaking.

Tanner glowered at her, Aranthus chewed his lower lip, and the king nodded as he prowled about the room. Occasionally he plunged his hands into a pile of coins or jewels and let them trickle through his fingers.

Anson, to the head treasurer's disgust, choose to speak. "I can get you the original records, Your Grace, so you need not rely on copies which may or may not have been transcribed correctly."

"Thank you. Your cooperation shall not be forgotten," the duchess replied.

"We do not need more security. As I stated before, the king and I are the only two people who hold keys to the vault," protested the treasurer, shooting a glare at his assistant.

"I must disagree. It is too easy to grab handfuls of coins, gems, or sacks of spices with no one the wiser," the advisor replied, "especially when there is more than one person in the vault at the same time."

"I fail to understand how my wealth could be made more secure. Or how it has dwindled so much." Maceanas puffed out his chest. "The piles should be taller than I."

Blithely the duchess explained in more detail what she meant.

Tanner stewed. *Dratted woman! Redesigning means royal guards will be present to keep any workers from stealing. It will make it harder for me to funnel my share away.*

The king blinked in startlement before a pleased smile split his lips.

"And you say these . . . improvements . . . will keep those craftsmen needed for them occupied the rest of the winter, thus effectively paying back the crown's charity of housing and feeding them during these dark times," the king stated.

"Yes, Sire."

"By royal decree, let it be so. I give you full authority to do what you must. Treasurer, I hereby command you relinquish your keys to the duchess."

"I'm sorry, what?" Tanner spluttered in offense.

"You dare to question your sovereign?" Anger suffused the king's face with red. "Think first and tread lightly with your response." The warning was dire as Tanner was about to offer a rebuttal.

The treasurer's nostrils flared, lips tightened, eyes narrowed as he gave a stiff, formal bow. He thrust his clenched fist toward the advisor, keys jingling on the iron ring. She wrapped her hand around the key blades, making them clang. Tanner and the duchess exerted equal but opposite force for several seconds before she ripped the ring with its keys free.

His eyes watered with pain, not having expected her to possess the strength she did. A brief smirk flitted across her face, further heightening Tanner's rage toward her.

The king gave one last look around, clapped his hands once and then rubbed them together. "Advisor, I will leave the rest in your capable hands. Aranthus will make sure as we leave all here are aware of my wishes."

He turned while motioning to his guards. The three members of the treasury bowed to the king's retreating back.

Bitch! You think you can just meddle in my domain? I see now what kind of menace Lord Nicky was right to complain about and try to contain. The head treasurer's thoughts were bitter.

"Your meddling, instead of ensuring the funds remain safe, will only provide a greater opportunity for stealing," Tanner groused.

"I have complete faith you will be certain to inform His Majesty if your fears manifest themselves—if only to gain a measure of revenge, however small—for the insult done toward your supervision." The advisor turned her back on him in dismissal and addressed the clerk who had accompanied them.

"Copyist, what is your name?"

"I am Kevayne, Your Grace."

"Those desks and chairs"—she gestured to the furniture in the center of the room—"are they bolted or can they be moved?"

"They are moveable," he promptly replied.

She made no indication of approval or disapproval at his answer, only swept the room a last time with a piercing gaze before gesturing to the men to precede her outside the treasure room.

The men did as requested, Tanner taking the opening to hiss at his second-in-command when he thought they were out of her hearing range.

"Just what the hell do you think you're doing, Anson? We have a good setup and you're putting it in danger."

"Maybe I think it's time you joined Nicky."

"You fool! You think you can take my spot? Take over my idea? Take my money?"

"Why not? You think I don't know you've been cheating more than just the crown, but me and the others who help you?"

"If I go down, you will fall with me," Tanner threatened.

Anson snorted in reply as they watched the advisor relock the doors and come within normal hearing.

"What do you wish us to do now, Your Grace?" Tanner barely kept back his contempt.

"We will return to the main room, where my questions shall be answered. Proceed," she ordered the three workers.

All but four royal guards had been left behind. Illyria motioned six of the eight to escort the men while two were left behind to guard the doors. The traps remained disabled.

Tanner and Anson found themselves forced into separate corners of one of the outer rooms, a guard on each as the duchess called the lowest-ranking workers into the head treasurer's office for questioning.

There must be a way I can frame my underlings and Anson. Surely I shall have enough time to think of a plan while she is busy.

* * *

Tanner swaggered into his office with a small, self-satisfied curl to one side of his mouth. He was the last person the advisor needed to question. She was tired from being awake most of the afternoon, even with being indoors and shielded from the weak, winter sun. Illyria never had managed to work out a way of draining and storing Nicky's blood from him before the immortals, with her help, had killed the former advisor. Eron had yet to let her drink from him. When he was her consort, was the answer she consistently received. Respecting the bargain and the man's wishes instead of forcing what she wanted from him, was becoming harder to resist. She would have to dispose of the king soon. Earlier that day, Eron passed on information he'd gleaned from the physician. The man only had enough herbs to keep the king complacent for another two weeks at the rate she was having him doused. The minds of the clerks let her know there were problems. She needed the actual books, both sets, as proof for the king while continuing her charade.

Just hold your temper a little longer, she reminded herself. Lull the people into complacency before loosening the final blow.

"Why are the chests not locked? Nor the barrels secured?" the duchess snapped out, the shutting door behind Tanner adding punctuation to her question.

The treasure paused to process her words, and she watched his smile widen as he replied.

"There is no need. As has been pointed out earlier, there are only two sets of keys. His Majesty holds the other set," Tanner answered.

"Why is there no order?" She mixed her questions up, hoping to keep him off balance.

"His Majesty spends so much, there is no point, as it doesn't stay long before being sent back out."

"A poor excuse. How much of what should be here will I discover to have been stolen when we are done?"

"I'm sure I don't know what you mean. How can anything be stolen if the books balance?" the treasurer asked of her.

"Are you positive you have never . . . loaned . . . the keys to your assistant in the past, perhaps when there have been extraordinarily busy times?"

"Those keys never leave my possession. I do not recall ever having been consciously lax to allow such to happen. Today has been the first and only time anyone other than I have held them, or been alone in the vault." Tanner forced a mixture of insult and outrage into his tone. *And the last, bitch.*

"Would you be prepared to swear upon your life?" Her Grace quietly, calmly replied. "Just because Rablias is gone and there is no replacement doesn't mean lawbreakers won't be punished."

Tanner sneered, but the quick lick of his lips and shifting away of his eyes as he answered told her the man lied. "I will swear what I say is true."

It will take at least two months, working eight to ten hours each day, to do a thorough and proper inventory. If need be, I can be gone before then.

Illyria needed him to think of where he had placed the stolen goods, or else drink from him. She let the silence continue as she sat staring, evaluating.

He managed no overt fidgeting, only a minor shifting of his weight from one foot to the other. Tanner left off staring back to let his eyes wander about the objects in his chamber.

"Very well. I shall send for you and the others when I am ready to begin reconciling the books with what is inside the vault. Until then, you and your compatriots can consider yourselves on temporary leave."

"Doing so will bring the kingdom to a halt. There are expenses which must be paid. My clerks and copyists don't receive coin unless they work. They won't be able to feed their families or buy wood." He stabbed a finger toward her in emphasis. "Some concern you show for the king's citizens. I can't wait until they learn how little you really care about them," he gloated.

She stood, leaning her fists on top of the desk. "This can all go away if you admit your guilt and return your ill-gotten gains."

"I have no guilt, nor stolen goods, to be worried about being discovered by the likes of you."

"Keep lying, and instead of rotting in the dungeons, your corpse will be hanging from the palace wall. Consider my offer, and send me word when you are ready to be reasonable," the advisor pleasantly replied. "In the meantime, enjoy your night off."

Their eyes clashed a moment, then he leaned forward and deliberately spat upon the floor. "That's what I think of you and your offer."

He wheeled and stomped out of the room, pausing at the main entrance to rake his eyes over the guards and the rooms which comprised the treasury.

"When you are ready to apologize to me for your insinuations, Duchess, I will remember. I will more than remember; I will see you toppled from your position." He made a low bow, insult in every line of his body, before leaving.

"Guards, we shall lock up. I leave it you to decide how you will divide the hours of insuring no one other than the king or I attempts to penetrate these rooms while I investigate. I want two people on duty all day and night until I say otherwise."

The men cast glances at each other, a few shuffled their feet, but they all mumbled assent.

CHAPTER EIGHTEEN

The slave escorted a burly man into his master's study. The visitor paused a moment to scan the room before seating himself.

"Ale?"

"Thanks."

After the drinks had been brought, they toasted each other and drank, waiting for refills and the slave to leave before getting beyond superficial subjects. The swish of snow and wind could be heard against the outside of the brick and plaster home.

"Has that bitch visited you again?" Tanner asked.

"No. But I heard she questioned all the clerks a second time, with some of them more than that. She had some of them arrested and tossed into the dungeon. Seems a few of our workers were also running concurrent scams, piddling enough we would never have noticed. I say we leave now. There's something not right with that woman. How was she able to break Lord Nicky's hold?" Anson grumbled.

"Don't be stupid. If we leave she'll know we're guilty of something whether or not she finds proof. Just keep your mouth shut." Tanner scowled as he drank more ale.

He too had heard about the clerks, and while he wouldn't show his concern to his underling, the head of the royal treasury had already put in motion his plan of making the man before him a scapegoat. He gazed in satisfaction at his study. It was simple, but richly furnished, including the rest of his house. His family dined well, and wore clothes and jewels to rival the richest of merchants and minor nobles. He was not about to let anything ruin him.

"I am wondering if the rumors of the prick being a warlock weren't real after all. Maybe she is a witch." Anson continued his musings. "We don't need those kinds here. I say we join forces with the storehouse master. He said she's poking her nose in his records too."

Tanner shot the other man a look. "Hell, that damn woman is prying into all the royal accounts."

"So we join forces."

"What good is it gonna do? The king ain't gonna listen to us."

Anson scowled at his superior. "I say we run while we still have a chance. Take what we have. You have contacts at the docks; when's another ship coming in?"

"Look, I told you. We aren't running. We have a good scheme going. She's not going to find proof. My work is solid, my skills beyond compare. Besides, I'm the only one who knows where the real books are stored." Tanner seethed, jaw clenched.

"Yeah, but if she's—"

"Don't be stupid!" the royal treasurer bellowed. He squinted his eyes as he gazed at a spot on the wall, thinking. "Look, isn't the madman who found Nicky speaking out against her? Doesn't he go around town, preaching against her?"

"Huh?" It took a moment for Anson to understand to whom his superior referred. "Oh, yeah. That crazy man. Calls himself a priest or some such nonsense. Always standing around ranting and raving about the 'Death Lands' and evil beings and begging for handouts. What about him?"

"We can use him."

"How? He doesn't trust anyone he can't convert."

"I'll send a slave with some stuff, food, wood, whatever; tell him it's a donation for his work and have the slave mention some choice 'gossip' about the bitch and how it might be beneficial if he can continue denouncing her from outside her own gates." Tanner smiled broadly.

His underling pulled at his lip, worry creasing his brow. "I don't understand how it's going to help us."

"Idiot! Think! The more he rails against her, the more people will start to wonder, and question what she's doing. The merchants and the nobility who don't want a female advisor will become more strident in their opposition." The royal treasurer rang a bell for his slave. Plotting was thirsty work.

Anson still sat with a creased brow, unease in every line of his being. The minutes ticked by, Tanner rang for the slave again.

What was taking so long? If he didn't come soon, he was going to get a beating he wouldn't soon forget. Just when Tanner was about to stand and yell for his slave, the door to his study opened, and he wished it hadn't.

The look of shock and panic on the faces of the two men before the duchess caused a small, smug smile to her lips. She held a pitcher in her hands as she advanced into the room, kicking the door shut behind her.

Tanner figured he wouldn't get another opportunity, and with a bellow he charged, reaching behind his back for his dagger. He felt himself fly past the spot she had been standing. His momentum was such he barely managed to turn. His right side crashed into the door, his shoulder taking the brunt of the collision, causing pain to shoot down his arm. Tanner barely had time to register the pitcher being swung his way. Ale washed over his head and face, blinding him, and a sharp, immediate pain at the side of his head dropped him, stunned, to his knees. He was barely aware of the shards of the pitcher lying around him.

Anson was still frozen in shock at the sudden attack, and had yet to leave his chair. Blazing golden eyes turned to him as his superior dropped in a heap on the floor.

"Advisor!" he squeaked, bouncing out of the chair so fast it tipped backward, thudding behind him.

"What have we here? Two people who think they are the foxes, not realizing they are the mice."

The man's brain whirled frantically. *Kneel, stupid*, it shouted at him, and he dropped to one knee, bowing his head. "Your Grace—"

"Tut tut," she interrupted him. "No speaking unless it is the truth. I know you two are actively plotting, and have been cheating the crown since His Majesty's father so unwisely placed you both in charge of the royal treasury."

The kneeling man hoped she was bluffing; he flicked his eyes to his groaning superior on the floor. "I am unaware of what you refer to."

"How disappointing. For once, it would be nice if you blots on humanity grew a pair, and just admitted your wrongdoings."

He trembled at the calm tone, but responded anyway. After

all, he didn't have the real books. "I am not lying, Advisor. I am willing to help you in any way I may, for the chance—"

"Do not attempt to bargain with me, worm. Nor placate me with false promises." Her tone was still smooth and controlled. "You wasted your chance of any clemency when you lied to me earlier today."

Menace filled the room, sweat forming on the underling's brow. He noticed behind the duchess, his superior overcoming his stupor. The man still clutched his dagger. In a sudden move, he brought it around to plunge into the lower leg of the woman within reach. The *thunk* of the dagger sinking into the wood floor reached both men's ears a second before a grunt of pain. Tanner's head hit the floor, blood leaking from his nose and mouth. He didn't move.

Anson couldn't bring himself to look up at the duchess's eyes. He swallowed, wondering if he would have better luck stabbing her, then discarded the notion as his main plan.

"Let's have a chat, you and I." She walked over to him, and the underling felt five iron-hard digits and palm press into his shoulder.

He was boggled at the impossibility before the pain of bone grinding upon bone wiped logical thought from his mind.

* * *

A strange buzzing noise in his ears and the feeling of swimming upward through molasses made Tanner aware he wasn't dead . . . yet. His face and head ached with pain, made all the more intense because the side that had taken the blow lay pressed on the floor. He could barely feel the blood which trickled down. The royal treasurer groaned as he attempted to roll onto his back. Even a little movement caused the room to spin. He closed his eyes and fought back a wave of nausea. When he was able to open them, Tanner cautiously sat up, again waiting for the dizziness to pass.

The room was empty. Where was Anson? Where was the duchess? Did she have his assistant and was questioning him? Maybe this meant he would live, if his subordinate could keep his mouth shut, or lie if he couldn't.

Tanner realized he had heard more than the buzzing inside

his head as it faded. The sounds of voices: some of them shrilly female, pounding, and booted feet. He managed to stand, rage pushing the pain aside. The man cast about for his dagger, but it was gone. He would have to try and make it to his back up dagger underneath his pillow, or his sword, also in his bedroom. The royal treasurer opened his study door to behold two palace guards, one to either side of it, in the hall. Their halberds crossed in front of the doorway. They turned to face him, eyes glinting with purpose.

"Sir," barked one of the men as they both brought their halberds around to block forward movement. "Stay inside the room. By authority of the Royal Advisor Illyria, in accordance with His Majesty's proclamations, you are under arrest for crimes against the crown."

"The hell you say!" he barked. "I demand to be taken to His Majesty! This is outrageous! I am innocent! There is no proof!"

The weapons stayed firm, the guards' expressions tightening more, expecting trouble.

"Stay inside, sir." The first guard repeated his warning.

Tanner debated fighting, but a new set to the men's jaws he had not seen before when he'd had dealings with the royal guard had him discarding the thought. Perhaps they would be open to a bribe?

"Now gentlemen, let's calm down and think about this a moment, eh? I know how much you men earn. It's a paltry amount considering all the hard work and royal demands which have to be met. What if I could see to the both of you getting a higher pay? In return, you escort me to the palace, and make sure the king will hear me out."

Tanner could see the men wavering. "Here, I'll even give you an additional bonus out of my own pocket right now."

He slowly reached for the money pouch on his belt and drew out four silvers for both men. The treasurer held the coins in his outstretched palm. One of the guardsman licked his lips and shot a quick glance to his fellow guard. The man was reaching out when a cold voice interrupted.

"Allen, Allen . . . taking bribes?" Her Grace commented.

Both Allen and Tanner froze. A look of instant regret and

shame flashed across the guard's face. He didn't fight his fellow men as they clapped him and Tanner in manacles and chains.

"You have no proof!" Tanner struggled, repeating his mantra.

"Anson was wise enough to rethink his position. He has agreed to testify against you in exchange for a reduced sentence," the duchess informed him.

"But you have no proof! Neither of you does! I will be pardoned! Just you wait and see!" the head treasurer yelled as Allen was led away, presumably to the dungeons.

"Tanner! Tanner! I demand to see my husband!" his wife screamed from somewhere close by.

The sound of scuffling and more hysterics from his family came to the treasurer's ears as the duchess shoved Tanner inside his office, the manacles and chains making it hard for him to keep his balance. He fell, butt striking the rug-covered wood floor painfully.

"You monster! You leave my wife and children alone." The royal treasurer struggled to stand, but a booted foot on his shoulder kept him in a kneeling position.

Her Grace rested a forearm on her upraised thigh, bringing her face close to his. "Unlike Nicky, they will come to no harm from my hand." She paused. "Assuming, of course, your wife is indeed ignorant of your perfidy."

Her shark's grin made sweat pour down his back and face. He didn't believe her, saying as much.

She finally removed her foot from his shoulder, and it burned with pain from being used in such a manner. Tanner didn't hear any footsteps. He craned his head to see where she went. The duchess sat in his chair, riffling through the drawers.

He refused to kneel before the bitch. After a brief struggle, knees creaking in protest, he managed to stand.

Her voice, a whip, cracked out, "Defiant to the last. Normally I would applaud, but given you are a liar and a thief, I find it tiresome."

Tanner cast about for something to use as a weapon, finally settling on an ornately decorated and painted vase. His onrushing charge was abruptly stopped by his own momentum as the back of the chair in which she sat slammed into his gut. He pitched sideways, vase slipping from his hands to shatter as he scrambled to keep upright. Without giving himself time to stop and think on the impossibility of how fast the duchess eluded his attack, the royal treasurer grasped the back, meaning to batter her with the chair.

Instead, Tanner found his head painfully yanked by his hair so he stared up at the smoke-stained ceiling. The new abuse on top of the old caused him to yell in pain and let go of the chair, his hands reaching instead to loosen her grip. Dimly, he was aware of his yells turning to horror at the sight of the two ivory fangs among the duchess's gleaming teeth. In a moment, they pierced his neck.

Pain lanced through his veins as his struggles grew more frantic, rising in intensity the more he fought.

Gold, jewels, precious spices. All left in heaps in the treasure vault. Why should he and his family exist on the paltry pay he was allowed as head treasurer with the wealth of the kingdom at his fingertips? It was laughably easy to steal what he wanted. The only hitch was Anson, whose greed slowly grew to match Tanner's as the years passed and they remained uncaught. Even the advisor, when he found out, had let them be. He only asked certain boons in return, which Tanner was all too happy to grant. But now . . . now Nicky was gone, and in his place an implacable enemy who would not be gainsaid.

Pain overwhelmed Tanner's ability to think. He was just a screaming, struggling mass of flesh, bone, and blood. "Make it stop! Make it stop! Pllllleeeeaaaasssse!" He wanted the experience ended.

"It will never end. Not until I get what I want." A cruel voice lanced through the pain, searing into him with an even greater intensity.

Tanner knew if he gave up his secrets, he was dead. *But the pain.* He didn't think he could take anymore.

"Please, stop," he begged, his voice weak.

"Tell me what I want." A soft voice caressed his mind, bringing a cessation to his agony.

I mustn't, Tanner repeated to himself with slipping conviction. At his rebellious thought, the pain returned. It didn't just race through his being, but searched and sheared, destroying who he was.

The head treasurer felt a spectator in his own life, rendered useless as bits of his memories ripped away from him. Each one left an abscess of acid in its place. Gone, his knowledge of his father, mother, brothers and sisters. Gone, his first crush. Gone, his first time lying with a woman. On and on, relentless.

"The cellar! It's in the cellar! Behind the vegetable bins!"

Tanner woke, lying on his side, vomiting bile upon an icy stone floor. He heard screams, mad cackles from the darkness. Panic engulfed him as he realized he must be in the royal dungeons, his own screams of horror joining, mingling with the others.

CHAPTER NINETEEN

Raina and Viscount Martin stood at the top of the bridge, exchanging pleasantries when they heard the far-off sounds of shouting. The palace guard poked their heads out of hastily erected huts. Another blizzard had passed by, leaving more death and devastation in its wake. Homes and businesses weakened by the fire, or of uncertain construction to begin with, collapsed under the weight of more snow and ice. Many who had been inside were crushed or left with horrific injuries. Not a few people ran out of wood or food and froze. Those who made it through, and didn't think they could survive another storm with what they had, showed up at the palace with all their goods, begging for shelter. The small shanty encampment outside the palace walls grew daily. Despite the cold, the stench of unwashed bodies, booze, and misery permeated the air.

The small group still couldn't see what or who caused the commotion. The weak sun did its best to shine down. The noises got louder, and people who had volunteered to go out and cut wood for fuel to keep the homeless warm, appeared.

Behind them, men limped or were half-carried by friends. A few bodies lay still on top of the logs, blood soaking in and dripping down the sides. Bringing up the rear was another cart with people inside. The group began the climb up the icy bridge as the patrol stepped outside, waiting for them.

"What happened?" called out a guard.

"Damn bandits attacked us! Must have thought we had supplies of food. Killed a few of our good men. We captured those we didn't fight off, and some of our boys went after the runners. Found a bunch of their slags and kids, and figured if we took 'em prisoner, that'd keep the others in line." A large man with snow-covered beard and hair spoke.

"Dunno what you want us to do with 'em; we barely have

room for our own."

"Toss 'em in the dungeon, let 'em rot," advised the lead man as he continued on up the steep hill.

The two young people watched in shock as the cart full of captives passed, mostly women, children, and elders with a few young men, all shivering, emaciated, and barely clothed in rags.

"Pardon me, Mistress Raina, but this seems to be a matter which will require my presence at the palace." Lord Martin bowed good-bye, doing his best to hurry up the slippery hill.

Raina turned to the remaining guard. "What if they're not bandits? What if they're really poor farmers?"

He sneered at her. "Don't matter now, do it? They shouldn't be attacking people. If they're starving, they can sell themselves to the people who need and can afford a few more slaves." He paused to spit on the ground. "Now go on with you. It isn't any concern of a woman what happens to them."

The young woman compressed her lips, scowling, turning toward the old Fishton Manor. She didn't trust the duchess, even though Her Grace had been the one to appoint Raina as the new royal treasurer, including a raise in pay, but knew of no one else likely to care what became of those poor people.

I should just mind my own business. After all, no one came to help Hilel and me when the bad things happened.

The guards admitted her through the gates, escorting her to the front of a small house. Raina had enough time to glance at the bulk of the mansion, the structural work suspended until it became warmer. The young woman could still hear the *chink* of iron on stone as someone worked, probably on areas independent of needing the correct temperature. She sat waiting in the simple parlor, hands wrapped around a cup of hot cider, feet stretched toward the warmth of a crackling fire. Eventually, the inner door opened, and Her Grace entered.

Raina stood and curtsied, but was waved to sit.

"I did not think to see you here again." A brief, amused smile curled the older woman's lips up.

The young woman's scowl said it all. "I would not be here; however, there is a subject which I feel you should be informed of."

A brow raised. "More stealing of the royal funds and food stores?"

"No. At least, not that I have come across again, yet." Quickly she told of what had transpired outside, afraid if she gave herself time to think, she wouldn't mention it at all. Raina took a sip of cider when she was done.

Her Grace sat silent, eyes narrowed before speaking. "His Lordship is a fine man, the same in temperament and ideals as his father. I am sure he will make the proper inquiries and see the prisoners are fairly treated."

"My apologies, Your Grace. I do not doubt what you say is true. However, he does not have the respect . . . he hasn't earned . . ." She broke off, cursing softly under her breath. "His own mother works against him. I have accidentally overheard some of the things she says to her friends without realizing I am around."

"Lady Elizabeth has many faults. I do not recall abject revenge toward her only son and heir to be one of them. Not when rumors say he is her favorite."

"I would not know. I only know what I have heard with my own ears. I wanted to make sure the king's advisor knows what is going on in the town."

Another smile crossed the elegant woman's face. "Ah, in which case, I thank you." She stood to go, motioning for the girl to stay seated. "I trust you are settling into your new position, and your brother is doing well?"

"Yes, Your Grace."

"Very well," she replied before exiting the room.

* * *

Viscount Martin slowly rode down into the town proper; thin streams of smoke rose from hearths and chimneys. Before he had gone far, a small crowd of women, children, and elders gathered, arms out, pleading for food.

He shook his head sadly at them. "I only have coin." He offered what he had on him, not much. A few snatched them, others cursed or spit on him. "Go to the palace; you will be taken in," he urged them before moving on.

The young man knew that many, with their deep distrust of the king and the traitor Lord Nicky, would rather starve and freeze first. *How is it none of us saw the depths of evil in the former advisor?* He turned his chestnut mare into the sheriff's office training yard, seeing the recruits hard at work. It seemed to him the group had grown. He handed his reins over to his groom, and walked through the dirty slush to where his father and Saizar stood giving instructions.

"Father, sheriff."

"Afternoon," the men greeted him.

Martin asked if they heard about the attack, proceeding to tell them what he'd discovered, which wasn't much. The prisoners refused to speak with him. He concluded by saying. "I suppose I should inform the duchess."

"I will handle it," his father said, "or Saizar, for it is clear any other such parties will be needing protection. I only hope the farms have enough security, as they will no doubt be attacked next."

* * *

Sydney wrapped his cloak more tightly about him as he descended the dungeon stairs after the head clerk. The walls bore a thin layer of ice, and he could see where ice had been chipped off the stone stairs and floor to allow safe passage.

The fire pit in the guard's room did little to dispel the chill. The men huddled so close, they were in danger of catching fire themselves.

What must the prisoners be suffering if the guards themselves cannot even keep warm? he wondered with dread.

There was grumbling from the new head guard over having to leave the comfort of the fire, and he didn't bother masking his annoyance.

"They ain't gonna talk. They wouldn't fer the last guy what came here."

"His Majesty commands me," the earl lied, which made the man fall quiet as he escorted the noble to a cell.

Sydney peered through the grill set in the door to the new

arrival's cell. He could barely see inside and asked for entrance.

"Damn king and nobles, why you all gotta be bothering with scum when our town is suffering?" he mumbled under his breath as he worked the key.

Finally, the door unlocked and swung open. The guard thrust his torch inside to provide more light. Those inside and nearest cringed, hands up to their eyes to shield them.

The earl entered with his torch, heart seizing at the sight. Ice coated the walls and ceiling thinly, which barely cut down on the stench of human waste and unwashed bodies packed tightly inside. Moldy straw littered the floor. The cell was made to hold maybe four people total, but he counted at least a dozen.

Eyes glittered in faces little more than flesh-covered skulls.

"When was the last time these people were fed?" he quietly asked the guard.

"Last night. They only get one meal a day. We haven't the stores for more," the head guard explained, while his tone implied even if there was, the prisoners wouldn't be given extra food.

Sydney addressed the group. "If any of you want to have a fair hearing and escape hanging, now would be a good time to speak up."

He waited while most turned their eyes or heads away from him. A few stared mutely, eyes dull.

"Please," he began, "if at any point you want to speak with me, I will come. At least consider it for your children, if not for yourselves."

He stepped back outside, the guard following and locking up.

"Told you theys wouldn't talk." The guard couldn't help himself as they walked back to the main room.

"I want to know if any of them want to speak with me. I don't care what time of day or night it is."

"Why's a noble like you care? You people never do," the guard questioned, not caring he could be punished for talking thus with a member of the nobility.

Sydney handed the torch back before replying, "Changes are being made, whether we like them or not."

"I thought you supported, I mean . . ."—the guard realized

he was straying into territory best left alone—"Her Grace."

"She is a woman of infinite kindness and wisdom. She can see the good in a person that others overlook. Even those accused of crimes." He didn't know why he answered, or explained his position, to the crown's servant before him.

The guard snorted, the look on his face clearly saying he didn't trust or believe the noble before him but wasn't going to be stupid enough to argue further.

Sydney took his leave, thoughts heavy with what he had seen and wondering what Lira would do if she knew about the situation. He debated with himself, and decided she ought to know. With this thought in mind, he made his way toward her mansion. It was late enough in the day the duchess would be home and not at the palace on business.

CHAPTER TWENTY

Bre and her mother worked together to clean the inn's guest rooms, a task the few slaves the Thorns owned would typically do. There usually weren't many stay-overs during the winter months, but since the initial raid and fire, a few of the traveling merchants had decided to become citizens. Because of the early, brutal winter, and a shortage of building supplies, they had no choice but to continue to stay at inns or with other guild members who would host them. A cold gust of wind rattled the glass panes, and voices drifted through from the street.

The young woman glanced out the window as she dusted, then stood and stared. A small crowd of people had gathered around two men in brown robes. One of the men, whose long hair and beard tossed about in the wind, gesticulated wildly.

"Stop staring at whatever is going on out there! Mr. Jersen will want the use of his room soon." Her mother's voice intruded on her thoughts.

"Sorry, Ma," Bre apologized. "There is something strange going on. Is that not the crazy priest who saved the former advisor?"

Her mother walked over, arms heaped with used linen as she peered out. "Hrmph," was the only comment she made.

Bre gathered up the cleaning supplies, following her ma back downstairs and stowing them away before she washed her hands. She placed an apron over her dress, and began to help her mother finish dinner.

The Thorn family sat to dinner late, having finished serving the last patron. The family was a jolly lot; there was much chatter, laughing, and ribbing among the siblings and their parents.

Trey, the sixteen-year-old, called out, "Da, Her Grace is hiring more help!"

"Just figured that out, dummy?" their older brother jeered.

"She being advisor now and all with an entire kingdom to help the king run, it's to be expected."

Trey glared back. "Dummy yourself. Not for the kingdom, for her! As part of her household."

Nathan sopped some sauce up with a piece of bread. "You wouldn't be thinking of trying to find a way around my orders to not become a soldier, would ye? Because I won't put up with you learning to be a personal guard." He nailed his son with his gaze.

His two little sisters beside him giggled as they whispered behind their hands in between pretending to feed their dolls.

"I knew it!" his mother shrieked. "What is so wrong with being a respectable and prosperous innkeeper like your father?"

"Yeah. Besides, I'll be needing help once Da retires and I fully take over," the eldest brother retorted between mouthfuls of meat.

"Exactly!" Nathan replied, giving Levi an approving nod.

"Girls, stop feeding your dolls. You're making a mess," Mrs. Thorn reproved her daughters.

Bre sat quietly and ate, thoughts churning inside her. She remembered the conversation she'd had with the duchess when Her Grace first came to live in their town.

Trey continued bullheadedly. "I could be a butler! Or even first footman," he insisted over the scoffs of Levi, and leaned over his plate to deliver his impassioned plea to his father. "Just think of it, Da! Isn't that as prestigious as being an inn keep?"

"Firstly, you don't know anything about buttling. 'Tis a lot different than serving in an inn like ours, no matter how fine the Silver Thorn be," Nathan lectured, his knife waggling as he did so. "Secondly, advisors come and go."

"But not duchesses," Trey protested. "And I can learn to be a butler."

"From whom? You'd have to go to the great houses and be taken on as a mere lowly footman first. It'd be years before you got enough experience, and by then she'll have the spot filled," Levi scoffed.

Trey pelted his brother with a crust from his bread. "What's wrong with me trying? It'll be years before Da retires."

Nathan continued to eat, and caught his wife's eye. He

knew the look she was giving him. He sighed around his mouthful of food as the two brothers continued to argue. He believed everyone had his place, whether they had been born into it or not. He saw no harm in at least trying to better oneself.

"Knock it off, you two!" the inn keep bellowed at his sons. "Trey, if it means that much to you, you may apply to be a footman. However, if you don't get it, I expect you to return to your work here. Understood?"

"What!? You know he won't get it! He doesn't know any more about being a footman than he does being a butler!" Levi protested. "Then he'll just mope around here and be useless when he doesn't get a spot."

"I promise, Da. Thank you." Trey puffed out his chest smugly as he shoveled more food in.

* * *

After dinner had been cleared away and Trey finished his chores, he carefully washed and groomed himself, putting on his best suit of clothes. He was surprised to find his sister waiting at the back door for him.

"You don't mind if I come along for luck, do you? Besides, it would be nice to see what the inside of a duchess's house looks like."

"I don't want it to look like I need a minder," he protested with some heat. "I want her to think I'm mature enough to do the job."

"Please? Besides, I did perform guide service for her. I can be your reference, let her know how well you do your work here." Bre stated her case.

She waited while her brother's brow creased in thought. Finally, he nodded and they stepped out into the dusk together. Snow crunched beneath their boots as they rounded the corner of the inn and crossed the courtyard. As they stepped outside the gates, the crazy priest was still ranting and raving.

"Why don't the guards do something about him?" Bre whispered nervously as they navigated their way around the group of ragged townspeople who stood listening. Many shouted agreement or shot glares toward the town homes lining the street.

"I dunno, maybe the nobles haven't complained enough yet. Maybe they think with the changes going on, it's okay."

"Don't let them see us," Bre breathed out as they gained the opposite side of the street. "I just have a bad feeling about him."

The two siblings paused a moment to turn and look at the crowd around the man. They listened to his ravings, then slipped inside the partly closed great gates to the duchess's mansion. A small line waited outside one of the cottages. They took their place at the end of the line, huddled in their cloaks, each lost in their thoughts. Despite the length, the line moved at a more or less steady pace. Trey and Bre were sixth to enter when slaves came out and replenished the wood in the braziers Her Grace had provided to help keep those waiting somewhat warm and to illuminate the darkness. She or someone in charge had also sent several slaves out with trays of hot cider for the people. Slowly the line moved forward. Snow was beginning to fall when Trey and Bre were admitted inside a small front room to join other applicants. Some sat around a crackling fireplace, chatting or pacing as they waited.

Bre looked about avidly, a bit disappointed the mansion wasn't rebuilt enough for use. The sitting room was rather plain and homely in her eyes, better suited for a farmer than a powerful and wealthy duchess. Her brother greeted the others, and as was his friendly nature, joined in on the conversation. She added her own brief comments when able. After a bit, her brother was admitted through the inner door and new people joined the group inside.

It seemed time ticked by, and Bre became worried when her brother didn't come back out, even though others had gone in after him. When the slave appeared, she was startled to hear her name being called.

"Yes, I am here." She popped up and followed the man through the door. Anxiety made her insides feel as if they twisted.

She was surprised to find herself escorted into the duchess's office and before she could protest, the door shut behind her.

"Hello Bre." Her Grace smiled warmly as she stood and

gestured for the young woman to seat herself before the worktable as she retook her own chair.

"I'm sorry, I think there's been a mistake," Bre apologized.

"I should be disappointed to learn if there was," came the smiling reply.

Bre's heart beat faster. "I was merely wondering what had become of my brother. We arrived together and I have not seen him since he was admitted."

"He has joined a few others on a tour. I believe he will be heading back to the inn soon enough. Are you sure that is the only reason you have come? I am sorry to say I do not require your guide services at this time. Perhaps there is another job I can offer you which you would be amenable to doing?"

She blinked and her answer came tumbling out before she thought. "Beyond my guide skills I only know how to help run my parents' inn."

"You are the eldest female, correct?"

"Yes, Your Grace."

"I would imagine your mother has taught you how to keep a pantry stocked, how to order the supplies needed, how to manage the slaves working for you along with the linen and dishware?" the duchess asked.

A crease appeared between Bre's eyes. "Yes, of course, Your Grace. Not to be rude but I—" Her words were waved off.

"It occurs to me the skills your mother has instilled in you are not much different from those used by a head housekeeper."

The young woman's eyes widened. Surely she couldn't be hearing the duchess correctly. "That is true; however, I have not much experience to go on. I have always had my mother to rely upon. She would correct any mistakes I made before they could become real problems. I have also never had a hand in buying new slaves or selling those who were disobedient."

It was as if the grand lady before her didn't process what she was being told. "My staff is small. I will not need more until the mansion is repaired enough to be livable. That may be at least another two years. Surely it would give you ample opportunity to settle into the position? I am willing to consent to the experiment as long as you agree any situation which you feel is unmanageable is brought to my attention." Her Grace paused before continuing. "You will be given a suite of rooms for yourself, uniforms, and what I believe you will consider a fair wage." She named the price.

Bre couldn't help but sit and blink in stunned shock. She would have a safe, steady job outside her home until she was ready to marry which wouldn't rely upon guide jobs.

"I—may I have a day to think over your generous offer?" Bre cautiously held her breath.

Her Grace inclined her head. "Of course. I shall have Susafan show you about briefly." She rang a small bell on top of her desk and after a few moments the door opened.

A middle-aged woman peered in. "Susafan, please show Bre about. She is considering the head housekeeper's position," Illyria commanded.

The woman's brows rose, but she merely motioned to the young woman to follow her. Bre blushed, partly in embarrassment, partly in anger. She followed Susafan down the hall and through a rough doorway which looked as if it had been cut between two different dwellings on the grounds.

"How old are you, girl?" Susafan bluntly asked, stopping in the middle of the deserted hall.

Bre prickled at the tone. "Eighteen. I have lived and worked in my parents' inn since I was five."

"Psh! 'Tis not the same at all. You won't have a mother to answer to, but Her Grace, and any mistake you make can be costly and bring disgrace upon the whole household."

"I appreciate what I'm sure you mean to be kind advice, but I have asked for a day to consider," Bre replied stiffly.

The lady's maid looked her up and down, contemptuously it seemed to Bre. "You're young enough to marry, almost past the stage for it. This position may well put any end to those hopes you may have. You won't have time to be gadding about or entertaining suitors, so just forget those thoughts right now."

The opposition she was encountering—for a job she had not even intended on applying for—made her determined to consider the offer more seriously than she had been planning on.

"Thank you for your concern. I shall reflect upon it properly when I am home," Bre coolly replied. "If you would be so kind as to finish showing me around?" She straightened her already perfect posture, looking the older woman directly in her eyes. After a moment, they continued on.

* * *

Bre eased in the back door to the family side of the inn, hoping not to be noticed. A celebration was currently going on, and the youngest children were allowed up past their normal bedtime. The small parlor was cozy with a fire burning and lit by numerous oil lamps. Her youngest brother minded a kettle of corn, and she could smell ale and wine.

"Bre!" her little sisters squealed, jumping up and down, giggling wildly for no apparent reason.

"Sis! Where have you been?" Trey called out. "I looked everywhere for you once I was done!"

She gave a strained smile and a poor excuse. "I saw a friend there and we were chatting. Sorry, I didn't realize how much time had passed."

Her mother *tsked*, but handed her daughter a glass of wine. Bre took a sip, expecting it to be watered, and nearly spluttered upon finding out it wasn't.

"To my second son, for becoming a footman in a duchess's household," Nathan toasted.

The family raised their glasses and toasted Trey, who, despite his obvious embarrassment at the attention, shone with pride. The impromptu party lasted for another hour, then their mother took the younger children upstairs and tucked them into bed. Bre's father motioned for her to clean up.

"I want to talk to you about your tardiness when you are done."

Bre's parents were sitting by the fireplace when she had finished cleaning up. She stood before them, hands clasped before her waist.

"Trey's situation has made us realize you, too, are old enough to be starting a household of your own. However, your actions earlier were not very responsible—and foolish, given any man can walk about this street at this hour unchallenged since the raids," her father added sourly.

"I'm sorry. It shan't happen again." Bre apologized, heart beating hard.

"I should hope not," her mother lamented. "You will only have tomorrow at breakfast to spend with him. He will begin his position afterward, living at the mansion."

"Even being just across the street, he won't have time to stop and spend with you the way you two do," her father warned her.

Bre licked her lips, bowing her head in understanding briefly. She decided if she were going to seriously consider a position of great responsibility, she should start acting worthy of the honor shown her.

"I know my lack of concern for the family's feelings when I failed to return in a due manner was selfish. I apologize. I, too, have been considering my future. I know most girls my age have been married since age sixteen or fourteen, and have given birth to several children. With that in mind, I also wish to ask you both for counsel," Bre said.

Her parents stared at her as if they had never seen her before, then exchanged glances. By the way they shifted positions, she could tell her tone alerted them this was no ordinary request.

"Of course you can." Her mother's smile was fearful.

"Best have a seat," her father added, and waited for his oldest daughter to do so. "Now what is it you seek?"

"I want to first say I had no intention of seeking out for myself what I am about to tell you. I was waiting for Trey when Her Grace asked for me to speak with her. During our brief conversation, she mentioned she was looking for a housekeeper." Bre wet her lips. "She thought the skills I am learning under Mother would transition to working for her."

For a moment, there was silence except for the crackle of flame. Her parents sent questioning looks to each other.

"Bre, dear, are you sure you heard her correctly? Are you sure she said housekeeper and not housemaid? 'Tis an easy enough mistake."

"No, Mother. Her exact words were 'head housekeeper.' She understands I lack the life experiences an older woman will have." Bre continued, summarizing the conversation she'd had with the Duchess Maison du Corbeau.

Once more, silence filled the room; her parents appeared shocked, and not a little dubious. Bre felt a growing certainty inside herself that she didn't want to miss out on the opportunity. She stated her case to her parents of why she could succeed. When she finished speaking, they protested, but it was for form's sake only. The three understood Bre was right.

Her mother sniffed and hugged her daughter. "I wish you well, and . . . well, if the two years don't quite work out, there is no shame in returning to the inn."

Her father squeezed her tight and his voice was gruff with suppressed emotion. "You make sure you do your best, understand? I won't have it said my daughter failed because she didn't give her all to the job. You show them all wrong, and succeed."

"I will." Bre swiped at her tears as she stepped back.

Her mother sighed and fussed with her daughter's braid. "You have considered you may not have any chance at marriage if you succeed at this post?"

A nervous giggle slipped out. "Her Grace's body slave said the same thing as well. I am sure should the chance arise, Her Grace will not deny me the opportunity, not when she is so open-minded already."

A watery smile from her mother was her reply. "Things change. There is no constant. As long as you are aware and have considered if you can be happy with the life you choose, should that opportunity never occur."

"Yes, I have." Bre assured them both with more confidence than she felt on that particular subject.

"Well, we should all get some rest, then. Tomorrow always comes earlier than we want," her mother said.

CHAPTER TWENTY ONE

"Victor," the drawling voice of the marquis brought his slave's head up. "How long has it been since we had one of our special parties?"

"Not since your masque, m'lord."

"I think it is time we had another."

"But where? The hunting lodge . . . in this snow?"

"Naturally, not there. You will make inquiries of Madam Breck, say, to be held in three days' time. She is to supply me with my usual request."

He scribbled a note and sealed it before handing it over to his slave.

"For Madam?"

"No, you will take that to Gri. I have a surprise for my guests he needs to supply me with."

"Is refusal an option?"

"No."

"As you wish, m'lord."

"Oh, and Victor," the marquis drawled out, making his slave pause in the doorway. "Find a way to shut that damnable priest up, one that won't have the new sheriff sniffing around."

Victor gave a deep bow, a sly smile curling his lips up as he left the room to do as bid.

Kendall lit a cigar, estate books and business papers spread across his desk. His office sat in flickering shadows, and occasionally a cold draft caused the heavy gold-brocaded velvet drapes to move. His plans of becoming advisor had been momentarily squashed by that insidious woman and the honorless earl who'd betrayed him when he made his bid for Nicky's position.

It was abundantly clear to him, the earl seemed to have a fondness for women who kept a tight grip on his balls. He should have known better than to think the coward would be able to help elevate him to the status of king's advisor, which he desired and deserved.

The marquis fingered the note delivered by a freezing, snow-covered slave earlier this morn. A cruel smile caused his lips to curl upward. He'd sent his reply back with the slave who delivered the note. Abruptly he stood, walked to the fireplace, and tossed the note into the flames. He then continued out and up to his wife's sitting room.

The white painted and gilded wooden doors were closed but not locked, and they flew open to bang against the wall, startling the occupants inside. Anne's already pale countenance turned even whiter as she unconsciously shrank farther back in her chair.

Her slave hurried to kneel on the floor, with bowed head.

He savored the scent of fear and strolled farther into the room. "Leave us," he curtly commanded, and the slave scrambled to do his bidding.

Kendall sat across from his wife, who had yet to speak a word. She appeared frozen in place. He took a second or two to puff on his cigar and survey the room.

It was not changed much from his last wife, as he had forbidden his current wife to make changes without first asking him. She had tried at the start of their marriage until she learned her place. The walls were papered in white- and black-flocked silk. The black marble, gold-veined fireplace was carved with satyrs and nymphs. The furniture was delicate, gilded wood. Even the heavy velvet drapes drawn shut across the window were black.

Sitting in the midst, his wife appeared a thin reed, trembling and swaying whichever way fate, or his fists, blew her.

"Tell me, Anne, how is your friendship with the duchess going?"

Her breath whistled in and out, eyes growing so wide, they looked as if they would pop out.

"Anne," he warned her in a low growl.

"My-my friendship? You said I was to be polite and welcoming. You did not say I was to become friends."

"I've changed my mind. You will go visit her, tomorrow."

"What-what if she-she is-isn't there?"

He gritted his teeth at her stupidity. "Send a note telling her you will be there."

"What if—"

"Dammit, woman! Did I say this is an option for you?"

Tears leaked out, her chin quivered, and he felt disgust coil inside.

"I'm sorry, my lord. I will do as you say."

"Good." He sat and smoked.

She bowed her head, hands clenched around her embroidery, wrinkling it as she fought back her tears. He hated when she cried for no reason, and she didn't want to set his temper off.

Please leave, she thought. *Why do you continue to sit there?*

"You know, you are looking rather thin. I will have Cook prepare you some food. You will eat it." His silky voice broke the relative silence of the room.

Anne nodded her head in understanding, and couldn't keep from flinching when his fingers caressed the side of her face. She almost expected him to hit her, but then the feel of his flesh left hers and she heard his voice ordering her slave back inside, and the door closing. She breathed a sigh of relief. If only the rest of the day and night would pass without him noticing her.

* * *

Even though it was the middle of the afternoon, the dark, lowering clouds made it seem closer to twilight. Anne stepped from the carriage, shivering despite the mounds of blankets, the hot brick at her feet, and the fur-lined cloak she wore. A slave stood holding the door open to a small house for her.

The woman took a moment and looked around her in interest; the mansion glowed with light, and one side of the double front doors stood open to allow workers to freely come and go.

She stepped through the open door of the cottage, only to be led farther inside and to a small back parlor, where a fire crackled. The young woman handed her cloak over to a slave and sank with a sigh on the couch which had been placed facing the grate. Shortly thereafter, the duchess came in, gowned in dark midnight blue velvet, heavily embroidered in silver, and sparkling from small gems sewn onto the fabric. White fur encircled the neck, wrists, and hemline.

"Hello, Lady Anne." She greeted her warmly and sat beside the woman.

A timid smile was all the marchioness could muster. *I can't do this! But I have to! If I don't, he will take his displeasure out on me.* She felt dowdy sitting next to the glamorous older woman. There was no reason she should; the marquis made sure she was dressed in the height of fashion, and had jewels to match. *Like a toy*, she thought bitterly.

The door opened again, and Anne could smell food. A slave came around the couch and set a loaded tray on a small table before them. Without asking, she proceeded to place items on a plate and handed it to the guest, along with a mug of what smelled like hot cider.

"Oh." Anne was distressed. "You-you should not have gone to the trouble. I know you are busy with the king's requests. I-I had not planned on staying long."

"Nonsense," was the reply. "If I am needed, the palace slaves know where to find me. You and I both know your husband is a sadistic brute who starves and beats you when he thinks you have committed some perceived slight on his part."

Anne felt the blood drain from her peaked face, and a buzz started in her ears. She began to hyperventilate.

"There is no need to worry anything we speak of here will get back to him. Eat, drink, and please try not to pass out."

The young woman took a tiny sip of cider, let its warmth flood her being. When she felt calm enough, she picked delicately at the food, even though she had a gnawing ache from lack of sustenance.

She didn't know how to say what her husband wanted her to. She had nothing in common with the duchess the way she did with the other noble ladies. It seemed she would not be expected to talk . . . at least, not yet.

"I do hope the snow isn't causing problems for you. Lady

Lily mentioned the other day that if it weren't for her duties at the palace, she would not get out at all. The Sydneys have sent word of Lady Sally's engagement. I hope to see you at the party. I do not recall having ever met the man she is to marry."

Anne nodded and made noises indicating she was listening as she filled her stomach while the woman before her continued to make small talk. Before she realized it, the marchioness was replete with food. She felt warm, cozy, and safe, a feeling she had not felt since before her marriage.

"Lady Anne, forgive my intrusiveness, but I know you did not come to hear me prattle."

"I . . ." Anne couldn't breathe, sudden terror flooding her brain.

"Please, I don't mean to upset you. I shan't let on to the marquis that I know he sent you for a reason. What is it he wishes me to know?"

"I . . ." She struggled to get the words out, misery at having to be a part of her husband's deception bringing tears to her eyes.

"He-he wants me to invite you to supper. A-a special supper."

One elegant brow arched upward. "When?"

"Tomorrow."

Except for the crackle of the fire, no other noise was present.

"Very well, I accept."

Anne let out the breath she had unconsciously been holding. She began to babble her thanks, but a raised hand cut her off.

"None needed. I suspect any other answer will cause your husband to take his ire out on you."

The marchioness blanched; her chin trembled and then she swallowed, unsure what to say. She felt miserable for the part she was being forced to play in Jenabram's deception.

Her Grace reached over and gently touched the back of the young woman's hand. "If at any time you wish to sever ties with your brute of a husband, I shall be only too glad to wield my royally appointed powers and make it happen."

Mutely Anne shook her head, a near inaudible denial

slipping out. "No one can help me. He will kill me, and any who try to help."

A brief knock sounded on the door, and the duchess called out for the person to enter. A slave walked over and bent low to whisper in Her Grace's ear, then left with her reply.

"Please keep my offer in mind. If you will excuse me, I have palace business to attend to. Please feel free to stay as long as you like, and order more food and drink if you want."

"Oh, no. I can't. I mustn't." Anne cried in panic. "He will be waiting for me, and-and your answer."

"Then your coach will be made ready. I will send a slave in for you so you don't have to wait out in the cold."

Before Anne could thank her again, the duchess had risen and swiftly left the room.

CHAPTER TWENTY TWO

The line of displaced, starving townspeople snaked out the palace gates and down the street. Many had little more than the clothes they wore, and for most, their outfits showed the ravages of many washings and patching. Farther back, the slave traders fumed with their wares, people of all ages chained together and shivering violently as many went barefoot and dressed in scraps of cloth. Darkness slowly descended on the land, the wind picking up in force as yet another storm bore down on them. Saizar and his men patrolled the length of the street, making sure no fights or stampedes broke out.

"Sir," Guts addressed his superior, "the people aren't gonna wait nicely no more. They've been here all day, most of 'em."

"I will try to find out what the holdup is," he replied.

The sheriff walked as quickly as he dared on the icy stones, stopping to reassure those in line he was working on getting them inside faster. He got to the gates; only one side stood open. Two shivering clerks, Will, and Panja, sat at tables taking down names, ages, and occupations while tired guards milled about. The man he looked for was not immediately noticeable, so he went and banged on the barracks door. A recruit opened it and ushered him inside where the captain sat.

"Captain Mathias, the line is moving entirely too slow. The people are ready to riot."

"I have my orders, same as you. We're going as fast as weather and time permits."

Saizar shook his head. "I suggest, sir, something more be done."

Mathias ran his hands through his hair and over his face. "I cannot do more."

"I can't accept that. We can at least get them inside the gates, set up braziers outside for people to warm themselves by while they wait."

"His Majesty—"

"—is too busy cowering in his rooms to give a shit!"

The men glared at each other.

"May I remind you, such language is enough to mark you as a traitor. Old spies are replaced with new, and those who will take the opportunity to improve their lives through careless slips of the tongue."

"Her Grace, the advisor, would agree with me." Saizar leaned his fists on the tabletop.

Mathias grimaced, muttering, "Bloody woman! Even the king with all his demands doesn't give me half the trouble she does." Louder he said, "Then you find her, and she can damn well help instead of prancing around giving orders."

"So be it," the sheriff gritted out and stomped from the room, back to his men. It was a little harder to get out the gate, as people were now bunching up, complaints getting louder and the nervous palace guard fondled their sword hilts or pike handles.

"Merrit!" he bellowed, and the man trotted over.

"Sir."

"I need you to quickly find Her Grace. Try her mansion first. Tell her we need her at the palace; a riot is threatening to break out."

"Yes, sir!" the man barked out and half trotted, half slid down the hill.

Saizar went over to the people bunching up. "Come on, now. We're all cold, tired, and hungry, but this isn't helping. Form the line. Come on."

He received grumbles, complaints, a few held fists up. Long, tension-filled moments passed by before a whisper ran up the line.

"She's coming!"

"Look at those manky whores, thinking they're guards."

"You bitch, you said you'd help us! This ain't it! We're starving and cold!"

"Let us in! Let us in now!"

Her Grace caught his eye and indicated with her head he should follow. Surrounding her was a squad of women wearing leather armor and carrying weapons so shiny, it was doubtful they had seen battle. Leading them was a dark-haired and -eyed man. She was not riding her stallion, but a bay mare. The horse's hooves threw slush balls out, and she used the bulk of the beast, along with the novelty of female soldiers to move people out of her way so she could enter the courtyard. Saizar nipped in behind her and held the bridle as she dismounted.

"You"—she pointed to a guard—"get me Mathias, and you, get me Aranthus. Saizar, bring your men in." The force of her commands had the three scrambling as she handed the reins over to a palace groom and stalked toward the gates.

"How many people have been processed through?" she demanded.

"Since word first went out and the line formed, about a hundred," Panja snapped back before returning her attentions to the man and his family before her.

The duchess took the few steps needed to reach the guards still manning the gates and spoke quietly with them. They nodded, eyes widening a bit in fear, but created a line to prevent anymore coming in. By now, Mathias stomped over, scowling.

"My men. . . "

"Who set this up?"

"I did."

"It's a piss-poor job. Are you trying to make them riot?"

He opened his mouth for a hot rebuttal, but she continued with her dressing down. "There is an entire courtyard going to waste. Send some of your men to have slaves bring out wood and get bonfires started. Those two can stay at the gate; have the others stand watch around the perimeter and the admitting door." She turned away from him, ignoring his sudden swearing, but he didn't dare disobey; not after the king's tantrum over complaints about her.

"Panja, and you—"

"Will, Your Grace."

"Yes, take your stuff over by the admitting door. Quickly now." They scrambled to obey.

Aranthus came huffing and puffing, his staff bobbing by his side.

"My dear! I thought . . ." He leaned over, wheezing for breath. "I thought something serious was happening."

"It is. Where are those who have already been let inside?"

"In . . ."—more wheezing—"In a side room."

"Tell the kitchen staff to start boiling large quantities of water and find empty barrels which can be used as baths. Have them gather up all the soap, towels, and grooming implements they can find. I want two rooms, for men and women. Their clothes are to be taken and boiled clean. The great hall can be used for feeding; have some sort of a simple meal made ready," she continued on.

Aranthus stood there with his mouth hanging open in shock.

"They are filthy! If they won't bathe, they can sleep in the outbuildings. I will not risk infection or disease setting in." She turned away from him, walking toward the two people who had reset their tables, telling them what she wanted passed along to the townspeople.

The voices outside the gate had reached a pitch loud enough to be heard clearly. The duchess signaled to Mathias.

He lifted his horn and blew three short blasts. When the babble quieted, the commander shouted instructions. "Keep order! No pushing or shoving. You will be admitted inside the courtyard, then the palace, as rooms are made ready. Failure to maintain order results in arrest."

Mathias then signaled for the waiting people to be let back through at a trickle. Illyria stood before the door, on the stone landing before it. The man and women with her formed a half ring around the stone stairs. The citizens first in slowed from their run to a jog at sight of the line of shields. They did their best to re-form some semblance of a line. However, some people still outside had other ideas, rushing the opening. The royal guards struggled to keep a grip on the gates The men braced their entire bodies against the wood, and two more rows of their fellow guards added their weight to help. A group of men, the instigators, rushed in, some slipping and falling. They ignored the shouts of outrage from their fellow citizens and continued at a run, desperate to gain entrance. There were cries from those who were shoved aside and fell to be trampled underneath.

"ORDER! YOU WILL KEEP ORDER OR YOU CAN TAKE YOUR CHANCES BACK OUTSIDE!" Illyria's clarion voice rang out strong, the force of her command making itself felt.

She gave an almost imperceptible nod, and the soldiers with her took one step forward, locking shields.

The men had almost reached the line when their commander, Eron, bellowed. "Brace!"

The first desperate row of men made no attempt to stop. They were pushed violently forward by those behind who didn't think the rank of soldiers would hold. The men slammed into the line of shields. Grunts rang out, both from the soldiers, and from those who collided with the metal.

"Push back!" Eron called as the women gave another grunt and shoved together as one.

"Close the gates!" Illyria yelled.

The royal guards heaved as one and managed to decrease the opening.

"Form up!" Eron yelled as he used his shield to bash a man away.

He could smell the scent of fear and desperation. It was only the fact the men were half-starved and thus weak, which gave the women an advantage. Even so, a few lost their footing on the slick cobbles and broke rank. A few of the men managed to get through before the women scrambled up. By the renewed grunts of male pain, he figured the females had rejoined the line, forcefully. A sardonic smile tugged his lips up.

Panja and Will watched in barely concealed horror, bracing themselves to slip under their tables if needed. But the men ignored them, and leapt up the stairs where they shortly found themselves sailing backward in the air. Their screams of pain as they landed, along with the sounds of bones breaking and blood splattering brought a quick end to any further attempts of rebellion.

Those who saw what happened shouted the news to those outside, and the rush slowed to a steady flow. People broke off to the sides as they came inside, many craning their necks for a glimpse of the wounded men. When it seemed order had been restored, Mathias signaled for a few of his guards to drag the men off to the dungeon. The rising buzz of voices fell to a murmur. The townspeople, realizing the advisor would not hesitate to toss everyone back outside, even if it meant doing the job herself, made sure to keep order. A few glanced nervously at the dual sword handles poking up from the back sheaths she wore.

"ATTENTION! I NEED YOUR ATTENTION!" she called again as they all continued to filter inside, trying to keep some semblance of obeying.

"In a moment we will have fires going to help keep you warm. Everyone will be given a spot inside. We will do our best to keep families together; single men and women will be housed separately. Food and drink are being prepared for you. Due to the close living quarters we shall all have to endure, it is vital for anyone wishing to partake of the king's generosity to bathe themselves before being assigned a living space. Those who do not wish to comply can leave now. Furthermore, if anyone is in need of medical attention, you will make it known. Am I understood?"

The refugees glanced at each other, the ground, the guards or toward her. A few nodded or voiced compliance; some tried complaining but quickly squelched it as her fierce gaze landed on them. When she was satisfied they would listen, she motioned for Panja and Will to begin their assigned tasks again. People scrambled to form a long, snaking line which crisscrossed the space as she verbally remanded those whose actions or words showed them to be recalcitrant. Slaves came out, lugging the heavy brass braziers and fuel.

Soon, patches of heat and light dotted the courtyard, and people shivered, taking turns to warm themselves, mindful of both the duchess's watchfulness, and that of the guards. After giving name, age, and occupation to either Panja or Will, the person was allowed entrance. The duchess stood to one side of the landing, with an open door to the palace behind her. Many who passed her probing gaze on the way inside suddenly found themselves unwilling or unable to meet her eyes. Thus it was that most entered quietly, eyes downcast. Very few persons attempted to thank her. Those who did received a warm nod of acknowledgement.

"Duchess," Aranthus whispered as he came up behind her. She inclined her head enough to indicate she was listening and still monitor the situation before her. "I have done all you asked. The bath water will take some time, but until then, cold water basins have been set up. I also alerted the royal physician he would be needed, and Cook said he would have some food ready by the time the first people are settled in."

"Thank you, Lord Chamberlain. On another subject, I do not know if the local doctor survived the raid. If you would also be so kind as to have the physician set up a sick ward, I want those who are ill to be separated from the healthy. Tell him to err on the side of caution, and if any complain, send for me. When we can get the town physician up, he can take over."

"Do-do you mean to stay here? To personally oversee? My dear! No one expects it of you."

"No, but it may help. If you will show me the rooms set aside for use?"

"Of course. This way, please." He backed away with a small bow as she signaled for Eron to take her place before she turned and followed the chamberlain.

They were using one of the smaller side entrances which led onto a room with benches lining the walls. Townspeople nearly filled them as they waited to enter the next room. The two passed through the doorway into a larger area. The desk usually used by a clerk had been moved back next to the opposite door. Slaves were busy helping the refugees. Sounds of splashing and voices came from behind hanging bed sheets placed to provide small bathing cubicles. Aranthus continued the tour and they passed through into a hallway.

"Some of our lesser reception rooms, I took the liberty of ordering what straw and bedding could be spared to be placed inside. I thought since you want to keep families together, these will be perfect for them."

"Marvelous." She smiled at him and he puffed up before waving her on.

"The great hall, unfortunately, cannot seat everyone at once. We will have to have them eating in groups."

"Yes, I'm afraid some are so starved they may try to sit in on all the feedings. I advise coming up with a way of making sure it doesn't happen, so everyone gets food."

"Oh dear, that never occurred to me. Do you suppose we should post guards?"

"Leave it up to the townspeople to do the work, unless they are found to be too ineffectual."

"Very well. This way, please." He led them out the hall and down a short corridor to the grand reception hall. "Single women in here, and men in the ballroom, which is far enough away but not too much so."

They peeked inside, more slaves busy clearing out what furniture and rugs there was; others brought in straw.

"Is there an inside courtyard with a well?"

"Oh yes, indeed. Why?"

"I want their clothes to be cleaned too. It doesn't help to bathe and then live in the same dirty outfits."

"The laundresses can see to setting the area up and making sure the women are provided with what they need. Is there anything else I may have forgotten?"

"I don't think so. You have done an exceptional job. Shall we go back?"

Man and woman turned and walked toward the side entrance, chatting.

"Aranthus, has His Majesty said anything to you on the subject of the dungeons and the increased bandit attacks?"

"Oh, no. I believe he is hoping it will all sort itself out. Lord Nicky used to handle such things for His Majesty in his role of advisor."

"May I ask a personal question of you?"

"Ask away," he replied with a jolly smile.

"How is the king doing? I hope he has recovered from his fit."

The chamberlain hesitated, a plump finger held against his lips as he thought how to answer in a manner which wouldn't cast their sovereign in a bad light, should word trickle back. "He is doing as well as can be expected."

"Please, Lord Chamberlain, I must know the truth if I am to be effective in holding the kingdom together for his eventual return to the throne." The duchess's tone, while self-effacing, lurked with dark undercurrents.

Aranthus couldn't help the brief shiver at her words. He was beginning to believe Her Grace was content with their sovereign's state. "If he is not kept semi-drugged, or drunk, he reverts to lunacy. If the royal physician cannot cure His Majesty's affliction, and it gets out, there will be fighting over the throne and chaos."

"Pity he does not have any legitimate heirs," she mused.

"It would not stop those of the harem who have birthed sons, if they could gain enough support," Aranthus replied.

"Ah, say no more."

They arrived back at the entrance and stood to one side while a shivering group of people stepped through the door, clutching their meager bundles, heading for the bathing chambers.

"There is one other task in which your input would be helpful: asking the chef and each head of supply to make lists of how long their stores will last with the increase of mouths to feed, and what will be needed immediately," Her Grace requested.

"I shall attend to it personally."

"Aranthus! Aranthus!" a strident male voice yelled out.

The chamberlain groaned as an older man with a trimmed Van Dyke, carefully styled hair, tailored clothing and a big pot belly charged up to them. "I am the royal physician! I cannot treat anyone lesser! Who is making such ridiculous demands?"

"Why not?" Illyria replied.

The doctor glanced over, took a small involuntary step back before glaring at her. "You! You of all should know better than to ask why," he haughtily replied, hands gripping the lapels of his open jacket. "Aranthus—"

"You are refusing His Majesty's advisor?" The tone was silky-smooth, the dangerous undercurrent back. "I care not what Lord Nicky did or didn't do in regards to your position. The king does not require your services every moment he is awake—those very services which are paid for from the royal treasury, which in turn is supplied through taxes levied on those whom you refer to as lesser."

"Aranthus! I am not standing here to be threatened by-by some . . . trumped up foreign . . . duchess!" the man spluttered out as his face turned red. "Especially not one who overextends her authority while the king is indisposed!"

"Might I remind you exactly what my position entails? Advice. Such as who would qualify best to continue in their present roles for the glory and might of His Majesty's kingdom."

The physician ground his teeth. "You viper." He drew himself up, thrusting his chest out. "Might I remind you, I am the only qualified person who has been trained by the last royal doctor; therefore, it is easier for a troublemaking advisor to be replaced than a valuable personage as myself."

An amused smile played about her lips, and she lowered her voice. "No one person is so special they cannot be replaced. Consider your role temporary until we can find the local doctor, or herbalist. Besides, it doesn't seem your care is helping His Majesty regain his sanity."

He scowled. "These delusions take time to cure, and given the unrest the kingdom is suffering under your guidance, the king may be right to worry about his safety. Besides, I will not allow a witch to work her black magic while I live."

The duchess leaned closer, lowered her voice, and whispered something to him. Aranthus watched in fascination as the man's face blanched in horror. He strained his ears trying to hear what passed between them, to no avail. After a bit, the physician swallowed heavily and dotted at the sudden drops of sweat which had broken out on his brow.

"Your pardon, advisor. I-I will go now and see to setting up the sick ward." He turned and hurried away with unseemly haste.

Her grace ignored the pleading look of curiosity on the chamberlain's face. "I hope you will let me know if he gives you any trouble." She paused, standing aside to let more townspeople enter.

They looked out. It did not seem if the line had gone down at all.

"I will also send a few more clerks out. Thank you, Duchess. Shall I see you tomorrow?"

"Yes," she replied and the chamberlain walked off self-importantly, humming to himself with glee at thought of the battle he and the royal steward would have, and planning on how to worm out of the physician just what she had threatened him with to get his cooperation.

* * *

Panja sighed and shifted miserably, pausing after her last townsperson to hold her hands over the oil lamp's flame. She had been up since dawn, processing displaced townspeople. She blew on her icy hands, tugged her cloak tighter about her, before signaling she was ready. An older male stepped forward, a long line of chained slaves snaking behind. He tossed some parchment before her, sneering. Gingerly the young woman unrolled it and glanced down before back up.

"We are not buying slaves," she stiffly informed him.

"Not what I was told." He spat on the ground. "Total's on the bottom."

Her temper rose, but she kept her voice calm and authoritative. "You have been misinformed." A hasty thought struck her. "If your master wishes to relinquish all rights and responsibilities for them in exchange for a tax credit no more than forty percent of the total worth of all slaves present, then we will accept them. Otherwise . . ." She trailed off suggestively. *Hah! You can sort the mess out, high and mighty, Your Grace, Duchess Maison du Corbeau.*

"Stupid wench!" the man bellowed, causing a temporary stop in work around them. "We were told the palace was paying for excess slaves who could not be sold."

"We are not paying for slaves your master doesn't want to be bothered with feeding and sheltering," she hissed back.

"I didn't come the whole way up here, waiting out like the peasants, to treaty with a guttersnipe. I want a man what knows what's going on," his loud voice continued.

Some of her fellow clerks smirked at her; one spoke up. "I can help you, just let me send for the royal requisitioner."

Panja glared at his smug face, wishing she could slap him.

"No need," Her Grace called out as she reappeared in the open doorway. "What master do you work for, so I may have a word with him on the morrow about his tactics?"

"Er, um . . . Gri," he sullenly replied.

"Fine. Choice one: leave the slaves here and take the form of abandonment back, letting your master know I will come for it later in the day with his signature attached. Choice two: go back with the slaves. Or choice three: continue to be a problem and I will have you tossed in the dungeon for creating a public disturbance and the slaves will be your master's gift to the crown for your stupidity."

The man just stared at her flabbergasted, then he began laughing. "Ha, ha, ha, haaaaa! Whose gonna arrest me if I don't pick? You haven't got enough guards for it if you want to keep control."

She merely cocked her head to the side. "Is that your final answer?"

He continued to laugh. "You're all stupid wenches."

Those nearby sucked in breaths of anticipation, spats between slavers and nobles always a good source of entertainment. Heads craned as word quickly traveled, people trying to get a good view. The man looked around, flexing his muscles, preening as the duchess flowed down the stairs. He turned his gaze toward her, smirking broadly. She never broke her stride, just lashed out quicker than he could react before turning and resuming her stance before the door. His face turned red, then ashy gray as he slammed face-first into the ground. Blood spurted from his nose with a snapping sound. Immediate hissing noises, squirming, and clutching of delicate bits commenced from those males nearby in sympathy.

"Mathias, have some guards take this trash to the dungeon. Panja, continue."

The young woman blinked, working hard to keep the vicious smile off her face as she picked the scroll up and asked the first slave in line the pertinent details and matching it up with what had been noted, making corrections as needed. There were more than a few women who grinned outright, or tried to smother their glee. Two guards, one with the visage of a grizzled veteran, the other new, gingerly jogged over. They avoided the duchess's eyes, flipped the man on his back, and began to drag him past the whispering, goggling people.

CHAPTER TWENTY THREE

The palace had not hosted so many people, nor seen such activity, since the days of the current king's grandfather. More slave sellers had requested audiences with the advisor, and newly freed slaves joined the throngs inside the palace. Displaced people were still being processed through the outer courtyard, though over the past few days it had slowed to a trickle. Those who showed up were survivors from the outer villages and small towns. They brought with them horrific tales of bandits raiding and slaughtering before burning all they could. The people dragged in, exhausted, cold, and starving, many needing medical attention for a range of ailments, from frostbite to festering wounds received while defending their homes. They were met by a small group of men and women who had been appointed as official greeters. They helped the newcomers get settled in. Palace slaves came and replenished wood supplies, keeping the fireplaces burning.

A gong rang out, and another slave announced the first seating for breakfast. Tamzin slipped into line. Despite her bath earlier, her flesh still itched and prickled, as if the dirt and bugs from being a captive were still polluting her. She had wrapped a linen rag around her throat, draping it to look more like a short scarf. The iron collar which had identified her as a slave had been removed last night. The flesh of her neck still bore scabs and discoloration. After her breakfast, Tamzin sought out the rooms being used as a medical ward.

There was a line of hard benches, all filled with people with various ailments. She sighed and took her place in line. It was near lunch time when her turn came.

The doctor was a rotund man with a supercilious air. "Now what's the problem? You seem to be healthy."

"I need something for these scabs," she replied while removing the scarf.

His eyes narrowed, knowing the signs of a recently removed slave collar. No doubt the young woman before him had been in the group the duchess had "liberated" from some slaver.

The doctor lifted her chin up, doing a quick inspection. Finally, he let go and turned to a table covered in the instruments of his trade, including dirty bandages and bowls of water, along with jars of various sizes and material. He selected one, scraped out a paste strongly smelling of goose fat and put it in a smaller clay jar.

"Use this three times a day, keep the area clean and free of dirt. Next!" he called out.

Tamzin was not to be put off easily. "What's in this?"

"That, young lady, is not your concern. Do you want help or not? If not, I have others who are more appreciative and will use it if you won't. I'm not wasting my medicine on ungrateful former," he stressed, "slaves."

She glared at him, wrapping her hand around the jar and standing up from the stool. "If this doesn't work, I will be back."

He didn't even bother to reply, only beckoned impatiently to the person behind her who was waiting for her to leave. The young woman strode from the room, and joined the throngs of people flowing in all directions through the hallways, chatting away.

"The advisor has boards set up in the receiving rooms with notices for open positions needing workers."

"I told my daughter they wouldn't want women, but she defied me and signed up anyway."

"Disgraceful."

Tamzin scowled at the backs of the two gossiping women who walked in front, making it impossible for anyone to get around them.

"What's even more humiliating is they accepted her! I told her, I did, she was ruining her chances of finding a decent husband if she insisted on doing a man's job."

"They won't like that. A man wants a woman what will obey him, and keep a tidy home and bear his children."

Tamzin felt her blood heat up; she couldn't take any more of their chatter. "Excuse me! I need through!" She shouted behind them and shoved them apart.

They squawked in outrage, yelling after her about her rude behavior. The young woman ignored them, already out of hearing distance. She peeked into rooms as she passed, until she had found the area everyone talked about.

The white-blonde, blue-eyed female stalked inside, moving around those who meandered about. She ignored the looks sent her way, some admiring, some in displeasure.

It seemed every guild had a representative who sat behind tables draped in fabric, with their guild symbols displayed. Slowly she walked past, scrutinizing each one. They were comprised mostly of men who sat talking to potential apprentices, who had a tendency to deliberately ignore any female who approached looking for information or to join. Tamzin saw one of the parchment merchants, who was a guest of the duchess's, sitting behind a table. A small sign showed books, a quill, and ink pot. Small, neat writing underneath proclaimed: Colin Dugan, Professor of Learning, Royal Academy. Many people cast glances his way, with only a few of the more curious daring to venture over. As the woman moved throughout the connecting rooms, she saw one filled with artisans, which had a few females present. The last room was set apart, the royal weapons hall.

From inside came the clash and clang of metal, the taunts and yells of men, and a few women. Tamzin pushed her way through the crowd until she was a part of the front row.

A man with a luxurious white mustache stood on the room's wood platform against one wall, bawling out orders. Older men in rusted, dented armor performed mock battles.

"What's going on?" the young woman asked a mature male next to her.

"They're reforming the royal army, and looking for recruits. Rumor has it the officers' positions won't be filled by nobility alone. Anyone who proves their worth can be promoted."

"What about those others? In back?" She yelled to be heard over the roar of the crowd. She had to repeat herself as the man had turned back to cheering.

"Sheriff's office, royal palace guards, all recruiting too."

He ignored any other questions. After the current

demonstration, the white mustached man invited those interested to ask questions, to sign up, or to try their hand in mock battle, using wooden training weapons.

The crowd's blood was high with adrenaline, and thoughts of glory and heroism shining from many of the men and boys' eyes. The young woman ignored the group of females who gathered in a cluster to one side, giggling, whispering, and flirting. She sneered briefly, then weaved through the crowd to get closer toward the middle of the room.

A small group of six men around her age had picked up swords, shields, or staffs, trying to prove their masculinity against each other. The white-blonde observed them and the older men. The combatants had a mixed look of farmers and merchants' sons. After a moment, one arrogant guy managed to knock down the rest. He held his sword and shield up and bellowed in victory, preening for the ladies.

Tamzin saw a giant of a man approach behind him, at least two heads taller and a stone heavier, built of solid muscle.

"Try me, pup, and see if you'll be so cocky when you battle a real warrior." The challenger's voice was deep, with a thick accent.

"Sure, gramps," the youth sneered.

They faced off, saluted, and began. The youngster charged, and the big man stepped aside, applying a boot to the kid's backside as he flew past. His friends whooped and hurled taunts. The young man scrambled up, face red, anger sparking in his eyes. He tried a few different tactics, all easily rebuffed by the big man. After a few minutes, the watchers, along with the cocky youth, realized the older man was playing.

"You son of a bitch!" He finally yelled in frustration and let his rage loose. He hacked and stabbed in blind fury.

It didn't take long before he was on the floor, groaning in pain and hurling curses at his opponent.

The big man contemptuously turned his back. "War is not a game for untrained children, and those with more ego than talent," he addressed the crowd.

A few of the older men nodded, adding their support. Meanwhile, Tamzin had picked up a shield, and found a wooden sword whose balance wasn't too horribly off. She strode into the circle, stopping before the big man. His eyebrows raised in inquiry.

"Hahahahaaa! Hey, cutie! This ain't the place fer you. There're better jobs a good-looking young thing like you can do for the army."

"Stupid females. See what happens when a woman becomes advisor?"

"Get out of the ring before your pretty face gets ruined."

"You wish to fight?" the big man asked.

"I'm not here to look good," Tamzin spat back, taking up an attacker's stance.

"Wood weapons can still cause damage, and I will not pull my strength because you are a woman," he warned her.

"Shut up and fight," she answered, and feinted.

He batted aside her attack easily, and the force with which he did it had her boots sliding on the stone floor. A new circle quickly formed at their backs, bets, insults, and taunts flying fast.

Tamzin attacked again, once more easily rebuffed. The heckling grew louder.

"Come on! Finish this! He doesn't even have to try, and she's no good."

"Told ya women can't fight!"

"I got a better sword I can teach you how to use."

The young woman ignored them, as they were right, she was barely trying. But then again, she was trying to draw her opponent out. She made a few more incursions, barely missing a blow meant to knock the shield out of her left hand.

She set her face determinedly. She could see in the big man's eyes he didn't expect her to have more fight in her than what she was already giving, but he wasn't about to let his guard down either until their bout ended. Tamzin could respect that. It was more than most of the men she had fought in her brief life had given her. They usually were so arrogant and egotistical, not thinking a girl could beat them, they never treated her like a worthy opponent.

The white-blonde knew she had to end their fight soon. Her hands and arms ached from holding sword and shield, and absorbing blows. Then she saw her opening, sure the man didn't realize his mistake.

She launched a series of attacks, using not just the weapons, but her body as well. Tamzin saw surprise flit across the man's face, and let a small smile of satisfaction cross her lips. It was gone a moment later in a grunt of pain. Her shield splintered as she raised it to block a blow. She turned her face away and down while turning in a half-circle and bringing her sword around in an arc, the smack of it meeting flesh barely heard over the crowd.

The big man gave a grunt, arching his back while one leg went numb, causing him to slip to one knee. His sword arm came back as he used the flat surface of the shield to keep himself from crashing face-first to the floor. Tamzin's left arm collided with his muscular right, and she let hers slip under and then around, pinning his outstretched arm to her left side. She used the pommel of her sword to hammer on his wrist, causing him to drop his weapon.

A moment later, before she could kick his sword away, she found herself heading toward the floor. He had let himself fall on his left side and twisted his body to end up on his back. The move sent the young woman flying. Tamzin collided forcefully with the floor, and a wrenching in her right shoulder had her yelling out in pain. She was also facedown, with her right arm and sword trapped underneath her and his weight keeping her prone.

The men and boys cheered louder, and she could hear some calling for the big man to "finish her."

"Bastard," she spat, eyes flashing icy cold.

For a big man, he was lithe and quick. Before she could completely recover, he rolled off her and she forced herself to flop over on her back. Before she could contract her stomach muscles and get up, his booted foot landed on her wrist, immobilizing her arm. He leaned over, relieving her of the sword.

Tamzin wasn't giving up easily; she made a fist with her left hand, her right shoulder blade and arm grinding into the stone floor.; She half-rolled up and over to punch the side of his knee closest to her with all the strength she had. He yelled in pain and collapsed, further grinding her right arm into the stone. The man was splayed out on his left side, clutching his right leg. She couldn't pick the sword back up, unable to get her numb hand to respond.

She dragged herself up to a sitting position, clutching her right arm.

They were both breathing heavily, dripping sweat, staring at each other, the noise of the crowd around them hazy, far off, as if coming from a great distance. A slow smile curled the man's lips up, amusement glinting in his eyes, and he inclined his head to her.

"Shall we try round two? Or declare this a draw?" his voice rumbled out.

"Sign me on to the army, and we can have all the rounds you want," she replied.

He frowned while leveraging himself up, careful not to put too much weight on the leg with the knee she had punched. He held a large, callused palm out to her, helping her up.

"I'm Franz. It is not a wise decision, and I am not in a position to do such a thing. Besides, you would be the only female. You would not last a day once the men got ahold of you."

"Tamzin. I can handle myself. Let me worry about them."

He shrugged his massive shoulders and pushed through the crowd, making sure those gathered around let her through as well. It didn't take long before new combatants stepped in the ring, and most of the crowd ignored them. Her opponent led her over to the man with the white mustache. He was too engrossed on the current battle. The big man hailed him.

"Sir Dalton, I have found another worthy candidate who fights well."

Brown eyes regarded her disdainfully. "No females. I don't care how good they claim to be, or what that damn duchess thinks. There will be no female knights in my army. And if you dare suggest it again, you can find another job."

Rage boiled inside the woman. "Listen, asshole, maybe you can't see well. I fought him to a standstill—nothing those other pansy men trying out have been able to do."

The few men on the platform with him sniggered. He turned the full force of his gaze on her. "I said I don't take females, or pansy men. Now leave, before I forget you are a woman and have my men take you out back and teach you what happens to those who insist on joining groups where they are not wanted."

Tamzin opened her mouth again, but found herself being dragged off by the big man. "Get your hands off me or we'll have round two right now."

"I am saving you," he replied, managing to drag her outside the room before she stomped on his instep. His heavy boots protected him, and he slammed her back against the wall with one hand around her throat, insultingly easy. He leaned his weight into her to keep her from striking back.

"Listen!" Franz's voice rumbled menacingly. "You want to be a warrior that badly?"

"Yes," she gritted out, doing her best to master her rage.

"I know of a group. But it will not be with the army."

"What the hell good is that?" she asked.

"Maybe nothing, maybe another way in. What have you got to lose?" he asked.

She seethed silently a moment. "Fine, take me to them now."

* * *

Despite the horrid weather conditions and the fear of starvation, there was brisk movement up and down the nobles' street. Tamzin squinted her eyes against the sun bouncing off the snow and ice, not wanting to be blinded. As they approached the bridge, she reached out and yanked on Franz's sleeve.

"Hey! You said you were taking me to a female warrior group. Where the hell are they? In the woods?"

He half-turned. "You'll see," was his maddening reply.

Large wood and iron-bound gates stood open to the right. The narrow cart track chipped out of the high snow banks led past them. As they walked, they passed paths shoveled out to allow people and animal movement. What little could be seen of the dwellings did not inspire confidence. They seemed shabby, in desperate need of repair. Franz led her past a stone mansion, abandoned scaffolding hung with icicles, waiting for spring so repairs could continue. A strong crosswind buffeted them and brought the sounds of shouts. As the two rounded a corner of the mansion, a hastily erected wooden barracks could be seen. Before it was a frozen sea of icy mud. Farther behind them rose the mountain peaks.

She thought there were black dots scaling those sleek rocks, but couldn't tell for sure due to the sun. Women, in groups of twenty, went about various training exercises. The mud slush was further churned by a group attempting attack and defensive maneuvers. A tallish man with short cut, thick dark hair and deep brown eyes shouted out encouragement, advice, and occasionally a sarcastic comment. Franz led them around the edges, over to the man. Tamzin could see a fair number of the women wore slave collars. Her demeanor became wary, ready to run if this was a nasty trap.

Franz hailed the man, who made a gesture of acknowledgment, but didn't take his eyes off the group before him.

"Master Eron, I have brought you another recruit."

The man took his eyes off the women to give her a swift once-over before returning to the task at hand.

"Freeborn?" he asked.

"Yes," Tamzin answered, continuing on, "and I will stay that way."

The amusement in Eron's voice pricked her anger. "We have a mix of free and slave here. Those who are slave know they will have their chance to become free and are treated well. The free know they will not receive special considerations, and the slaves are to be respected. All the women must learn to work, live, and train together, no matter their status."

"Work? Who the hell has time for that? You can't be a decent warrior if you have to worry about providing food and shelter for yourself."

A smile crept briefly across the man's face. She wanted to punch it off.

"The royal advisor, Duchess Illyria, will be your patron, should you decide to join. She will provide all that is necessary. The only work she requires is what is needed to become a warrior."

"What's the catch? Come on, there's always a catch. I've already tried the royal army, and the asshole in charge made it very clear there will never be women soldiers," she persisted.

"The ladies here are preparing for a personal battle. Some of the nobles are training squads of warriors for a tournament in a year's time." Eron noted how her arms were still crossed beneath her breasts. "They will meet in battle. Whichever squad has the most members alive in the end will be declared the winners."

"Wait. So you're pitting women against men. How many squads of men?" she demanded.

"Ten squads total, including this one, made up of one hundred members. Still sure you wanna join?" A smirk curled one side of his mouth up, his eyes saying he expected her to refuse.

Tamzin swallowed hard. She wanted to be a warrior, defending against evil and wrongdoing. That meant battle, against real armies, not in some nobles' senseless tournament because they were bored. She cast her glance over the women. "What happens to the winners?"

"They gain their freedom, if slaves. The right to keep their armor and arms, and prize money."

"The losers?"

"They get turned over to the army, and become a part of it." Eron's smirk turned a bit twisted.

"That won't help the women if they lose. They'll be a constant target of the men," Tamzin spat out, the anger she always carried inside her at the unfairness of the world toward women slowly building.

He shrugged, as if it wasn't any of his concern what happened to them if they lost. "Or you could try and beg either the sheriff's office or the royal palace guard to take you on. But I doubt they'll be any more amiable to the idea than the army was."

"They any good?" Tamzin jerked her chin toward the women. "They have any chance of winning?"

"There's always a chance," his dark eyes turned enigmatic, "but the final outcome will only be decided on how much and how willing a person is to fight for it; even when the odds are unfair."

She looked at him then, and before she could change her mind, said, "When can I start?"

CHAPTER TWENTY FOUR

The marquis' mansion blazed with light, a bright beacon on an otherwise poorly lit street. Conveyances pulled up to the front, disgorging their heavily cloaked occupants.

Susafan fretted back at my mansion, worried I was being led into a compromising situation because of how the request to come dressed was worded. What she didn't know was I had a plan in place to mitigate such attention.

Slaves in uniform admitted me into the lamplight-filled entrance hall and took my cloak before escorting me to the receiving room. I could hear the sounds of conversation from down the hall.

The room to which I was shown only contained two women, one of whom was Anne. The young woman had her arms tightly wrapped around her upper body. The person she sat chatting with did not stir as the marchioness excused herself and came over to greet me. She had a filmy, white lace shawl draped over her shoulders which she fiddled with, trying to get it to adequately cover her. The rest of Anne's outfit consisted of a thin, round collared, maroon silk dress which ended barely past her butt. Garters held up silk stockings the same color, and she wore a pair of gold silk slippers. I saw her eyes widen as she took in my outfit.

"Thank you for joining us." Her cold hands wrapped around mine.

I could hear her rapid heartbeat, and her trembling grip upon me was tight. Her makeup was expertly applied, but was not a look she normally would choose for herself. *You should not have come. My husband means to ruin you.*

"It is my pleasure," I answered her.

She tugged gently on my arm, leading me toward the other woman. I came face to face with Lady Caroline. She wore even less than Anne. Her outfit consisted of a long strip of ice-blue silk that ran down the middle of her body. It barely covered her crotch. Another strip, only crosswise, just covered her nipples. The silk had been drawn tight, to help it stay in place, so the outlines of what it attempted to hide could easily be seen. She wore a pair of high-heeled shoes the same color, chased with silver. Her hair was in an elaborate style fit for court, with diamonds and pearls woven through.

She blinked in surprise, then her eyes narrowed in suspicion and mouth firmed in anger before she blurted, "What are you here for?"

"I might ask you the same question. I was unaware your parents had loosened the strictures they'd placed upon you. Country life can be a bit dull in winter time, can it not?" I asked.

"If it were not for you, I would not be banished. How dare you allude to your liaison with my father, tossing it in my face. You whore! You will pay for what you have done to me! I'll make sure he learns you were here."

I tilted my head to one side. "I am unaware of having a personal hand in your disgrace."

"Bitch! Deny all you want, but I know the truth."

Before she was able to continue further, a husky, weasel-eyed slave interrupted us.

"Ladies, we are ready for your presence in the dining room."

I barely felt the tremor which passed through Anne's body from where her arm brushed against mine.

"Thank you, Victor." The marchioness' reply was low. *Forgive me, duchess, for what will happen.* The subsequent thought came to me clearly.

Susafan would be part pleased, part furious, to know she was right with her warnings.

The slave stayed close behind us as Anne led us into a different reception room. I deduced from the gathering of men and women they were waiting for our arrival. The females wore outfits, if the scraps of cloth could be called even that, meant to show off their bodies, and give ready access. Many of the men had elected to wear tights with their shoes, and little else. Both sexes gleamed with jewels, elaborate hair and makeup.

"Bastard! I didn't think he could get her to come," one of the men murmured to the others while they thought we were still out of hearing.

"How much did you bet?"

"A hundred gold," came the disgruntled reply.

"A pretty price. But worth it if he can get her to stay."

"And participate."

"Freely?"

"I shall bet fifty gold it will be the usual way."

"I will take that bet."

They chuckled and watched us walk toward them. I felt a slight, frantic tug on my arm as Anne escorted me across the room.

I smiled broadly and inclined my head toward hers, as if sharing a bit of funny gossip.

"Please, Duchess, drink lightly of the wine," Anne squeaked out.

"Yes, Duchess, we wouldn't want anything horrible to happen to the king's favorite whore from an excess of alcohol," Caroline hissed as she pushed past us, showing the fabric turned into a thong in back which let her buttocks bob freely.

"Victor!" The sharp command and gesture from the marquis caused his wife to whimper in fear before she cut the sound off. Jenabram scowled at Anne as we came up to him while the slave clamped a hand around the marchioness' arm and forcefully dragged her over to a group of men who watched us.

Caroline preened next to him, a self-satisfied smile curving up her mouth, as if it was she who bore the title of marchioness, and not Anne.

"My Lord," I greeted him, "thank you for inviting me. In the months since my arrival, I have heard much speculation over some of your parties."

His eyes greedily roamed my outfit, which was an artfully arranged collection of numerous black silk strings, meant to show my marble-white skin. I had not even bothered with shoes, instead going barefoot.

Jenabram replied, "Have you now? Well then, it is good you took a chance and came. And even dressed the part."

"I would not want to disappoint," I teased with a sly smile.

The fool believed me. Personally, I was tired of getting blood on some of my dresses, and this gave a perfect excuse not to wear much of one.

He leaned closer a tad, and breathed in the musky, spicy-scented oil I had applied. His next words flowed out with his exhalation. "If only both our wants were so easily appeased. I hope the wait will have been worth it."

When we are done with you, you will be begging me to keep this night quiet, and for the position of advisor, I will. His thoughts flowed easily.

I kept the giggle of glee from slipping out. I wanted to tell him this night would indeed be memorable, but not for the reasons he was thinking. He would know soon enough.

Jenabram straightened and called out, "Let the feast begin!"

He gestured for Victor to lead the way. The dining room was brightly lit by a multitude of oil lamps, chandeliers, and fires blazing in the white-gold veined, carved fireplaces. The ice-blue, watered silk wallpaper stopped midway down the wall. Below it was wood paneling painted white. The chair cushions had been covered in a slightly darker blue, and the closed drapes a midnight blue velvet brocade tasseled in silver. The color scheme even extended to the extravagantly set table. Slaves of both sexes, wearing nothing but their iron collars, lined the walls. They stood straight, hands clasped before their genitals. From behind a folding screen painted with carnal scenes drifted a melody of string and wind instruments. I took an unneeded breath in, to scent the room. Anticipation, lust, some fear, and . . . ah, I had wondered if Kendall would. He had small incense burners creatively hidden about the room, which perfumed the air with the same drugs he had used for his masque.

There was no formal assigned seating by rank which usually accompanied such events. Just an unspoken understanding everyone sit alternating men and women. The slaves made sure the drink flowed freely. Anne started out sipping at her goblet. As the night wore on, I noticed she began drinking as heavily, or more than, her husband.

"I do not recall seeing you at any of Kendall's special soirées since you moved here," the man to my left said. "I am

Mercer."

"This is the first I have attended," I replied. "I am surprised, as rumor holds they are usually more . . . risqué."

He chuckled. "Our manner of dress is not enough for you?" His eyes darkened with lust. "We must have strength before we begin, and some do not care to partake in the entertainment."

"Why is that?"

A shrug was his answer. "They have no desire but to be a spectator."

Many hours flowed by as the humans feasted. Many of the men and women fed each other, or openly groped and fondled one another, the men I sat between never realizing I didn't partake of the sustenance. With their minds already befuddled with wine and other substances they had ingested beforehand, it was no challenge to redirect their roaming hands to the women beside them. The noise level gradually rose, along with the amount of imbibing. So too did the groping and fondling, as more than one person shuddered every now and again from orgasms.

I sat, pretending to sip from a goblet, eyes heavy-lidded as I let everyone's thoughts wash over and through my mind. I added to the atmosphere with my power, sending out waves of heightened lust. They were almost ready for me. I knew my eyes glowed honey-gold fire. Kendall stood as a slave rang a gong. Heads turned, eyes bright from drink, voices falling silent.

"We will commence to the postprandial, before beginning the night's special entertainment," Kendall boomed out, eyes glittering from excess of drink and repressed excitement. "Victor! The box if you please!"

The weasel-eyed slave stirred from his place in the corner, where he had been silently observing us. He walked up the length of the long table, a small carved, dark wooden box with brass fittings carried between his gloved hands. The man was the only fully clothed person present. He stopped next to Anne, bowing in a way which made what he carried seem as if it were an offering.

"Oh I couldn't!" she protested. "The honor should go to one among us who is attending for the first time." A shrill laugh of desperation slipped from her lips.

"Anne, my love." The jolly tone had dark undercurrents

and the excitement in Jenabram's eyes turned to a feral gleam. "It would not be fair to favor one above the many who may lay claim to that honor. Now choose." He spat the last two words out.

We all saw the violent shudder which accompanied her hiccup of fear. The marchioness' hands visibly shook as she lifted the latch and then the lid. The slave moved the box higher so she could not look down into it and was forced to reach up. Her left hand rested on the lip of the open box as her right dipped inside and scrabbled about for several seconds. I heard wood clacking together, before she withdrew something clenched in her fist.

She did not look at it, but pressed her spine firmly against the back of the chair. Her eyes closed as her jaw clenched and throat muscles rippled as she convulsively swallowed.

The slave ignored his mistress, and turned to the man on her left, presenting the still open box in the previous method. Whoever he was, darted his hand inside and withdrew it in a manner suggesting he had been bitten by something venomous. He looked at what lay in his palm, and a snigger of delight escaped as the slave continued left.

I observed the proceedings; some guests crowed, others laughed, a few made sounds of disappointment, but they all retained a frenzied eagerness. Soon it was my turn. I reached inside to feel cool, flat round objects. I plucked one from the diminished pile and following the lead of those before me, brought the disk below the level of the table.

Keeping my lids half-lowered, I cast a quick glance toward Jenabram. He avidly stared at me, waiting for my reaction to what I held. In my cupped palm was a wooden disk, with an image branded into it. I flipped the disk over, to see a second, different brand.

With a neutral face, I let my gaze dart to each guest before ending on the marquis' face. His manic grin had taken on a certain stiffness, and the blue of his eyes had darkened a tad in anger.

"Victor." The slave's name came out clipped, with none of the earlier bonhomie Jenabram had infused it with.

None of the others seemed to pick up on the change except for his wife, whose hands had risen to clutch across her mouth as tears made tracks in the rice powder covering her face.

Victor had since set the box aside, and now he walked to the elaborately carved, painted, and gilded double doors. He gave a stiff nod to the two slaves standing on either side. They opened the doors to reveal the hallway. During our supper, other slaves must have come and extinguished the bulk of the oil lamps which had previously filled it with light; for it now held wide pools of darkness.

"If you will please step through into the hall, one by one." Kendall gestured. "A slave shall escort each of you to a specially prepared room where you may enjoy your postprandial, and then the entertainment."

Titters and noises of anticipation greeted his words. I glanced around to see Lady Caroline lick her lips, avidly staring at the marquis.

"Anne, my love, if you will lead." His command held a thread of menace.

I heard her heart speed up, and smelled the wave of fear which washed over her as she silently stood and made her way around the table and toward the opening. Her arms hung limply by her side, fists still clenched, mouth slack. I noted the rapid rise and fall of her bosom, the terror which glazed her eyes.

The moment she stepped into the hall, a slave seemed to materialize from one side. His right hand closed about her left upper arm while his left carried a six-branched candelabra to illuminate their way. My dark-attuned eyes saw the slave yank Anne up and forward when she stumbled in a patch of deep shadow.

"Please, honored guests, if you will." Jenabram's tone was back to light and inviting.

Chairs scraped unevenly as their drunken occupants hurried to exit the room. I tried to listen in on the thoughts around me again, but received only impressions of lust and exuberance. Caroline sneered at me in passing as the room quickly emptied. I knew it was expected of me to follow, so I rose last and pretended to sway, as if I hadn't realized how much I had drunk.

To add credence to my act, I clutched the chair backs to either side, letting my disk fall upon the rug.

"Forgive me, I seem to have overindulged," I apologized.

"I don't think I shall make a merry companion for the remainder of the night."

Kendall hastened to my side with a rapidity which belied his own drunken act.

"Do not fear, dear Duchess, I will help my slave escort you." He snaked an arm about my waist, snugging me to his side as he tried to act like he wasn't trying to grope me.

Victor came over and knelt down to pick up the dropped disk. He stood, presenting it to his master. A brief, self-satisfied twitch of the marquis' lips at sight of what was branded thereon was all the comment he made.

I let Kendall guide me, hearing the slave's footsteps behind us.

We passed down the hallway and up the elegant, marble stairs. Shrieks, moans, and various other noises of both pain and pleasure could barely be heard behind the closed doors we passed. I was forcibly walked through an open pair of white painted, gilded doors at the end of the hall. I peeked over my shoulder to see Victor shutting and locking them, placing his back to the doors and taking up a stance which suggested he would be preventing any attempts at escape.

"Have another drink, Duchess." Kendall hadn't released his grip about my waist. He leaned over to pluck a goblet off a small table.

Except for the pair of lit six-branched candelabra which sat on end tables, and the fire burning in the hearth, the room was in darkness. My hearing picked up the sound of four separate heartbeats. I took the offering, pretending to sip while I covertly cast my eyes over the room. The walls were papered in flocked red and black. The floor a dark, almost black, stained wood. The centerpiece to the room was a massive carved wooden bed with posters rising almost to the ceiling. The carvings depicted lovers in different positions of copulation. Mirrors, in carved and gilded frames, had been evenly spaced upon the walls. The left wall had a black- and gold-veined marble fireplace where the glow of a banked fire shone.

To the right, a large square space of wall was covered with black and gold thread brocade drapes trimmed with gold fringe and tassels. They moved slightly, every now and again, and I could feel a swirl of cold air about the level of my ankles. The marquis' free hand, during my brief inspection, continued to roam up and down my side, stroking my skin.

"Perhaps you would care to sit?" Kendall's voice had roughened.

Again, it seemed he didn't care what my answer would be. He brought me to a low-backed divan placed before the fireplace and lowered me onto it. The branding on the disks, along with the behavior and thoughts of the guests at dinner, let me know what he was expecting. I was amused enough with his machinations to continue playing along.

I leaned back seductively as the strings shifted to show more of my marble flesh while bringing the goblet to my lips as he sat himself next to me. I stared at him over the rim, as Jenabram shifted up onto one knee. He was all but slavering as he placed an arm on the low back and leaned forward, reaching for a decanter behind me on the side table.

"Let me pour you some more." His wine-fumed breath flooded my nose.

Rustling and shifting from the direction of the bed let me know where the two other people hid beneath the generous bedding which formed a mound over the mattress.

"Don't bother; we are both more than ready for the entertainment to begin." I lowered my voice further. "Why don't you tell your friends to come join us?"

Puzzlement momentarily clouded his eyes before lust took over. He leered expectantly, flicking a glance behind my head and making a come-ahead gesture with the hand that had been reaching for more wine. He let it then fall to the seat beside my waist, shifting further so his lower half pinned me to the divan.

Two different hands and arms came into my sight line. One to take the goblet from me, the other to hold my shoulders down, as Kendall lowered his head for a kiss. Oh, this was going to be such fun! Before either man realized what was about, I bit down on the marquis' bottom lip. One fang pierced through.

At the sudden pain, Jenabram howled and reared back, nearly ripping half his lip off. His hands automatically came up to clasp over his mouth, feeling for the damage. Blood flowed freely down his chin. In a blinding burst of speed, I grabbed the arms of the man holding my shoulders down and yanked him forward. He slammed into the marquis. They both fell off the divan with yells of rage. I was standing behind the fourth person, so my sudden disappearance from the divan caused him to topple over the side table and onto my vacated spot awkwardly. His cry of pain brought a malicious smile to my lips.

"My lord!" Victor started away from the door, realizing their plans had gone awry.

Whatever else he was about to say, I choked off with my right hand around his throat as I "magically" appeared in front of him. The slave gurgled and found himself airborne before he could fight back.

I appeared at the end of the bed as he crashed down in front of me. Grabbing the dangling end of a silken rope tied to a bedpost with my left hand, and the slave's arms with my right, I restrained him, both arms bent back behind his head and tied with the rope. He was still recovering from his unexpected landing by the time I finished.

Meanwhile, Jenabram and the fourth naked man sprang up and away from the divan. Victor cursed and struggled with his bonds, causing the knots I had made to tighten further. The man who'd landed on the divan staggered to his feet.

"You bitch!" roared out the naked man as he charged me, drink and overconfidence in his abilities making him reckless.

I stepped aside and tripped him as he flew past, and he windmilled his arms, trying to keep his balance. I grabbed one of the appendages with both my hands, lifting, heaving, and turning in one smooth movement. His howls of rage turned into pain as I flung him to bounce off the wall next to the fireplace.

"Get her!" came the command just as I felt a scoring across my back as a crack reached my ears. I turned to see a thick, braided black whip recoil past me.

The third man came toward me in a manner suggesting he meant to tackle me. The marquis readied to lash out with the whip again as I tossed my head back, laughing while subtly shifting. The charging man's snarling face as he sailed past me in a midair dive changed to panic. I didn't bother watching where he fell, only felt the heavy thud and scream of agony when he landed. The thong, fall, and popper of the whip, meanwhile, came at me like lightning. I lashed out and let the length snap and coil around my arm. I ignored the pain. As he was not expecting such a response, Kendall was not ready for my move, thus he still had the handle gripped tightly. My yank sent him crashing into the divan. His weight caused it to tip over, both landing with a jarring thud on the floor. The thong loosened as he lost his hold on the handle. Now I was in control of his weapon.

"You, bad, bad, bad man," I purred. "We will indeed have fun tonight—though," I gave a mock sigh of disappointment, "you may think otherwise by the end."

Kendall was climbing to hands and knees, rage distorting his face. He was inebriated enough to ignore the feelings of danger I projected along with my unnaturally blazing eyes.

"My lord!" Victor's voice held frustration.

"Silence, slave!" I didn't bother turning around, letting my voice castigate him. "Speak without my permission again and I shall rip your tongue out."

The marquis' eyes flicked to his struggling slave, then over to the naked man prone on the floor. A dark liquid oozed out from underneath where his head and face rested on the wood. The arm I had used as a fulcrum was perpendicular to his body, with a slackness and misshapen look about the shoulder area which meant it was both broken and out of joint. His eyes then flicked to something behind my shoulder.

Kendall gave his own laugh, albeit silent. "I knew kitty would like to play. But it is you whose claws will be clipped when the night ends."

I contemptuously tossed the whip toward the entrance of the room, my return smile feral, eyes golden flame. "Then let's play, puppy."

CHAPTER TWENTY FIVE

Jenabram found to his shock he was flying across the room. He'd barely moved toward his prize. He crashed into the center of his great bed. He had enough presence of mind to slip a hand beneath one of the pillows, where he kept a spare dagger.

A wicked-sounding laugh, along with a long scream of agony, came from the third attacker. The marquis rolled off the bed, landing in a crouch on the floor. His bed sat high enough that he had a clear sight line toward the feet of the duchess and his crony in their ongoing tussle. By the time he crept close enough to ambush the woman, a pool of blood and guts spilled out of his friend's ripped-open abdomen.

The sight enraged him; who did she think she was? He came up fast and, he thought, silently. A sharp crack, along with the sensation of briefly flying, barely had time to register as Kendall crashed onto his bed. Before the marquis could react, his arms, including the now-broken one which had held the dagger, was viciously yanked up and out. Silk ropes bound his wrists, then his right leg. His left was free, as the cord which was usually used currently held his slave to the bedpost. He yanked hard with his good arm, fighting the nauseous swells of pain radiating. His body bucked, but the knots only tightened.

Jenabram gritted his teeth, lip throbbing in time to the pain of his arm. He blinked sweat out of his eyes, raising his head enough to see where the bitch hid herself. Pools of wavering light and shadow meet his gaze. No sound of a door opening or closing came to his ears, so he knew she was still in the room.

"Master," Victor panted out, "please, we need the slaves to help subdue her." The sounds of him coughing competed with the crackle of flames in the fireplace. "She-she isn't drugged like the others. Why isn't she drugged?"

The heat from the fireplace intensified the coppery scent of blood, along with the thick stink of spilled bowel. Jenabram swallowed convulsively before he managed to tamp down his rising fear.

"Idiot slave! Your inability to follow orders is our problem. I told you to make sure the wine meant for her was drugged." The marquis hissed in rage.

"Master, I swear I did as you commanded," the slave protested from his position on the floor.

Kendall managed to sneer despite the growing waves of pain from his busted arm. He went to lick his lips, cursing when his tongue hit the spot she had bit. He knew he could talk his way out of his predicament.

"It seems my slave failed to heed my orders. The other men were not supposed to attack you. We're just playing games, kitty. Untie me, and I promise, together, we can discipline him."

A sinister chuckle came from the darkness, along with curses from his slave. The shadows moved, the pale oval of Illyria's face and blood-streaked body, eyes glowing honey fire, stepped toward him. The sight thrilled him, excited him.

"Discipline? My dear marquis, we have already begun. You wanted this to be a special party. The best one you've ever held. Trust me, it shall be talked about for some time."

He couldn't help himself. "You won't keep that milksop earl when he learns of this."

Jenabram blinked more sweat out of his eyes, unconsciously recoiling as the duchess appeared beside the bed. The movement sent more pain shooting up his abused arm. She leaned over him, roughly shoving pillows under his upper body to raise him. Her lips hovered over his. "Who says he will know I stayed after?"

Victor snorted from the floor. "He shall know. My master and I will make certain of it."

Without moving, she replied, "I did not give you permission to speak. And when a slave is disobedient, he must be punished."

Jenabram felt a chill of terror race up his spine as the shadows wavered and parted as if made of mist, and the duchess appeared at the end of the bed to stand before his slave. The slap rang throughout the room, along with a howl of pain.

"Enjoy your preview, gentlemen."

Illyria thrust the double doors open, candlelight flickered throughout the hallway. The sounds of sex filtered from behind closed doors.

"You bitch! Get back here! It is my right to have you first!" Kendall screamed, his fury overriding good sense.

She ignored him, stepping outside the room and turning right, toward his wife's room. He could only listen in impotent anger at what went on.

The double doors into the marchioness' room flew open to slam against the walls. The lady herself was being used, two men sitting and drinking wine while watching, and two buried deep in her flesh.

"Come on, quit being so damn lifeless. You don't want us to have to punish you further do you?" one of the men grunted out.

The sitting men lazily called out without looking. "Shut the door and wait your turn."

Please let this end soon. I wish I were dead. The thought was repeated endlessly by Anne in her mind. The vampire picked it up.

She came up behind the two men on either side of the couch, who drank and masturbated while waiting their turn, and calling out things they wanted the other men to do to the woman. Illyria grabbed the sides of their skulls, fingers entwined in their hair, using her strength to bash their heads together. They tumbled off the couch in an unconscious heap, wine glasses spilling and shattering on the floor. The vampire advanced without pausing to the big bed, black string skirt fluttering around her blood speckled legs.

"Sorry boys, playtime's over." The words came out in a rough purr.

"W-whaaa . . . ?" The man sodomizing Anne gasped out, almost at completion. *Wait! Why am I sailing across the room? The dog has never been that great a lay.* His befuddled thoughts were cut off as he slammed, back-first, into the marble mantle.

Sudden pain brought him out of his erotic haze, his moan of pleasure turning into a sudden shriek of agony. He slammed face-first into the floor. His nose and teeth broke, lips split, warm blood gushed out.

The second man had just climaxed when he was ripped away from Anne, his fingers leaving marks on her wrists. He looked up dazedly from the floor, not understanding how he had ended up there, or why there was another woman with flames for eyes standing before him. He had started to raise himself from the floor when a foot slammed into his chest, forcing him flat.

"Oohh baby—" His leer and suggestive words quickly dissolved into wordless screams of terror and pain.

He had a brief moment to see his genitals in one of her bloody hands before she forced his mouth open and rammed them as far down his throat as she was able. His arms and hands automatically came up to claw desperately at his blocked esophagus. While he suffocated, he barely felt her sharp nails carve lines into his chest. The pain and shock overcame him quickly, causing him to lose consciousness while he bled out.

Illyria grabbed the arms of her first victim, hauling him to the end of the bed and laying his limbs straight by his side. The pool of blood from his wounds smeared across the polished hardwood. The man who'd hit the fireplace was trying to lift his upper body. His back spasmed with pain, and he had difficulty breathing through the ruin of his nose. "I can't feel my legs!"

His words came out garbled, but the look of horror in his eyes at the sight of his friend spoke volumes. "What the hell are you?" he whimpered.

"What am I?" The duchess smiled, a hint of fangs touching her bottom lip.

"'E never said this was another costume ball," the man before her sobbed around the excruciating pain of his broken back.

"Who said anything about costumes?" she asked, one arm snaking out lightning-fast.

The man couldn't help the cry of agony she tore from him as he found himself bent over backward, face toward the painted ceiling. He flailed about with his arms, hoping to bash her. He heard a crack of bone breaking, and registered dimly that it was his arm. Honey fire consumed his gaze as he felt two hot needles stab into his neck. He felt himself being drained of what made him: his memories, dreams, and fears.

Illyria let the body drop, not concerned with drinking down his essence, his "soul." She just wanted a quick snack. Like the first man, she dragged him to the end of the bed, laid him out the same way. Then she ripped his genitals off, cramming them inside his throat and mouth and carving the same words on his chest.

The last two men in the room had woken dazed; one immediately scrambled for the door, while the other attempted to fight back. He found his efforts to be all for naught as he soon joined the other two dead men on the floor. The final man screamed out warnings, pushing open doors that hadn't been locked as he fled down to the first floor, unmindful of his naked state, trying to yank the locked front door open. He wasted precious minutes scrambling to unlock it. The door swung inward in a blast of icy wind and sleet. He'd just stepped on the landing when a hand closed around the back of his neck and left shoulder, yanking him inside. The door slammed shut, locking of its own volition.

"No, no, puppy. There's no escape here. Take your punishment like a man."

"Bitch! Whore! When the king hears of this, you will be stripped of your title; you won't be an advisor anymore."

The amused laugh sent shivers down his spine; her hands, hard and cold as metal, crushed both his shoulders. The hallway spun and he found himself captured by the duchess's glowing eyes. His arms felt like unwieldy weights hanging from his mangled shoulders. The fourth man who had waited to assault Anne blinked in disbelief as it seemed the walls moved downward. He turned his head just enough to realize he and the woman were flying. The man struggled, trying to kick her, but only felt his feet and ankle bones shatter as they made contact with her flesh.

"What the hell are you?" he screamed, repeating the question which had been asked before, as they flew down the hall toward the marchioness' bedroom.

"Death," echoed in the air around them.

Illyria stood and surveyed her handiwork, dimly aware previously locked doors were starting to open down the hall, their occupants peering out. Now with the screaming ended, a few ignored the commotion, continuing with their pleasures. A few cautiously crept out.

"You assholes!" Kendall howled from his room. "Untie me! Help me, and I'll make it worth your while."

Lady Anne still lay sprawled on her bed where she had landed after the vampire ripped her attackers off of her. She had the appearance of a broken doll, and the abuse she endured daily at the hands of her husband, along with the more recent from her rapists, could clearly be seen. She breathed shallowly, still trapped inside her mind. Behind Illyria, feet ran down the hall and into the master bedroom. She paid no attention when several pairs stopped outside Anne's room.

The shrill female scream of terror brought her around. She coldly assessed the small crowd growing outside the doors of both their hosts' rooms.

"You monster! What the hell you'd do to 'em?" a man accused her.

Illyria let their thoughts wash over her.

"Shit! I was supposed to have the marchioness next."

"Hope it was a good last fuck."

"Twisted bitch! Ain't any of the men or my sister whores that perverted."

"Death is not worth staying for a free fuck. I'm leaving!"

The crowd flinched back at the sudden, evil smile which creased the duchess's face. A moment later, a wind tore through the hall, extinguishing all the candles and oil lamps. Chaos reigned as the partygoers tried to get free of the tight clump they were in. Those who fled blindly, arms out, stumbling and falling down the hall, felt a wave of pure terror wash over them.

Illyria didn't care to feed, she only wanted to kill and maim the sheep before her. Those who were standing inside the doorway found themselves slamming off the walls before death claimed them. Her eyes glowed as crazed streamers of flame, the only light to be seen as she moved preternaturally fast. The marquis thrashed in impotent rage as his two closest cronies tried to undo the knots which bound him.

They couldn't see what happened in the darkness filling the hall. Screams of fear and the sickening crunch of bones made them all wonder if it wasn't worse that way. The marquis finally rolled off the bed, staggering a little as blood rushed back to his extremities.

"That bitch!" he growled, flinging open a wardrobe. He yanked a shirt out, using it to bind his broken arm against his upper abdomen. Jenabram reached back inside to extract a sword. "Grab the poker, Zeck, and Tully, take my dagger. We'll teach the whore manners."

Crazed with pain, wanting revenge, Kendall never spared a glance for his slave, still sitting on the floor at the end of the bed, tied up and making strange noises. If he had, he would have noticed the obvious deformity to the man's jaw. It spoke of being out of joint, and broken.

Kendall paused motioning with his sword for Tully to grab up a branch of candelabra with one taper still alight. "Afraid to be seen in the light, kitty? You want to fight like a man, you whore? Then test yourself against one!" he screamed in rage.

"Uh," began Zeck, but was hissed to silence by his friend.

The screams and unnerving sounds of people meeting their deaths petered out. A deep silence filled the mansion, heavy with terror.

Kendall sneered, "Bah. I won't let some whore of a duchess destroy everything. It's just tricks on her part."

He took a step out into the darkened hall and immediately stumbled over a body. "Damn it!" He swore as he righted himself and shook his hair back out of his face. Kendall wanted to stride purposefully, but the light wasn't adequate.

"We need to see!" Zeck instructed Tully as he cast about for an oil lamp or another candelabra.

The two men didn't have a chance to do more than grope about. A sudden hissing intake of breath brought their heads toward Kendall. Before him stood a nightmare vision of the duchess. Her skin glowed luminescent beneath the black string dress she wore. They could see the bones of her skull, her arteries and veins a roadmap of red and blue beneath her flesh. Her eyes glowed as honey-gold fire in dark eye sockets, hair writhed in an unseen wind. Her ruby lips parted to show two vicious-looking fangs.

"Cowardly worms! Bow before the Raven Queen. The Empress of Death."

"By the Undying Lands! You're not real! You can't be real!" Zeck stuttered out. *It's tricks, it has to be. Just like Lord Nicky and the grove. It's all just tricks.*

Kendall's momentary disbelief grew into a howl of rage. He thrust forward with his sword. It passed through the spot where she had been standing. He whirled around, enraged, to see Tully being consumed by a vast shadow. An abrupt, choked sound came from where he had stood. The marquis lunged forward into the darkness again with his sword, hoping to impale the bitch, not caring if he got his friend in the process.

A thud and a brief scream had him whipping back around. Zeck lay beneath the corpse of Tully, who appeared bleached of color.

"The bitch isn't natural!" his friend yelled, frantically hauling himself out from underneath the body. "He dropped from the ceiling dead!"

"YOU DARE CALL ME A COWARD?!" Kendall screamed, "WHEN IT IS YOU WHO CHEAT!"

An evil laugh echoing in the hallway was his reply. Zeck jumped, thinking he felt a cold breath on the back of his neck. He swung the poker about, sweeping curios and other objects off the nearby tops of hall tables before stepping on a body and twisting his ankle. He fell to one knee, breathing heavily.

"Fuck this! Let His Majesty deal with her murdering ass!" Zeck panted out. He was standing when he felt his head yanked back and a white blur crossed his vision.

He felt teeth close around the side of his throat, tearing and ripping. His body dropped to the floor a moment later. Kendall swung around just in time to see the duchess lift her head and look at him, her mouth, chin, and throat coated in crimson. He tried to stab the bitch, who was clearly insane, but once again met air.

A moment later, his good hand went numb from a blow. He found himself being dragged back to his suite and tied to the bed once more. His left leg, which had previously been left free, was tied to the bedpost with the intestines of his dead friends. The flames in the fireplace flared brightly, fresh wood feeding them.

All the candles and oil lamps in the room suddenly blazed alight. The marquis could hear the frantic gurgling sounds his slave made as the duchess walked toward him.

"The king will hear of this! You don't dare kill me, not if you care for your position." Kendall threatened, straining against his bonds. "You can't kill everyone who knows you're here." The last filled with uncertainty.

She made no reply, only yanked his slave's broken jaw open. His screams were cut off as she held up something long and pink. Her left hand rose, holding the poker Zeck had tried to use to defend himself. Illyria placed the object against his slave's forehead, driving the poker through it, the man's head, and into the bedpost behind.

Kendall's mouth snapped shut upon viewing the sheer impossible feat she performed in the mirrors hanging around the room. A fresher scent of blood and excrement mingled with the old. His eyes grew wide as Her Grace leaped onto the bed at his feet. The marquis didn't even feel the mattress sink under her weight as she walked up before crouching over his waist. Despite his situation, he still found the sight of her blood-coated body erotic.

"Tricks. I'm not afraid of your tricks. Nor was I of Nicky's." He spat.

She just smiled and using her blood-caked nails and hands, ripped every piece of clothing from him by shredding it. He tried to sneer. *Why unclothe him if she didn't mean to have sex with him?*

Illyria gave a wicked laugh, as if she had heard his thoughts. Then she began to carve words into his chest with her razor-sharp nails, humming as she did so. At first he clenched his teeth, determined not to scream. By the third word, he was making a high-pitched keening noise.

Kendall felt sweat pouring off his body. It stung the fresh wounds. His unbroken limbs trembled from the effort of trying to yank free of the binding silk cords. His broken arm felt dead. He watched the duchess place his sword's blade in the flames. She strolled back over to him, a tiny wicked smile playing about her mouth. The duchess leaned in close, stroked his sweat-matted hair off his face and forehead, leaning in to whisper in his ear. As the sword heated, she drove her fangs into his neck and fed. After the first few minutes, Kendall lost track of time. He felt a searing pain at his groin, smelled burnt flesh and hair. A small, wet sack was placed on the middle of his abdomen. The marquis felt her breath on his ear one last time, whispering, bringing his fears to life in his mind. He passed out from terror and exhaustion.

Illyria held her hands over the flames in Kendall's fireplace, let them burn off the blood and flesh clinging to them. She used the rags of his clothes to clean her body of blood. The duchess walked into Anne's room, adroitly avoiding the blood and bodies littering the hallway and both bedrooms.

"Hello, Anne. I'm sorry I couldn't help you sooner. I'm here now." She spoke kindly to the young woman who stared without really seeing, using her vampiric powers to find the thread of the marchioness' consciousness and gently tease it to the surface.

Lady Anne's body was a mass of new and old bruises, much like Mary Elana's had been before Illyria had bought her from her parents. Her arms and legs appeared stick thin. Each rib and knob of bone on the marchioness' spine stood out, skin taut.

"You appear uncomfortable. I'm going to move you." So saying, the duchess gently turned Anne onto her back, composing her limbs by her side. She propped the woman's head up with a pillow.

Anne blinked, tears leaking out her eyes, streaming down the sides of her face. She mouthed words soundlessly, but Illyria could read them from her mind.

I want to die. I can't live like this anymore. He will never let me be free.

"He will have no choice but to do what he is commanded. I would not worry about your husband. I had a talk with him; no one defies my will."

A small head shake was all the movement Anne made, mouth continuing to move, forming words she couldn't speak aloud. *Please. Let me die. I have no will to continue on. If you truly want to be my friend, grant me peace.*

Illyria was gently brushing the young woman's hair,

smoothing the snarls out so it lay shining and golden about her. "Death . . . your death, is permanent. I am offering you the means to break free of him and remain so without ending your life."

The duchess retrieved the pitcher of water and the basin which stood next to it behind the privacy screen; along with a cloth and a small bar of scented soap. She gently bathed Lady Anne, then dried her off.

Please. I have not your strength. You have been one of the few women to be kind to me and genuinely mean it.

Illyria stood, retrieving a ball gown, including undergarments and shoes, bringing them back to the bed. It was a confection of pink silk, white lace, gold detailing and puffy underskirts. She dressed Anne with care.

Please. Why would you be cruel and make me beg after all your kindnesses?

"As you wish," Illyria replied, and finished preparing Anne by putting a thin layer of rice powder and blush on her face and cheeks, along with a dash of the young woman's favorite scent at temples, ears, and wrists.

She sat beside the marchioness, leaning close to her ear, speaking both out loud and inside Anne's mind. "Think of some happy event before your marriage. Hold on to that thought. There will be one last tiny prick of pain, which I can only apologize for. Are you ready?"

Illyria didn't wait for a reply; she bit firmly but quickly into Anne's jugular. A small shudder was the only movement besides the breathing the marchioness made. The duchess found the happy thought Anne held onto, using her powers to enhance the memory as she drained the young woman's life. She left the marchioness' mind alone except for the help to the happy thought. She had no need to take the young woman's essence.

The vampire heard the thudding of Anne's heart grow weak, and yet it made one last fluttering attempt to hold onto life. *Let go, Anne. It is time. Go to your happy memory. You are alive in it. Nothing, and no one, can ever hurt you again.*

Lady Anne's heart beat once more, and a last gasp of air, sounding as a happy sigh, left her lungs as Illyria stopped drinking and erased the marks on the woman's neck with a small drop of her own blood. She placed the marchioness' hands one on top of the other across her waist. The vampire retrieved two gold coins, breaking the locked coin box hidden in the marquis' room, and placed them on Anne's eyelids, helping to hold them shut.

"Fare thee well, Lady Anne." She addressed the corpse.

Illyria strode purposefully yet soundlessly from the room. She firmly closed the double doors behind her.

CHAPTER TWENTY SIX

Saizar gazed dazedly at the remains of the marquis' dinner party. A woman's shrill hysterics penetrating the closed door of the receiving room. Behind him, his men shifted and muttered among themselves.

"Uh, sir, are we um, uh, gonna do anything?" Frog tentatively spoke.

"I hardly know where to start," the sheriff said more to himself than his men. "Guts, go get Earl Sydney and ask him to come and bring his secretary with him. When you have done that, bring Mathias here. We will need help. The rest of you, shit . . ." He trailed off on a curse.

The front door opened and closed after Guts who ran to do as bidden. Saizar rubbed a hand through his hair, head swiveling as he once more took note of the wreckage. "Cregan and Merrit, go around to the servants' entrance. Gather all the slaves still alive and hold them in the kitchen. Toras, see to the woman; try and get her to stop screaming. Gordy, stand guard and don't let anyone but the earl and his man and the captain of the palace guard inside. Frog, we must find out if his lordship is still alive."

Carefully the two men started up the marble staircase, skirting dried blood, and bits of bodies.

"What or who, did this? It's like some wild animal attacked."

Once at the top, the pools of blood were wider, and not completely dry near the centers. There were also more bodies lying about, limbs contorted unnaturally, faces a frozen rictus of terror. The majority of victims were nude.

The sheriff recognized a few faces from his visits to Madam Breck's. He didn't relish the visit he would have to make in his official capacity. The bloody footprints on the outside stoop, sidewalk, and street, marked the flight of survivors.

Most of the doors remained partially or fully open the entire length of the hall. Saizar and Frog glanced in at the gruesome tableaux as they passed. Their goal was his lordship's chamber. Once they knew his status, then they would delve farther into each room. Two sets of double doors, one cutting off the end of the hall, one set to the right, were the only closed pairs.

Gingerly, the sheriff turned a knob on the pair of doors at the end of the hall, and slowly opened it, watching where he stepped.

Malodorous scents assaulted his olfactory ends. From the near-complete darkness came unintelligible babbling and maniacal laughter. A faint outline of daylight on the right hand wall suggested windows hidden behind drapes.

"Sir," Frog tapped his superior on the shoulder, and passed him a candelabra he had found on the floor. The candles had been half-used, but the wicks had not been soaked in gore and thus could still be used.

"Thanks," Saizar answered, and carefully negotiated farther inside, toward the drapes.

He had to avoid shattered, bloody pieces of furniture. Frog followed close behind, and when they got to the covered windows, the apprentice lawman parted the drapes. Daylight flooded the room, the stark winter sun harshly illuminating the space.

The marquis lay supine in the middle of his great bed, forming an X. He was naked, arms and legs tied to the posts. His lordship's right arm looked broken and mottled a deep black. Blood had run down his chest from lines carved into it. A strange, blood and hair-covered sack-like, thing, sat in the middle of his abdomen. The bedding beneath his groin was also black with blood, and the scent of charred flesh came from the area.

His slave was tied to a post at the end of the bed, mouth gaping open, a fireplace poker had been shoved into his skull with a piece of meat dangling from it.

"Is that . . . his tongue?" Frog ventured closer to study. After a moment he said, "Yup."

Meanwhile, Saizar had approached the bed. "Your Lordship? What happened?"

"Golden flames! I display my shame! I am a worm! A

sadist!" Jenabram screamed and thrashed before laughing maniacally.

The thing on his belly landed beside him. Frog had come to stand on the opposite side of the bed from his superior.

"Uh, sir. I do believe that is his . . . uh . . . um . . . nut sack," he finished lamely. "And, uh . . . um . . . whoever did it cauterized the wound. So . . . you know, he wouldn't bleed out."

Saizar pinched the bridge of his nose; he was not a man given to drink, but dearly wished for one now.

"Frog, you are to remain silent on what you have seen. We all will have to. I dare not move his lordship without the advice of a physician. Let us check the other room, and then see if there are any servants left alive we can send to fetch the doctor."

They exited the room as carefully as they had entered it and stood before the right-hand set of doors which were also closed. The sheriff mentally steeled himself to find more horrors.

Luck was not kind to him. The mutilated bodies of four men had been laid out in a row at the foot of the bed. Each of their chests had carvings on them, hard to read with all the blood. Their cheeks and mouths bulged from their genitals being stuffed in them.

Behind him, he heard Frog gag and retch, followed by a splash of vomitus landing.

Saizar ventured farther inside, trying to contain his own nausea. He placed his sleeve-covered arm across his nose and mouth. Sweat dotted his brow, and the room felt hotter than it had a moment ago. The outlines of a fifth body could be seen on the bed under a sheet.

It was incongruous, given the way the other bodies had been left lying about; as if they were trash. The sheriff took several shallow breaths, then with both hands, folded down the sheet so he could see who it covered.

Lady Anne was the victim. He lowered the sheet farther, past her toes, puzzled. She had been laid out already for burial. Her hair was neatly arranged underneath her and looked to have been brushed. Her face had been carefully enhanced with cosmetics, the new and old bruises on it faintly seen. Her lids had been closed, a gold coin laid upon each to keep them shut.

The marchioness' hands had been clasped across her abdomen. She wore a pale pink, lace-edged ball gown that only accented the whiteness of her skin. Matching shoes had been placed upon her stockinged feet. There were no immediately obvious signs of what might have killed her.

"Who—who would do such a thing? It's right creepy, I say. She-she looks as if she smiles," Frog softly exclaimed from beside Saizar as he made a gesture of warding away evil.

"That is what makes it all the more gruesome. We will find she had no lovers who would dare go to these lengths inside the marquis' home. Nor outside of it."

"But the bodies on the floor . . ."

"I do not understand that part of the mystery. Let us hope any survivors will be able to shed some light on what happened last night. Come." Saizar replaced the covering, just as carefully, he imagined, as it had been drawn up by whoever killed her.

* * *

Mathias stepped into the front hall of the marquis' town home and blanched. The last time he had seen so much gore had been during the bandits' raid. He let a few of his hand-picked men inside and gave his directions.

"No one is to speak a word of what we do today. Should I catch any man discussing these events in a public setting, or with those of us not directly involved, I will fire. The sheriff's office shall be helping our endeavors today, so I also expect cooperation on all sides. Saizar has already sent for the royal advisor, so be sure you grant her entrance when she comes."

He then rapped out instructions, and his men started on their appointed tasks. Mathias was about to head into the receiving room when the front door opened again.

Earl Sydney stepped into the hall, stopping short at the sight. "What in the Dark Lands is going on?"

"My lord, we were alerted by one of Sheriff Saizar's men. I have been told there are a number of problems to contend with."

"Such as?"

The captain of the guard, while not afraid of battle, dreaded what was to come. Still, he tried his best.

"The marchioness is, unfortunately, one of the victims. The marquis has been injured, there are a number of nobles dead as well, and then there is the matter of Lady Caroline."

"I'm sorry, what? Surely you are mistaken. My eldest resides at our country estate now," Sydney barked out.

Mathias cleared his throat and coughed. "The receiving room, my lord, is where you might want to start." He bowed respectfully. "I shall be upstairs." So saying, he made his careful way up.

Sydney, for once, found himself nonplussed. His eldest couldn't be here. She wouldn't dare! Would she? It was too much, considering how he believed Illyria's love for him had cooled. What time she spent at the mansion was occupied with royal business, with barely any left for him. He turned and strode down the hall, paused outside a guarded door a moment. The man bowed, a mix of pity and scorn in his eyes as he opened the portal.

The earl could only stand in the doorway in shock, then rage flushed his features. He firmly shut the door behind him. A lawman knelt beside a body, with his back before the drawn drapes of the room, as he murmured details to a nearby scribe. A second naked body, with a face which bore the remains of heavy make-up which the wearer had used in an attempt to make herself appear younger, lay sprawled in a pool of dried blood. The third body belonged, indeed, to his eldest daughter.

Sydney's body sagged a moment, then he staggered a little before dropping to his knees with an audible thud.

"Uh, sir . . ." began the guard as he glanced over at the sound, only to be interrupted by a keening noise.

Sydney felt his gorge rise; he just wanted to leave and try to forget this new dimension to his personal nightmare. But he had been called upon in his official capacity, and he must not shirk, no matter how distasteful the revelations in his deceased daughter's behavior. Only he couldn't seem to make his body obey him.

CHAPTER TWENTY SEVEN

Chadrick dismounted, body and mind numb. A silent, tear-stained slave led his horse away. Behind the earl, the cart containing his daughter's body creaked down the drive toward the back entrance. He had sent instructions for only the basics to be done. In a daze, the earl stood in the entrance hall, eyes wandering over the portraits of his ancestors. He didn't even hear the frantic steps coming his way, or notice his son beside him. Martin was talking, begging . . . something. Chadrick took a step, staggered, and collapsed to his knees on the dark wood flooring. He bent over, face hidden in the crook of his elbows, fingers laced together over his head, the sounds of his keening echoing.

Martin left his sire where he was. He didn't relish having to tell his sister or mother the news, since it seemed his parent was incapable at the moment. They had to know before any more time passed. Firmly his feet trod upstairs, and to his sister's guarded door. He motioned, and the man asked respectfully before opening the door:

"Is it true, my lord? Lady Caroline was found dead, in unpleasant surroundings?"

"Lukas, I forbid any mention of the conditions of my sister's demise."

"Yes, my lord," the chastised slave replied, lapsing into silence as the young master entered the room.

Martin listened to the door softly shutting behind him. His sister and her body slave stood at one of her bedroom windows. They had the curtains twitched back, gossiping, craning their necks to see into the courtyard.

"Sally." He had to call her name several times before she half-turned to him.

"Is it true?!" she asked, sounding more breathless with excitement than grief.

"Our dear elder sister is dead," Martin confirmed.

Sally exchanged glances with her slave, then came away from the window to stand nearby, with Crystal a step behind. "But, brother, the rumors. Are they true? The slaves say she was found naked at the marquis' mansion, in a compromising manner."

"Sally!" Martin was shocked into shouting his sister's name in disbelief.

She didn't heed him, but prattled on, cheerfully, "Oh, honestly, Martin. You forget Lord Nicky made a real woman out of me. Although, according to custom, I will be unable to marry now for at least a year."

Her words became a buzz inside his head. He felt disgust and revulsion rising in his gorge. It seemed his hand raised of its own volition, and delivered a stinging slap to the side of Sally's face.

His sister stumbled back in shock, one hand raised to her cheek. She stared at her brother a moment in silence, then launched herself at him, a fury of slaps, bites, screams, and hair pulling. The two siblings struggled together for several moments before Martin managed to shove his sister away and to the floor, his hair and clothes in disarray from their fight. He quickly strode to the door and opened it, pausing only long enough for a final comment.

"Your marriage will still take place before the spring planting. You will remain confined to the house."

His sister's screams of rage followed him down the hall. Martin paused briefly inside his room to repair the damage wrought. He continued downstairs, his father still on his knees, grieving. The butler slid noiselessly into the hall.

"My lord, the slaves are gathered downstairs, as requested."

"Thank you."

The two men descended to the kitchen environs. The slave's hall was crowded. Some wept silently, others gazed stone-faced, not meeting his eyes.

"I'm sure you've all heard by now, or seen, my sister Caroline's body. Your loyalty lies with the family. Caroline was murdered by bandits while on her way to visit my mother. Any other word—any other hint—of gossip to the contrary, and the perpetrator will be sold to work on the barges. Am I understood?"

Martin glared at each slave, waiting until they had all murmured acceptance, and made obeisance. "You may continue with your duties."

He wheeled around on his heel, and stalked back upstairs as the front door bell jangled. The upstairs staff following in his wake. Martin entered the front hall as the butler let his mother in. She swept past him, face tight in fury and disgust. Lady Elizabeth stopped five steps from her husband, her lips curled up in contempt.

"How dare you?!" Her enraged screams filled the space. "How dare you! If you had just let me handle matters with our children the way I wanted, we wouldn't be facing this disgrace. This is all your fault. You think you can just tell a pretty lie to cover it up? If our slaves know the truth, so does every other slave of our peers. Do you know how much more honor we have lost because of our daughter? How much standing?"

"Mother, please. Father couldn't have known Caroline would disobey."

Martin's ears were left ringing from the force of his mother's slap against his face.

"Don't you dare contradict me!" she coldly informed her son before turning her fury back onto the curled figure of her husband. "I have had enough of your nonsense. You will move back to your home. You will do what I say. You will not go near that foreign whore ever again."

Elizabeth whirled on her son, face red, contorted in fury. He felt a trickle of fear worm down his spine.

"Mother," he tried again, "please."

"You. You will do as you're told. You are not old enough, nor have the aptitude, to be called the head of our house."

Martin felt his own temper rise. He glanced down again at the pitiful spectacle his father presented, so lost in his grief he'd never heard a word his wife castigated him with.

"Carn," the young man addressed the butler, "please have my mother escorted back to the dowager cottage, and kept there until she calms down. It seems her grief has driven her temporarily mad."

The butler murmured a response, and signaled to the slaves

who had crept toward the front hall upon hearing all the commotion.

Elizabeth gave a scream, and charged her son. He flinched, arms up while trying to ward off her attack. Strong male slaves managed to pry his mother off him before she inflicted too much damage.

Martin continued with his commands over the sounds of his mother's shrieks. "Also, please see if the royal physician will send something to help keep her calm. Have the steward alerted to attend me at once, and see to it the house is dressed for mourning."

Carn bowed again, beckoning to slaves and instructing them in a low voice. His mother could still be heard, albeit faintly, as the slaves dragged her out of the house by way of the back. The young man walked over to his father, and knelt beside him. He placed a hand on his sire's shoulder, and squeezed lightly. Eventually, the keening tapered off, though his father still knelt, curled over himself.

The earl's body slave entered the hall, and between the two men, they managed to get the elder on his feet. Sydney stumbled between the men as he was led up to his bedroom. Once inside, Martin let the body slave take over, and descended to his office. There, both the estate and house stewards waited for him. They bowed and, at his signal, seated themselves before his desk. The two men waited for Martin to speak first, out of deference for his recent loss.

He opened his mouth, then closed it several times, searching for the words he wanted. "I'm not sure what you may have heard concerning my sister's death," he began.

The young man mentioned what he wanted the official record to be. Caroline would be interred in the family vault as soon as the body was made ready. The affair would be private. The household staff would observe a two-week mourning period. His sister's wedding would not be put off. Lastly, he sent a note to the advisor.

* * *

Martin stood nervously in the entrance hall, snow swirling

inside from the open front door. A week had passed since Caroline's death, cremation, and interment of the ashes. The door slave waited for the elegantly cloaked figure to mount the steps. Behind, in the street, a groom waited with the advisor's horse. The woman paused just inside the threshold.

"Am I welcome?" she asked.

The young lord took a step forward. "Greetings. I bid you to enter, Duchess."

She lowered the hood of her cloak, then unfastened the garment before handing it over to a slave. "I heard of your recent misfortunes. Again, please accept my condolences on the loss of your sister."

"Thank you," Martin replied with a wan smile.

She gave a regal inclination of her head. "Is there anything I may be of assistance with during your mourning?"

"I should hope so. My father has taken Caroline's death hard. He will not respond to any of us, even his own body slave."

"I am not sure how much help I will be, if he won't respond to his own kin."

Martin paused, not sure how to say what he wanted without insulting her. "I am hoping that your . . . special relationship . . . with my father will enable you to reach him."

"Very well. I shall try my best, but I make no promises."

"Thank you, Your Grace. If you will please follow me." The young man turned and mounted the stairs. He had to glance back to make sure the duchess followed, so silent were her steps.

Martin paused outside his father's room and knocked. There was no answer, so he turned the knob and swung the door inward. Most of the drapes remained closed, except for one pair. The outline of a chair blocked the bulk of the winter sun. Illyria placed her hand on the young man's arm.

"Please, let me try alone." She smiled to take the sting out of her words, and then swept inside the dim room.

His lordship closed the door, then slumped down against the wall beside it. He didn't know what else to try to breach the self-imposed exile his father wallowed in.

Illyria paused inside the earl's bedroom, taking a moment to scan the surroundings with her senses. She could feel the regret, shame, and grief which permeated the room. *It's good I drank from Eron before coming, else I would not be able to tolerate so much direct sunlight.*

Her footsteps were noiseless; she paused by the side of the chair. Sydney stared blankly out the window. He had a view of the back garden, stables, and the mountain rising behind all. Since the death of his eldest, the earl had closeted himself away from everyone. The duchess noted how suddenly the earl had aged from his grief. The silver wings at his temples had grown upward, so that only a thin strip of black hair remained on top of his brow. His once-piercing sapphire eyes had a dull, grayish look to them, and had sunk slightly into his orbits. What wrinkles he possessed stood out as deep grooves. Illyria could tell by the fit of his clothes that her lover had lost weight. She leaned close to his whiskery cheek, and gently pressed her lips to the sagging flesh.

"Chadrick." She spoke low, power flowing behind her words. "Will you come back from your grief, just for a moment, to speak with me?"

The duchess caressed his brow with her left hand, and gently squeezed her right over his hand, which felt delicate and knobby, where it lay on top of the armrest. She kept up her low flow of words, a murmur for his ears alone.

"My love. My champion. Come back to your family, to me. Come back to us."

She noted tears which leaked from the corners of his eyes, and his hand trembled briefly under hers. Illyria tried once more, not wanting to break the tenuous connection his mind had with reality.

"Chadrick . . . my love . . . Chadrick."

The earl took in a long, quivering breath, his eyelids squeezed shut, then opened. He turned his head toward her, slowly, as if in physical pain.

The vamp kept her expression serious, tinged with sadness. "My love, Chadrick, I have not the words to express how sorry I am for the loss you and your family bear. Your son is so worried about you, he sent for me. Shall I stay? Or would you rather I go?"

His eyes roamed her face in a manner suggesting he didn't know where to focus. The earl's dry lips parted, and his tongue darted out in an effort to wet them before he rasped out, "Why did you wait so long to come? Do I mean so little to you? Does our love?"

"I do not deserve your forgiveness, nor your love, for staying away when I knew you would need me most. I only thought to spare your family my presence."

"My family?" Hurt clouded his eyes, crumpled his face. "My family?"

She waited patiently by his side, kneeling so they were eye level. His hand trembled under hers. He began to cackle, then ended in choking coughs. She turned, spotting a water pitcher and goblet nearby. She poured and brought it over to him, raising the rim to his lips and tilting it so the earl could drink. He wrapped his trembling hands around hers, then let her set the empty goblet back on the side table.

"I am done with them. I don't care what Elizabeth thinks, nor says. I will not suffer a moment more with her malice and hatred of me. You claim you love me, yet you abandoned me when I needed you most."

He abruptly withdrew his hands from hers, and turned his face away so he once more stared out the window.

Illyria stood, feeling his despair, self-loathing, and rage boiling inside of him.

She hesitated a moment, then withdrew a scroll from inside the bodice of her dress. The duchess gently laid it down on Sydney's lap. "You shall always have a place in my heart, and home, for however long you wish," she replied with a last kiss to his lips before leaving.

* * *

Martin looked up from his contemplation of his clasped hands, and thoughts, at the gentle shutting of his father's bedroom door.

"Walk with me, please," the duchess requested.

He scrambled up, the plea for information unspoken in his eyes. They began the long trek back to the front hall.

"Your father roused enough to speak briefly with me. It

seems the manner of your sister's death has proven to be more than he can handle. I am aware now is a poor time to speak of your father's and my personal matters. I feel I owe you the courtesy of informing you nonetheless. How aware are you of the state of your parents' marriage?"

"Enough to realize he is miserable, and as the years pass, my mother becomes less and less able to tolerate his presence and attentions. And her . . . rejection . . . of him leads him to find temporary, physical solace in other women."

She nodded once, sharply. "Your father has requested on more than one occasion I procure a divorce from His Majesty for him, so he may be quit of your mother. Please do not think it is his grief speaking."

Martin swallowed before he spoke, weighing what he wanted to say as they continued walking to the stairs. "Has he mentioned . . . I mean, what will he . . ."

"Chadrick did not tell me. I did not ask. I know your mother opposes your father's wishes. I am telling you this now, so you may prepare your family."

"Now? He spoke of that now?" Martin's voice rose in disbelief and disgust, stopping and staring at the duchess.

"No, the king has finally signed the divorce decree, and asked me to deliver it in my official role as advisor."

In his current state, the young man didn't think to censure his next words. "My sister is dead, her manner of passing a disgrace to the family name, and you think now is the time to bring more dishonor upon us all? I am beginning to think my mother was correct in her estimation of you."

A thin smile from the duchess, a glinting of dark amusement in her eyes, made Martin realize what he had said.

"Thank you for your honesty. Your family doesn't have to like, or approve of it; know that it has happened." A thread of steel entered the duchess's voice.

The two paused at the bottom of the stairs, facing each other. Martin clutched the newel post. Did she really not understand the trouble his father's divorce would unleash?

"There is no happy ending, Martin, not for either of your parents."

"Then why do this? Why make Sally and me suffer through the fallout? Through the social stigma? No one divorces!"

"I fear your father's health will deteriorate, and he will let himself die rather than remain unhappy a moment more."

"And my mother? What of her health? What of her feelings?"

"Even if I had never become involved with your father, someone else would have. How long such a state of affairs would have lasted before coming to this point, I do not know."

Martin barely heard her replies, his hands white knuckled fists. "You are destroying my family!"

"No, that happened long before I arrived. I am merely finishing what was begun the day your parents married."

"You—"

"Ah, ah, ah," she tutted, "some states are worse than death. Your father is suffering through one now. May you never be brought to such a position as he."

"Vile! Home wrecker!"

"You should ask your mother a question. If Chadrick was the type of man she wants him to be according to her view, would she enjoy her life lived the way Lady Anne did? If she says aught but yes, then she is a hypocrite."

His lordship's mouth dropped open in shock. "Lady Anne was forced to endure abuse, and endless humiliations, and now she is dead! I find your comparison distasteful."

"Perhaps, yet it is true. Would your mother rather be dead instead of divorced? Or a widow, after she finishes driving your father to his grave. Think about it."

"I beg of you, do not do this to my family, not now."

"But it has already happened. I need only inform your mother."

"Stay away from her."

"I cannot ignore a command from our king." She smiled gently. "I have already held off on performing my duty. Your mother will not admit me, but her slave can accept the document."

"I thought Lord Nicky the cruelest person in the kingdom, but you are not so much different."

"Perhaps one day you will understand, and think

differently. Good day, your lordship."

The door slave scrambled to get the portal open, trying to pretend he hadn't eavesdropped. Illyria swept past him, leaving a furious Martin behind. The young man dearly wished he had someone he could trust to confide in. Instead, he slammed his fist into the newel post, and then stomped back to his office.

CHAPTER TWENTY EIGHT

The throne room was packed with people, and more waited outside in the cold, huddling together for warmth. Braziers were placed at intervals, and great gouts of flame blazed as the wood within was consumed.

The royal court had been in session for several hours. For once, the crimes and sentencing of prisoners were held out in the open. To the left of the great doors giving entrance into the royal presence, a chopping block sat in the snow. Blood lay in deep, frozen pools, and the bodies had been stacked to one side like a pile of cordwood. Four men, of various heights but all highly muscular, who were rumored to have been paid handsomely for their jobs as executioners, sat beside a bonfire huddled in their cloaks. Each of them was cleaning and honing his weapon of choice, two with great axes, two with heavy swords. No one knew for sure who they were, as each wore a black hood over his head, the eye and mouth holes all that could be seen of their faces.

Despite the serious nature of events taking place, a festive air permeated the grounds. Enterprising merchants moved about the crowd or stood beside carts, selling a variety of food and drink. A few people performed simple acrobatic acts. More than one petty thief and pickpocket slipped amid the crowds, liberating coin purses, watches, or jewelry when possible.

Inside and outside the throne room, many different conversations took place, rumors and gossip flying, the currency of the day.

"I can't believe there were so many prisoners inside."

"Who are half of them? I barely remember what they did."

"The sheriff still doesn't know who killed all those people at the marquis' party. Including the marchioness and Lady Caroline."

"Lady Elizabeth is looking more haggard than normal."

"That uptight cow! She deserves all her humiliations and more. I always said them nobles ain't any better than us."

"I can't believe the earl divorced her! And their daughter not long dead too!"

"I can't believe he waited so long. I bet Her Grace used her new position to force it through."

"They'll never be received together in public."

"The youngest is still going to be married. They're not even going to wait the proper length to mourn."

"Hmm, maybe she's with child, despite what they say."

"Ohh, I don't think the king will take well to the news, if the rumors of the father are true."

"The Great One save us! Do they mean to empty the entire dungeon? Does this mean they're cleaning it out for more prisoners?"

"How can they have gotten the truth out of those who were arrested after the head questioner was found dead? How can they trust anything of what those criminals said?"

The onlookers commented on the proceedings. Most people whispered to each other or their neighbors, not wanting to miss hearing any of what was taking place at the base of the throne stairs.

For once, His Majesty was not sleeping, or distracting himself with his harem, of which only two attended the king. They knelt at his side, occasionally reaching up to wipe long, glistening strands of drool from his mouth.

"What is wrong with our king?"

"I heard from my sister who works as a scullery maid, he's mad. The physician has to keep him drugged; otherwise he runs screaming throughout the palace, believing he is being chased by assassins, and ordering those he runs across to be put to death as traitors."

"I bet Her Grace loves it."

"If he doesn't get better, who will be our king? Those damn nobles will fight over the right, and it's us who'll suffer the most for it."

Most of the people noted the marked difference in the king. His head lolled about, as if he could not lift it up. When Maceanas did briefly look up, his face seemed wan and the skin sagged. Those closest could see a fine tremor which constantly made his hands and arms shake. His Majesty had yet to speak.

Aranthus stood halfway down the stairs, in his best court outfit, staff polished to a high shine. The entire royal guard unit lined the perimeter, and formed a boundary across the front of the room to prevent anyone getting too close to the open space before the dais stairs. Outside, the sheriff and his lawmen, now numbered at two dozen, patrolled.

To the left of the dais, facing the crowd, sat a mixture of nobles of both sexes selected at random. To the right, the same for the prominent townspeople, guild and artisan members. The royal advisor stood at the bottom of the stairs, in the center position. Her crimson and silver outfit, black leather pants, and dual swords, along with the faintly foreboding aura around her, kept the proceedings continuing smoothly with a minimum of chicanery. The two groups had heard the evidence and any testimony from accused and witnesses, if they were alive and available, the week before. Today's final was the culmination of their decisions for each case, with the royal advisor and the king being rumored to have the final, deciding vote for or against any punishments.

Even the townspeople noticed how the nobles frequently snuck glances toward His Majesty.

"Is he truly mad?" Baron Stavic whispered to his seatmate.

"So **she** says," he replied with a subtle nod to the advisor.

"You don't think . . ." Stavic said.

"That she's poisoned him? Not with his personal physician overseeing. I heard those two arguing. They hate each other. He won't let the duchess do anything other than inquire about the king's health. Nor will he leave her alone in His Majesty's presence."

"Does she really think the king will let Sydney, a divorced man, marry her?"

"Shhhh," someone behind them hissed, "do you want her to hear?"

The nobles stopped gossiping long enough to focus on the next prisoner.

"We will now hear the case against Tanner, former royal

treasurer in charge, and those workers under his supervision who participated in his crimes," the chamberlain called out, banging his staff against the floor.

The whisperings rose along with townspeople standing on their toes, trying to get a good look at the people being led forth from a side chamber.

The prisoners were all males, ranging in age, filthy, gaunt, and pale from their weeks of incarceration. They were barefoot, collars around their necks from which chains had been attached to both sides linking them to the person next to them in line. A chain at the front of the collar ran down the length of their bodies, connecting the manacles at hands and feet together.

"The High Lord Treasurer Tanner is found guilty thusly: abusing the trust of his appointed position which he was placed in by our late king's father; stealing funds from the royal treasury for his own personal use; conspiring with certain men of his office under his supervision to hide said crimes; the planning and intention of escaping with his ill-gotten gains."

The accused man held his head up defiantly, eyes glittering with rage.

Aranthus continued reading from the scroll he held. "Evidence has been given by Anson, the second-in-command to the treasury, and by the other co-conspirators. Additional proof was found in the traitor's home itself, where he'd hidden what he stole, along with detailed accounts of how much he stole."

The crowd pressed forward, eager to hear the punishment. Those at the very front were roughly pushed back by the guards and sharply reprimanded.

"As justice for their crimes, they shall pay thusly: the clerks are sentenced to work as slaves collecting trash and night soil and the disposal of such. Any remaining funds which they received for their roles will be seized by the crown. If no such funds remain, the amounts shall come out of the auction of any personal property or possessions bought by said funds. "

Several wails rose up near the back of the hall, along with a few shouts of anger or sadness as the families of the men learned the fates of their loved ones.

"The second in command, Anson, is to be branded a thief

and become a barge slave for the duration of his life, his thefts of funds to be repaid in the same manner as the clerks."

Another wail was heard, which dissolved into hysterics and largely ignored.

"High Lord Treasurer Tanner: in addition to being stripped of your office, all your property and personal possessions are herewith seized by the crown. Your hands and feet shall be cut off, the wounds cauterized. You will be branded a thief, and placed in a hanging cage to die and rot."

The loudest scream to be heard yet rang throughout the room on the tail of the sentencing. A small pocket formed around the woman who had made the noise. She was Tanner's wife, and a passel of children stood around her, scared and crying.

Aranthus had to shout his last words in an effort to be heard over the noise the woman made. "All sentences are to be carried out immediately!"

The chamberlain banged his staff as the royal guards led their charges off, shuffling. There were stirrings in the crowd, as relatives of the condemned left the hall seeking a chance to speak with their loved ones.

"The position of royal treasurer is hereby formally conferred upon the Lady Raina Downton, Countess of Smirkin."

Outraged shouts, boos, and shaking of fists commenced at Aranthus's words, most of it directed toward the duchess. Slowly she turned her head, and each protester noted how her gaze uncannily found them in the crowd, a grim smile the only expression on her otherwise neutral features. She held a hand up, and the noise petered off to be replaced by an uneasy, waiting silence.

"If you continue to disturb the proceedings, you will be removed and barred from further attending. Those who have problems with the appointments may voice their complaints to me after we are done here." Her fierce gaze swept the crowd.

A nervous shuffling of feet and coughing broke out in the suddenly uncomfortable atmosphere. She turned and signaled to Aranthus to continue with the proceedings.

After the treasurer followed various other palace officials who had been revealed during the ongoing audits of having stolen funds, goods, or otherwise abusing their offices. They too were sentenced in much the same manner as Tanner and his clerks. The hall still held a fair amount of people, as they were in flux, dividing their curiosity between the executions outside and the events inside. Rumors were circulating since the arrests, as the townspeople and nobles understood positions of importance and power were opening up. Anyone with the knowledge, or funds, who thought they had a chance, had been doing their best to put their names forth for consideration with any noble or the chamberlain himself, whom they thought would advance their cause. As Her Grace didn't mention any more names for open spots, the people considered chance still in their favor.

Aranthus banged his staff yet again, and the king held a trembling hand up, signaling he meant to address his people. His head rolled back so he could look out upon his subjects. Those in the hall immediately sank in deep bows or curtseys. His voice came out slurred.

"My people! My advisor, the Duchess Illyria, will be in charge of interviewing and selecting those she feels are fit for the serious and demanding nature of the positions needing to be filled. As I will it, so it shall be. You will obey her decisions as you obey mine."

His head dropped back toward his chest, and Maceanas struggled up from his chair; a few of his guards rushed forward to lend their support. The two harem women wobbled under the weight of their king. The guardsmen reached His Majesty just as his eyes rolled back, showing the whites. His whole body jittered, causing the women to lose their grip. They all landed in a pile on the floor. Screams rose, a combination of dismay and fear.

Above it all rose the duchess's voice. "Get the royal physician in here now! As for the rest of you, keep order!"

The guards before the throne braced themselves as the crowd surged forward, hoping for a better look as their view became cut off by nobles and important townspeople standing, craning to see.

"What's going on?"

"Is he dead?"

"Did someone poison him?"

Dr. Greggson must have been nearby, for it didn't take him long to appear. He snapped out orders, the guards obeying. Aranthus hurried the few steps up to the top in time to see men trying to restrain the king's violently flailing body. Blood poured down his chin. After long moments, the fit ended. The physician turned the king's head to one side and pried his mouth open. Bloody saliva pooled on the floor. Next, he checked Maceanas's pulse and pupils.

Despite the noncommittal look his face wore, several small nervous tics gave away how serious the king's health was. The harem women still knelt on the floor, albeit to one side, clutching each other in fear.

The physician finally lifted his head, spotting Aranthus and the duchess. His nostrils flared briefly in distaste before he stood and approached them. He kept his voice low in an effort not to be overheard. The throne room had never experienced so much silence while packed full of people. Dr. Greggson's words could not be heard clearly, only the soft murmur of his voice.

"He has had some sort of fit. I don't know what kind, or why." The man paused to glare at the duchess. "It could have been brought on by the amounts of herbs you insisted he ingest, Duchess, to keep him calm."

"I insisted he be provided with a level of care to help him remain in such a state. If you have overdosed him because you are inept in your profession, then you will have to answer to a tribunal."

"How dare you cast aspersions upon my character? I recall quite clearly what you said."

She ignored his accusations. "According to you, the herbs would have run out a month ago. What have you been giving him?"

"Aranthus," Dr. Greggson turned to the chamberlain in an effort to dismiss the woman, "we must get the king back to his chambers immediately. I cannot conduct a proper inspection in these conditions."

The man ground his teeth in mute rage as the eunuch looked toward that wretched woman for direction.

"An excellent notion," the duchess approved. "Before you

go, if you could say a few words to ease the crowd's fears."

"I am not supporting your power grab," he spat.

"I am not asking you. I am telling you to give the people hope."

Dr. Greggson turned and looked out over the assembly. A mixture of fear, curiosity, and uncertainty met his eyes. He cleared his throat as behind him he heard Aranthus giving instructions to the royal guards.

"Loyal subjects to the crown, I cannot say for certain what caused the king's collapse until I further examine him. For the time being, he is alive. When I know more, I'm sure the advisor will be eager to share the updates. Thank you." He turned and walked toward the king's body, now loaded on a makeshift litter.

Behind, the noise of the crowd rose and swelled, many people calling out questions.

"Long live the king! All hail the king!" The duchess's forceful voice overrode all others as she called out from her spot in front of the throne.

The people had no choice but to follow her salute as His Majesty was carted off.

Before those gathered could devolve into idle speculation again, she continued to speak. "Good people, while Dr. Greggson works to restore the king back to his former health, it is important we all continue on with our jobs, and our roles to keep the kingdom running. As His Majesty's advisor, and the highest peer of the realm, I will be guiding our kingdom as we wait for the king to recover and take back up the mantle of his rule."

The voices rose in a buzzing wave of sound. Many of the men who'd hoped to bribe their way into a position appeared disgruntled. There were deep mutterings of displeasure at having a woman take precedence over them.

"Those individuals wishing to be considered for any of the positions available with the royal offices should have copies of their qualifications and any recommendations or references sent to my home. If any person has questions about what the posts are, or what kind of work is entailed, the descriptions have been affixed to my gates. I will be allowing one week for persons interested to drop off their materials before deciding on who will merit an interview. Thank you. If there are other problems or issues not dealing with the royal offices, I will be holding court from midday to dinner at my house. There will be a second court held from mid-afternoon until supper at the palace."

She paused to let her eyes rest on the crowd. Everyone present received the feeling she knew exactly what they thought, good or bad. The sensation intensified until many present dropped their eyes, unable to gaze upon her further.

"You are all dismissed," she commanded.

Rustling of clothing commenced as the people bowed or curtsied, and filtered out. Their voices kept to a whisper, many believing the itching between their shoulder blades was because they were being watched by Her Grace. Once outside, those who hadn't seen what happened called out for information.

The doorway soon became jammed. The nobles and merchants of affluence hurried to scramble from their seats and intercept the duchess. She moved forward with determined strides. The guards who were still in line snapped to attention as she descended the dais, and Eron slipped out from behind the pillar he'd concealed himself behind to join her. The guards formed a moving box around her, clearing space with their stentorian calls of "Make way for the royal advisor."

She continued on out of the hall, the jam seemingly melting away. The duchess stopped in the middle of the courtyard as the guards knelt around her.

Those townspeople outside bowed or curtsied as she briefly recounted what had happened to the king and reiterated her commands for work to continue.

CHAPTER TWENTY NINE

As the duchess crossed the courtyard, many people from both the town and the villages called out her name, begging and pleading for even a moment of her time.

"Celebrating with a group orgy instead of more bloodshed?"

"I have not ruled out the latter." She nodded and smiled to those kept outside the box formed by guards, but did not stop her pace. "Present yourselves at my home in two hours and I shall hear your pleas," was the only response Illyria gave to them.

Out of the corner of her eye, she spotted a few of her household standing in a group, observing everything. Because she turned her head slightly in their direction, she noticed Jenfry and Priester Joseph lurking not too far away. Once the noble party entered the palace corridors, the duchess dismissed the guards to perform the duties she had temporarily assigned them. She and Eron continued to the harem's quarters.

"Men are not allowed in." One of the eunuch guards spoke at their approach.

"Understood. He shall wait outside—if that is acceptable?" Illyria looked each man in the eyes, using her power. *The man is pacing the corridor, waiting for me to emerge.*

They bowed in reply, opening the doors, and she beckoned him in. Eron made haste, barely making it inside before the guards shut the heavy wooden doors behind them. An antechamber held four more guards, whom they disabled and left unconscious before passing into the hallway beyond. The long corridor was lined with many curtained openings. Farther down could be heard the chatter of female voices and children.

Eron took the left side, the duchess the right. Moving swiftly and silently, they yanked the fabric down. Most of the rooms were empty as they made their way down the hall. Only a few were occupied, mostly with sleeping younger children whom they left to their dreams.

The two burst into the central living chamber, evoking a number of screams.

"Silence!" the duchess's power roiled throughout the room. One by one the noise abruptly cut off.

The plaster walls were painted to resemble lush gardens. Wooden lattice work covered fenestrae openings framed by heavy green wool drapery. Braziers dotted the room, to help provide heat and light along with two fireplaces, around which were groupings of chairs, couches, and large pillows. The far right corner held a large loom, and across sat a group of women whom had been playing stringed or wind instruments. Most of the women, or youngsters, looked toward the intruders with wide, frightened eyes, except for a few who knew themselves to be held in higher esteem by the king.

"If you haven't heard by now, the king has suffered a seizure. Whether he will awaken and recover, or not, is unknown."

"He is not allowed inside. When the king learns of—" spoke a dusky beauty.

"I said silence." Her Grace cut the woman's words off. "The kingdom can no longer support the burden of such a large harem. Therefore, most of you will be leaving."

"You can't!"

"You bitch!"

A chorus of protests broke out only to be unnaturally silenced, many eyes now wide in fright at the unseen and unknown power which prevented them from talking.

"Much better," Illyria purred as she stood surveying them. "As I was saying, your services are no longer required. Despite the rumors, I am not insensitive to the harsh fate which will await many of you at being thrust from your home. Those with children, gather them to you now and stand to the left of the room. Those without, to the right, and those who are pregnant and haven't birthed, in the center."

She clapped her hands twice to get them to move, releasing her hold over the women. A scramble ensued, and after a few minutes, the women and children stood as told. Eron walked back to stand by the duchess, after helping some of the more recalcitrant choose a side.

"I have a list of jobs in and around the town and its environs which need filled. We will start with those better suited for you who don't have children. If you want the position, raise your hand." Illyria turned her head and nodded to Eron.

He, in the meantime, had taken a tightly wound scroll out of a case tied to his belt, along with quills and ink pot. The immortal swept a small table clear of its fripperies and used it for a writing surface. Eron called out the first job and what it entailed.

"Don't any of you bitches dare speak up." The angry command came from a woman who appeared to be in her late twenties. She stepped in front of everyone, fists clenched at her sides. "You do, and I will see His Majesty hang you as traitors." She leaned forward and spit on the carpet before the duchess. "That is what I think of you, and your attempts to usurp our king."

A few of the women gasped, while a slow murmur of agreement started to ripple about the room. Illyria appeared before the dissenter, a quick glimpse of silver flashed, then she was back to standing calmly in the same spot she had been. The rising noise abruptly ended as the woman crumpled to the floor. A dark spot of blood appeared on the front of her dress, which slowly grew and ran down the side of the body to make a growing puddle.

"Now then, who wants the offered job?" the duchess continued, not a shred of remorse on her features, her bloody sword held in her right hand, tip resting and dripping blood onto the rug.

It took longer than the hour's time she had allotted for the job, as many of the women had to be constantly prodded to pack up their possessions. Even her torching of clothes, and confiscating jewels, didn't help much. The women knew their lives of ease and luxury were over.

"I won't!" A beauty stomped her foot as reality impressed itself fully upon her. "We shouldn't have to work! Not after all we have endured, being ripped from our families and homelands, forced to service a selfish king. I won't become less than a peasant. I won't!"

She stared defiantly at her fellow harem women, using her

words to try and rouse them to rebellion.

The advisor's voice silenced the growing babble of dissent. "Very well; you do not wish to work, nor be slaves, then I release you from your burdens."

The protesting women eyed her and each other. The original starter of the fracas smirked, and looked smugly at her fellow supporters. The rest of the women had paused, and they stood uneasily around the edges of the common room. The duchess gave a single nod to Eron, and the two of them moved forward. It took mere moments for all the bodies of the rebels to fall down, blood flowing to soak the rugs.

"Does anyone else care to be relieved of their burdens?" the advisor asked, a cold honey fire glow to her eyes.

A long moment of silence ensued, then the survivors began to pack what personal items remained to them with no more voiced complaints.

The eunuch guards had long since recovered, and been cowed by Her Grace when they tried to protest. After seeing her kill several of the more enthusiastic guards who attacked her, the others happily decided it was far better to help. Eron spent his time briefly speaking with, and separating out, those slaves he felt couldn't be trusted to properly care for and look after the royal bastards. The eldest child was six years old, yet the sight of his mother leaving him behind brought on shrill cries.

His tears and screams caused the other children and infants to follow suit. Illyria and Eron had never been more relieved to leave the noise behind them. The eunuchs stayed to guard the wing, which had now been repurposed as an orphan's home.

The advisor and Eron herded the remaining women outside, many sullen and resentful. Large wagons awaited them, along with half the royal guard. With their task done, the eunuchs trudged back inside the harem wing. A pile of bodies needed to be burned, and the rooms cleaned.

Baen, a large, ruddy-cheeked man, boomed out instructions. "Right then, those of you heading outside of town will go in these two carts." He pointed to his left. "Those of you staying in town, go in that one," he again pointed, but this time to his right.

His men helped the travelers up; most sank down on the

layer of straw covering the rough boards. They clutched bundles, sobbing or numb of all emotion.

"'Tis a bold move you make, Your Grace," Baen rumbled to her, his version of a whisper. "When His Majesty finds out . . ."

"He will no doubt have fun choosing new women to service his needs."

The man scratched beneath the knitted, wool cap he wore. "Eh, not to be presumptuous, but, uh . . ." He searched for how to make his question less offensive. "You wouldn't by any chance be reviewing the guards, would ye?"

"Is there a need for me to do so?"

"Mmmm, ye might wanna. Not to go behind me commander's back 'n all, but there are some who aren't happy the old advisor's gone. They keep their opinions mainly to themselves or others of like thought, and away from Mathias's ears, but I wouldn't trust it to last long."

"Thank you, Baen. I will take your suggestion into consideration."

He bowed, seeing the carts were loaded and ready. "Most of 'em are part of the night watch, Your Grace." He turned smartly and called out to the drivers, "Get 'em moving! Night'll be falling soon." He accepted the lists of where the women were to be delivered before walking over to mount his horse.

As the cavalcade slowly rolled out the side courtyard, a black and silver coach was revealed to be waiting. Two liveried footmen jumped off the back rumble seat, opening the door and extending the steps.

"Come along, then." The duchess gestured to the small group which hadn't boarded either wagon.

The three women and four children followed obediently. They handed over their bundles, which a footman secured to the top of the coach while the other handed them inside. Domiano rode up, leading Gray Ghost and Striker.

CHAPTER THIRTY

The elegant turnout stopped at an intersection in the poor part of town.

"Your Grace, it's too narrow for me to risk taking the coach down," Harbo called out.

"Remain here; I'll send Eron back for the occupants in a moment." She slipped off her mount.

The immortal followed, handing the reins of Striker over to Domiano.

The coachman inclined his head, trying to huddle farther inside his cloak as the duchess and the man with her walked down the side street.

Nighttime was fast falling, all the crofts were shut tight against the cold. Scents of burning wood or peat, along with food, dimly masked the strong odor of manure, animals, and close living quarters. As they approached a croft halfway down, Eron broke away, swiftly moving along a narrow footpath which would lead him behind the row of cottages. He snuck through the dirt yard of Priester Joseph's place, hearing the sleepy cluck of chickens. Eron placed his back against the outside wall near the kitchen door and waited.

* * *

Illyria pounded on the cottage door with enough force to make it rattle in its frame. She could hear stirrings inside, and grumbling from Joseph. She repeated her summons, and finally the door swung inward. Thomas's greeting, along with his smile of welcome, abruptly cut off at sight of the woman.

"A-advisor," he stuttered in shock.

The duchess pushed her way inside, causing the brother to stumble backward and lose his grip on the door. She let it slam shut behind her. From the kitchen came the priest's crotchety voice.

"Who calls at this hour?"

An ice-cold finger pressed against Brother Thomas's lips before he could sound a warning.

"Choose your words carefully," she whispered to him before removing her finger.

"'Tis the advisor," the man blurted out.

Joseph hurtled into the room. "How dare you befoul my temple with your evil presence!" Any further words the duchess expeditiously cut off by grabbing the priest by the throat and slamming him against the partition.

"The kingdom has no need for the hate and bigotry you spew. Brother Thomas, you may gather your things and leave, or stay and share the priest's fate." She turned her head away from the struggling man, gazing at the acolyte.

The young man looked between Joseph, whose face was rapidly turning purple while he futilely clawed at the hand choking him, to the golden honey fire of Her Grace's eyes.

"You can't. The king—"

"—supports my decisions. Life or death, Thomas, which shall you choose?"

The oppressive air weighed heavy on the man. His eyes rapidly shifted from Joseph to the woman. "You can't; you just can't," he repeated. "It's wrong. You . . . you're no better than Nicky."

In an unseen movement, Priester Joseph lay dead on the dirt floor, his head and neck at an odd angle. A man appeared in the doorway between front and back rooms. He barely glanced at the corpse. One hand rested on his sword pommel. His dark eyes bored into the trembling figure before the duchess.

Will she let me leave? Will he? Where would I go? The people must know of the murders committed here.

Thomas swallowed, hands smoothing down his brown robe, fiddling with the rope tied around his waist. "I-I have no other home."

The duchess's companion suddenly moved, causing the brother to flinch backward in alarm. The man ignored the movement, opening the front door and letting it close behind him as he exited. Her Grace remained silent, regarding the trembling form before her. The two remained such. After a bit, the front door opened, bringing a blast of icy wind and a small crowd.

"Ladies," Her Grace greeted the newcomers without taking her eyes off the man before her. "Sleeping rooms are upstairs, access is through the kitchen. There is a hen coop out back, a well, and a small plot of land to grow food when spring returns."

A few low voiced murmurs of, "Yes, Your Grace; thank you," came from the women as they carried small children past and found the curtained doorway.

Two footmen followed a short while behind with the new residents' meager belongings, setting them down in a pile by the middle of the front wall before leaving.

"What? You can't. Who?"

"Herbalists. I doubt they will care to share their new home with a man just yet. They seem to have had enough of that with the king."

"Wha-what do you mean? The king? Are you suggesting they are-are whores?" Brother Thomas's incredulousness caused his voice to squeak at the end.

"They are former harem women, forced to submit themselves to His Majesty's appetites or face death or worse. What shall your decision be, Thomas?"

"But they are whores! Their very presence defiles this place. I have no other home." His plaintive wail trailed off as his eyes flicked toward the body discarded on the floor.

"You bore me, a state I do not care for." Illyria's voice held dark warnings.

"What did you wish to become before Priester Joseph took you in?" The unexpected question came from the dark-eyed man.

Thomas's eyes swung toward the man, confusion creasing his features. "I don't understand."

"Did you throw your brains out along with your ability to reason once you became a religious man?" The insult made the young man blink. "What other job did you want for yourself?"

"I . . . oh . . ." He paused to think, hands continuing their circuit of smoothing and fiddling with his robes. "I wanted to help others."

"Generally speaking, it works better if you try feeding, clothing, and housing the less fortunate instead of spouting platitudes about some nebulous god," Eron drily replied.

Confusion briefly creased Thomas's forehead. "But their souls . . ." He jumped in fright as the duchess appeared before him, her shadow looming large over him.

"You care for the wrong parts of them. I am tired of your mewling."

Behind her, Eron silently cursed and spoke. "Either stay and help the women, without your preaching unless they specifically ask for it, or die and experience the afterlife."

The brother's breaths came short and fast, while a strange buzzing started inside his head, and the edges of his vision began to darken. "I-I . . ." He couldn't take his eyes off the honey-golden fire consuming what remained of his sight.

"I will stay and be a servant to those-those . . . women," Thomas finally gasped out, clutching at his chest through the robe as he fell back against the flimsy partition.

The duchess's cold gaze raked him, and he shuddered in fear at her departing words: "Do not think to mouth empty promises and get away with them. Understand I shall always know what you think, whether you will it or not."

The man with her grabbed the corpse by its legs and dragged the body outside. He left it sitting against the wall as a warning, before catching up to Illyria, her long coat train smoothing out the snow behind her.

"Harbo, you may take the others back with you, and stable the horses. I shall not need the coach for the rest of my rounds." Illyria commanded while mounting Gray Ghost.

"Yes, Your Grace." The man touched the brim of his tall hat and clucked to the horses while popping the whip near their heads to get the conveyance moving.

The iron-rimmed wheels squeaked over the packed snow, accompanied by the thudding of hooves as the outriders and guards moved off.

"Bloodbath time?" Eron's breath steamed in the air as he nudged his mount to follow hers.

"I have fleas to squash," she replied.

* * *

Light and sound from the Bloody Knuckles greeted the riders on an otherwise dark street. Illyria noted the human rats who scuttled away from the half-burnt building, believing themselves to be invisible in the shadows. She was not here for them, not tonight, and they never realized the reprieve they were granted. Boldly, she rode her horse forward, past the charred posts which denoted the front of the building. Slowly, all noise and activity ceased as she used her mount to push people out of her way. Once in the relative center of the half-burned tavern, she called out:

"Jenfry Bartender! I command you to heed me now." The invisible compulsion flowed past patrons and into the kitchen, where the owner fumed.

Jenfry tried to resist the strange pull, but her efforts made it stronger. "Damn that whore to the Death Lands," she muttered. "You lot, keep working." The woman stomped out to the eerily quiet bar area. Her patrons, the worst kind of men and women, sent silent signals to each other. Why they hadn't pulled that damn advisor and the man with her off their horses and killed them, she didn't know.

"What the hell you be wanting?" Jenfry spat, legs apart, fists propped on ample hips. "I paid me taxes."

"Jenfry Bartender, I am here to exact retribution. You failed to follow my orders."

The older woman let out a cackle, showing rotting stumps of teeth. "You ain't no better than the whore slaves I own. You stole me daughter."

"I bought your daughter," the advisor emotionlessly corrected, "with the proviso you have no contact with her." A sly smile of self-satisfaction upturned the corners of her mouth.

The tavern owner mistook the sudden gleam which turned the duchess's eyes into glowing coals. "Well?" she berated her patrons. "What're you waiting for? Call yourselves warriors and fighters? Ya can get outta my place if you haven't the guts to take on a whore who's stupid to ride on in."

"Oh goody, I was hoping she'd be stupid," Eron voiced for Illyria only, a sudden rush of adrenaline flooding his system. He felt a stirring, a whisper of displaced air and whipped his sword out and around the horse's flanks.

A clang of metal on metal reached his ears a moment before two figures hurtled themselves at the horse, intent on bringing the beast down. To Eron, it felt as if time slowed a notch. His foot and sword flicked out faster than he had been able to manage before drinking of the vamp's blood. The attackers fell back, but it seemed the signal the rest of the patrons waited for. Time snapped back to its usual pace. War cries and bodies flooded the two riders in an attempt to bring them down.

Illyria felt grubby fingers, and tips of weapons, brush within centimeters of her. She released her power in the manner of a bomb going off, with herself ground zero. The onrushing horde blew backward in a wide circle, the inner ring taking parts of the outer with them. She followed up the display by twisting in her saddle, and whomever her gaze landed upon, blood exploded from their orifices.

"Greedy bitch. Haven't you heard of sharing?" Eron grumbled as he set his horse in motion, forced to follow his prey, and hack them down where they landed.

Henrik stood stunned, pop-eyed at the impossible taking place, hands frozen around the mug he had been cleaning. Jenfry's derisive laughter abruptly stopped as crimson coated her.

"You ain't no different than Lord Nicky! Witch! She's an evil witch!" she shrieked.

"Run, little beasties. Run," Illyria commanded gleefully as she surveyed the chaos she'd created.

The smarter criminals had already heeded her words, fleeing in an effort to put distance between them and death. Those who were too stupid, or blinded by base emotions, tried another attack. They flew back to smash into the remains of walls and ceiling. Most had only the breath painfully knocked from them, a few felt bones break. None lived more than a few minutes after landing.

Throughout it all, the torches remained burning. A long shadow fell over the petrified form of Jenfry, her breath whistling in fear.

"I promised Mary Elana I would let no more harm come to her by your hand. I do so hate to disappoint the girl, especially after all she's been through. Besides, what sort of person would I be if I broke my word?"

Illyria held her long train gathered up in her left hand so it wouldn't become soiled as she dismounted and stalked up to Jenfry. Her right hand wrapped around the tavern owner's throat, and yanked the woman forward. Briefly, her gaze bored into Henrik's.

"Go away. This does not concern you."

The man felt his bowels loosen as he gazed deep into hellish depths. His subconscious pinged awareness the real ruler stood before him. "As my Dark Queen commands." He barely felt himself rise from his deep bow, or his legs and feet carry him into the kitchen, away from the tavern owner's fate.

CHAPTER THIRTY ONE

Dawn didn't rise so much as the past night reluctantly faded from blackness to dark gray. Slaves and other early risers discovered a new dimension to the problems plaguing Macinas. Their screams and shrieks echoed throughout the ruined town's streets, and the corridors of the royal palace. The cause for all the commotion soon became apparent as more and more townsfolk were awoken by the ruckus.

Bodies of the dead lay where once had been sleeping people. Half had stab wounds to the heart; others, only the tracks of dried blood from their orifices.

"Who could do such a thing?"

"The priest was right, we are harboring evil. We're all doomed!"

"Why, oh why? My Robbie never hurt no one!"

Voices rose with a mixture of emotions. It didn't take long for those who made the palace their temporary refuge to waylay royal servants, demanding the king come out and address his people.

For those who mourned, time seemed too fast, while for others it seemed too slow. Eventually, all were invited to gather inside the throne room. The king sat slumped to one side of his golden, gem-encrusted throne. To his right stood Aranthus; to his left, Dr. Greggson. At the top of the stairs leading to the dais, the advisor calmly waited. She had on the breast plate, bracers, and greaves made to imitate skulls, wolf heads, and snakes which formed the age-blackened armor. Her sword handles could be seen rising from behind her shoulders. The whole effect gave her a sinister presence. A pace behind, and to her left, stood a dark-haired and -eyed man.

They waited in silence, letting the voices rise and fall, reminiscent of waves. When the hall was packed with people, and more could be seen clogging the doorway and outer courtyard, she raised one arm with palm out.

"Silence." The sibilant whisper cut through the babble and she let her arm fall to her side.

Tension grew, not even coughs or rustles of clothing disturbing the stillness. Even the relentless winter wind failed to blow.

"Macinas has fallen, and all those harboring corruption who supported it. Do not despair. Illthanthia and new opportunities arise, and I shall lead. Bow before your Raven Queen."

The announcement stunned many who thought the days of fighting over the throne were behind them. Others voiced dissent.

"BOW BEFORE YOUR RAVEN QUEEN!"

The command rang out, cutting off the noise.

"BOW SO I MAY KNOW FRIEND FROM FOE."

Slowly, reluctantly, people did so singularly or in small groups, until more and more joined those on bended knee. The duchess, now self-proclaimed queen, waited a few more minutes. When no one else moved, her gaze noted all who elected to remain standing.

"Rise, with my thanks for your new loyalty. We will continue to rebuild the town, and our lives. Those who have died were traitors, corrupt men and women seeking only to profit from the subjugation of others. Those who devote themselves to the town and its peoples without thought of riches and glory will earn their rewards. Now go, and await my commands as you continue your lives."

All those gathered felt a compulsion to leave, and begin the day's work. Some gladly followed, some fought it, others remained unsure. Eventually, they all left the throne room, leaving behind both the old, and new, rulers.

CHAPTER THIRTY TWO

Nicky fought with all his strength against the invisible bindings. He couldn't see; darkness swirled around him. What felt like tentacles reached out for him as he hurtled toward some unknown destination. The boy tried screaming, but no sound escaped. Flashes went off all around him, briefly illuminating places and things no human had ever realized existed or even successfully accessed. He felt himself tumble around as he struggled to free himself. Behind, leading back into the darkness and a thick blue rope, was a silver line veering off the main strand abruptly ending in frayed tendrils. The kid put all his efforts into reaching back toward the snapped lines and managed to snag a stray thread.

His hand exploded in pain, racing up his arm and into his head. He silently howled, yet refused to let go. He would not go quietly, not even now.

* * *

"You know of whom I speak. Now I want to know where I can find her. I told you before—"

A mocking laugh interrupted him. "You want! Fuck you! Until you've upheld your end of the deal, you get nothing."

"I've done what you wanted . . ."

"You don't even know her name, do you? Or what she can really do."

Nicky gritted his teeth, "I gave you a way to insert trackers into our kind and not have them rejected. A feat a dumb ass such as yourself would never be able to think up, much less accomplish, on your own."

The older man's eyes narrowed, his scar making him more frightening. "Keep telling yourself that, brat. I know of someone who would love to get his hands on you."

A sneer crossed the kid's lips, "You're an even bigger idiot. My powers—"

"Charlatan's tricks. She thought the same and tried using her powers against me; yet she couldn't save herself from my . . . attentions. It was really quite entertaining, making her plead and scream while I used her as my test subject. I bet, if I used you for the next phase, you wouldn't last half as long."

"Tell me what I want to know, or you'll be missing your favorite body part," Nicky countered, forming the words in his head for a sunburst.

The anger and insolence dropped from the older man's face, replaced by a blankness and evil shining deep in his dark eyes. He leapt forward and sideways suddenly. Nicky unleashed the sphere he held in one hand. He knew the guy wouldn't attack straight on. The light burst, blinding the man and letting Nicky turn and run away.

* * *

"Insolent worm! You think you can escape me?"

Talons tore strips off his body, blackness oozed out as he screamed in agony. It was the sensation of all the pain he had brought to his own victims. The little boy felt what was left of him start to shatter.

No! I won't become nothing! I am somebody! I am the greatest immortal ever! I am Nicky!

"Yesssssss, this agony is just a taste of what you owe me."

The kid tried to ignore the mental and soul torture the demon flayed him with, to hold himself together. He had a feeling if he didn't, if he just gave up and succumbed, then memory by memory, he would be stripped bare, until all that remained was what the demon wanted him to know. The demon. The evil entity he had called up and shackled and forced to do his bidding. The one the little boy attempted to double-cross.

I am Nicky! My name is Nicholas. I was born in the first dark ages. I became an immortal. I helped topple modern civilization. I have done many wondrous, and near impossible feats. I AM NICKY!

The pain stopped abruptly. "Ignorant, evolution monkey!" the demon growled in his own language, which somehow the little boy understood. "You have no name but the one I give you."

The kid grasped tighter to the tendril which represented his life, reaching out his other hand for another dangling thread. It wrapped around his hand and wrist with the same sensation as the first. He felt a wrenching on his feet, the demon he had called DiJinn trying to loosen his hold on his broken lifeline.

I accept the pain. I accept what I have done and will do. I accept everything! Nicky used the last of his strength to pull himself closer to the dangling ends and his body.

He could feel himself stretching thin and thrashed in a last attempt to dislodge the demon as he plunged his face into the silver thread.

DiJinn's howling voice became a physical sensation, pressing and squashing his being in an effort to pound him into the individual bits which made him Nicky. The silver ends wrapped tight around his head, searing and lashing him. Memories became a storm cloud of lightning and thunder inside his head, each one an electric jolt searing his brain.

I AM NICKY! YOU WILL NOT CHAIN ME! I AM FREE!

The little boy let the pain overtake him, let it cause him to scream and thrash about, invading every part. He lunged once more, as images of a moonlit grove flashed by, hooking onto its memory strand.

"Noooooooooooo!"

Talons tried to grab his head and rip apart the lifeline which was now the only thing holding both pieces of him together.

Nicky kept wiggling forward, deeper into his thread, letting long strips of his numerous lives go, the sacrifice needed. He lost sight and feeling; he had won. The boy couldn't say how he knew, only that he was floating in warm darkness. A new pain took the place of the old. He could tell the difference immediately. The other had infused every molecule; this one was of the body. He had a body! He needed air!

The kid's reflexes took over, his lungs expanded, drawing

oxygen in. His nose and nasal passages exploded at the sharp, icy bite, nearly causing him to stop breathing again. He fought past the sensation, taking another big inhalation and exhaling noisily. Nicky cracked his eyelids, what illumination was left in the wan light causing him to blink at the stabbing sensation. When his vision adjusted, he tried to wiggle fingers and toes.

His extremities burned at the movement, protesting, stiff and slow. It took a while before Nicky realized he had landed in the grove, his grove. The one he had used to slaughter people so his demon would have food. How much time had passed? Trees which had once been burnt lay moldering on the ground under a covering of snow. New growth, dormant, poked up from the remains.

"Ha! Bastard! No one defeats Nicky!" His voice was a thin, reedy strain, throat feeling raw from all the screaming he had done. He gulped more air in, his limbs tingling as he forced them to move. How long had he been dead? Trapped between worlds and planes?

"Damn it!" Nicky spoke ritual words meant to provide illumination and heat, which no one else would be able to understand if they overheard him. He didn't feel his power, his magic, responding. He tried again. Nothing.

"No, no, no, no, NO! My magic! I didn't sacrifice my magic! Not that! Never would I sacrifice that!" He howled, tears leaking down his cheeks. "You bastard demon! I'll get you for this!"

After a few useless minutes of cursing, crying, and trying every bit of magic he knew to no avail, did the boy realize it was completely gone. The one other thing he had feared happening, had.

"I will get it back," Nicky muttered determinedly. Now—now he had to get up before he froze. He set himself grimly to the task. It took longer than he liked, his body feeling heavy and dead, but he managed to turn enough on the rock altar, and let gravity take over.

The face-plant into the remaining drifts of snow were unpleasant and painful, further chilling his naked body. His muscles shook from the strain he placed upon them. His head ached and throbbed, and more than once he vomited up bile before he stood upright. The boy leaned, panting from effort, on the icy stone. It seemed he would be learning how to move all over again. He tried to think of how to walk, and in fits and starts managed to get turned around. Nicky let his eyes rove around; where was the path? Denuded branches from trees, bushes, and vines which had grown in the passing of time obscured all marks.

Nicky closed his eyes, visualizing how the grove looked before his sojourn in the Afterlife. When he thought he had the image firmly at the forefront of his thoughts, the boy opened his eyes. It disconcerted him, seeing what had been overlaid on what was like a ghost image. He was forced to slowly shuffle forward, using his cold hands and feet to push through the plant matter which had reclaimed the grove. His mind and body had lag between what he wanted to do, and when it responded. It took him longer than he expected to be able to accomplish any task.

"I will get my magic back. I will kill the fat fuck on the throne. I will kill that insufferably good Mica. I will kill—no, I will punish then kill—that damn duchess. I will make the town beg for my mercy."

Nicky kept himself moving with plans by talking, stumbling and pushing through the overgrown path toward his hunting lodge. His body finally finished with rebooting itself, the lag gone. The boy didn't even realize he had reached the lodge until he tripped over the edge of the stone terrace and fell.

"What the hell?" Nicky forced himself to hands and knees, craning his head back. His vision blurred from new tears. The vine-covered trellis had rotted and lay in a snowy heap on top of the terrace. Gaping holes spoke of where wood-shuttered glass windows had once been.

The boy gritted his teeth angrily, trying to hold back his sobs. His numb fingers clutched at the wall, dislodging crumbling mortar. Even though his feet were cold, and starting to burn, he forced himself to walk toward the opening which had once housed the courtyard gate. The stables had long since been torn down and carted off for their wood.

A litany of curses spewed forth as he cautiously stepped through the doorway to the slave's hall; even the door itself had been taken. Nicky eased down the hall, trying not to stumble on the debris-strewn stone floor. When he got to the entrance, the boy stumbled to a halt. The decorative marble, tile, and colored stone had been pried up and carted away, leaving gaping holes. A good portion of the marble stairs was missing as well. A hole overhead let weak rays of sun in. Rage replaced the cold. Nicky was forced to backtrack. Each once-elegant room bore testament to the scavengers. The walls and ceiling showed bare plaster, much of it having fallen from the walls and ceiling to show the building's structure. He climbed up the servants' stairs, testing each one of the wooden treads before putting his full weight on them.

The upstairs showed the same signs of the decimated ground floor. His once-ornate room had been stripped. Only the large, heavily carved bed and wardrobe remained. Both were coated in animal droppings.

He remembered the spells he had overlaid over the lodge and his secret workspace, meant to slowly kill intruders, whether they explored or left after a few seconds, or even minutes.

"After all, technically I did die, so it would all . . ." He trailed off as realization overcame him.

"Motherfucker! Son of a rotten, pus-dripping cunt! My trunks!" The outraged shout echoed in the dim chill. Any dreck of humanity would be able to open them, or to step anywhere inside his work chambers and disturb his books and materials and take them.

He had to get back to the palace; panic welled up inside. How long had he been dead? He could not lose his possessions; that was the main reason behind the secret chambers. Nicky clenched his teeth. He didn't expect the wardrobe to be full when he yanked a door open. He was correct. Most of the fine clothes had been taken, and only a few garments lay in a moldering pile. The boy gingerly drew them out, but saw an animal of some kind had made them into a nest.

The boy delicately reached in and felt around, prodding and pushing. Finally, the false bottom clicked free and after a moment of prying at the swollen wood, he was able to raise the lid. The shallow space had not been discovered. He took out the ornate silver and jeweled dagger hidden within, along with a small leather portfolio tied shut and a small bag which jingled. As he was withdrawing his hand for the last time, a splinter of wood stabbed him.

Hissing in pain, he spent several minutes working the shard out with the dagger, cutting himself in the process. Blood welled up and dripped down. Nicky didn't pay it any attention, gathering up his meager possessions. The dusty mirror hung on the inside of the door caught the last rays of sunlight. The cut was illuminated enough for him to see it hadn't healed. The boy stopped mid-step, mouth falling open in shock. He stared, astonished, brought a trembling hand up to the faint light, red rivulets staining his skin.

"Oh. No." He licked the blood off, examining his hand. Panic grew again. He started having trouble breathing, the room shrinking in, smothering him. "Nononononono . . ." It started low and monotonous, ending in a scream of denial. "NNNOOOOOOOO!"

His fist shattered the glass, sending cracks radiating out while a few chunks fell tinkling to the floor, with one largish piece embedding itself between the second and third knuckles. Nicky crumpled to the floor, crying and rocking in pain.

"Piss-filled dung buckets. Rotten cockroaches. Belly-crawling, dirt-licking worms." He swore old curses interspersed with new. "Fuck, fuck, fuck!"

The sliver came out with a minimal amount of tugging and force, more pain and blood welling. He tossed the piece aside, knowing what he would have to do, now that another unexpected, unwanted sacrifice had revealed itself. Nicky stood shakily, and groped for his things which he had dropped on the floor. He needed to get out of the ruined manor.

It was difficult to do now night had fallen. He felt something pierce the bottom of his foot and couldn't help the scream which rang out, snot and tears mingling, falling to join the dirt covering the floor. He kept going, limping down and outside the slave's entrance. He sat down on the cold stone, peering futilely at the bottom of his foot. His fingers brushed the object, sending a wave of pain through him. He grasped it and pulled it out and flung it far off to the side. Then he picked up his things, and began limping across the overgrown lawn and drive which led into the property, pain stabbing through him with every step.

* * *

The mare stumbled, nearly sending Nicky crashing into the melting snow drifts. He reined her in, letting the exhausted animal walk. It wouldn't do to ride her to death, because then he would be forced to walk the rest of the way himself. He'd had enough of that just getting from his lodge to the first farm along the track into town. Behind him, the night sky was illuminated from fire, and the scent of smoke rose and joined the night sky.

He hummed to himself, a nasty smile yanking his lips up as he replayed the begging, pleading and finally, screams of terror as he killed the stupid farmer, his equally stupid wife, and his family, after raping the daughter. The boy had gained entrance easily enough, his bloody wounds, naked body, and sobbing, terror-stricken act convincing. The wife and daughter cleaned and bandaged his wounds before feeding him. Nicky had been offered an old pair of pants, shirt, and cracked leather shoes along with a spot beside their son in the loft. He didn't want word of his return to get out, so he waited until the family was sleeping before murdering them. By the time he reached the edges of the town, dawn was breaking.

The former advisor used a little known path, which appeared more as a goat track, up the back of the plateau where the palace and nobles' houses stood. It ended in a small rock declivity. Nicky dismounted and sent the poor horse back down the trail, not caring whether it came across humans to take care of it, or fell to predators or the cold. He stepped inside, kneeling down on the frozen rock to light the oil lantern he had stolen from the owners and brought with him.

With the illumination provided, he ventured farther inside. He slipped and slid along the iced-over path, the rock walls and ceiling inches away, icicles forcing him to duck again and again. After about two hundred feet, the ice petered out into hard dirt. The opening was lost behind him to the twists and turns the tunnel made. A short flight of stone steps led to an abbreviated landing, an iron door prohibiting further access. Nicky put the lantern in a narrow niche carved out of the rock wall. The door would only open from his side by knowing the correct placement of the moveable metal puzzle parts making up the lock.

Nicky found himself grunting and sweating with exertion as he got the final piece into place. The cold, and rust had caused the metal to stick and a few needed the thin sheeting of ice broken. The wool gloves he had stolen were ruined. The young man took the lantern back up and pushed the door open. It groaned and scraped across the ground, then once he was through, shut with an echoing *clank*. He pulled the iron lever coming out of the wall, and barely heard the screech made by the plates moving back into the locked position. The air inside the tunnel was still cold, his breath came out in puffs. His shoes thumped on the stone floor as he continued along. The hallway slowly widened up enough for one person, even heavily armored, to walk without brushing the walls or hunching over.

It took a quarter of an hour to walk the secret passageway, false booby-trapped trails branching off to confuse anyone who didn't know the correct path, a last effort to save a fleeing royal family should it become necessary. He passed the room into which all the palace latrines dumped, the atrocious smell enough to make any person, even those reputing to have a strong stomach, vomit.

One last locked door greeted Nicky. He pressed various blocks of stone in the wall, heard a low grinding noise. The stone carved door opened a foot inward, then stopped. It had to be pushed forward several feet. Nicky emerged from the slim space created, and slipped around a seated figure of the first King Maceanas carved from rock. The current king would never make it through; he was too fat. The original progenitor of the ruling line, rumors had it, purposefully did that as a means of reminding his decedents to not get too complacent in their rule.

Forgot the most important part of your legacy, didn't you, Reginald? Nicky thought gleefully. *Even if you wanted to escape, not that I'll give you the chance, you couldn't.*

The boy turned and moved the stone figure's arm and hand holding the scepter, gears clanked and groaned in protest as the plinth with its seated figure moved back into place and locked itself. No one came down into the royal crypts unless it was to make ready a new burial spot. He walked around the carved stone sarcophagi holding the first king and queen of Macinas, and out the small space it rested in. A long, black hallway greeted him, along with the faint smells of rotting organic matter. The lantern illuminated other niches carved out of the inside the plateau's stone briefly as he passed by. Statues inside, if he cared to look, would show him a likeness of which king and his family's remains rested.

It wasn't long before he passed a space the current king would need. *And you can be damn sure I won't have any stupid carved statue of you put inside, you fat fuck. Lucky me you have no official recognized offspring, only bastards. I can have them killed and disposed of after you and thus no one to legally challenge my rule.*

Nicky passed the steep, worn staircase leading into the chapel of the latest fashionable god-of-the-moment, instead taking the secret one which opened out into the king's private audience chamber. Sweet, sweet, long-awaited revenge was about to be his.

EPILOGUE

Deep inside a mountain tomb complex, scars flared to life on vampiric flesh. The pain was so great, Illyria was forced from her deathlike sleep. She stared at the markings, glowing with the intensity of live coals.

"No!" The whisper held real terror, and disbelief.

She couldn't move; something beyond her knowledge held her in place. The space filled with ritual chanting in a deep, guttural voice, the voice of DiJinn and a host of other demons.

The connection broke, and Illyria's nature let her know dusk had fallen over the land. The glowing marks faded, their image burned onto her retinas. She strained every sense, yet nothing had changed inside her hiding spot.

Why now, after all the years which had passed since she and the immortals defeated Nicky, did the marks flare to life?

A conversation she had forgotten slammed into her consciousness.

"Time is fluid, ever-changing, mutating, as are the worlds and universes around us. The doors will allow passage between, and keep the realms separate. When they are broken, who is to say what shall happen?"

Illyria had a feeling she was about to find out.

Thank You for Reading

Connect with me online:

http://slfiguhr.com/
Twitter: https://twitter.com/SLFiguhr
Facebook: http://facebook.com/SLFiguhr.author

Send me feedback: If you have questions about the series, want to point out errors and typos, want to know how to become one of my beta readers or just embarrass me with totally undeserved adulation, I urge you to send me an email at

info@slfiguhr.com

I love to hear from readers and try to answer every email.

Follow my blog: The least amount of effort involved, the blog is at: http://slfiguhr.com/blog-2/

Click on the follow blog via email button, so you'll get an email notice whenever I update my blog.

Share your Opinion: If you enjoy the Immortalibus Bella series, please let others know, either by Twitter, Facebook, WordPress, blogger, or your social media of choice and recommend to your friends.

Write reviews: Most of the sites where you can buy ebooks or paperback copies have a way for you to post a review, so you can share with other readers whether a book or story merits their attention. The importance of reviews should not be underestimated. With over 350,000 new books published, it's difficult for writers to get exposure for their novels.